Darwin's Wake

Pete
Mitchell

Darwin's Wake

Publisher's Note: This is a work of fiction. Names, characters, places, and incidents are a product of the author's imagination. Locales and public names are sometimes used for atmospheric purposes. Any resemblance to actual people, living or dead, or to businesses, companies, events, institutions, or locales is completely coincidental.

Published by:

Madhouse Media Publishing | www.madhousemedia.com.au

ISBN: 978-0-6455695-3-7

Written and distributed by:

Pete Mitchell

petemitchell.com.au

Printed edition IngramSpark 2022

Dedication

To Connie, for so many reasons,
they could fill another book.

Acknowledgments

There are many people who have, intentionally and unintentionally assisted with the production of this book. To Connie McCafferty and Suzanne Zarach for their continuing encouragement and for patiently reading through far too many drafts. To Sunil Govinnage for first inspiring me to put words on paper. Thanks also to my editors and beta readers, Joanne, Sumudu Narayana and Ted Briggs and to the generous real authors who generously offered their assistance and realistic critiques; Jill Griffiths, Paul Hardisty, Julie Koh and Andrea Walters.

To the writers that continue to inspire me with their craft; Courtney, Green, Irving, Miller, Murakami and Winton.

To Geoff Hughes at Madhouse Media for bringing it all together. Darwin's Wake has been a bucket list project that you have brought to reality. I look forward to working on the next one with you.

Acknowledgements

Darwin

1. *A surname, especially referring to Charles Darwin (1809–1882), British naturalist and founder of the theory of evolution by natural selection.*

2. *The capital city of the Northern Territory, Australia.*

Wake

1. *To stop sleeping.*

2. *To make somebody stop sleeping; to rouse from sleep.*

3. *To be excited or roused up; to be stirred from a dormant, torpid, or inactive state; to be active.*

4. *To lay out a body prior to burial in order to allow family and friends to pay their last respects.*

5. *The pattern produced by waterfowl, boats, etc. crossing water in the shape of two lines that form a V with the object at the apex.*

1

Roland

Liquid dripped from the door. A halo of flies ringed the glistening puddle below. Wingtip to wingtip, they shivered as they gorged on the liquid. I waved my boot towards them. The flies didn't move. They were so captivated by the liquid that their primary instinct, ironically to fly, was ignored. I knew that anything that caused flies to become so obsessed could only mean one thing.

'You see sergeant, it doesn't look right, does it? First, the container's not on the manifest, and now it looks like something's rotten in there. It shouldn't be leaking like that. The manifest says it's full of furniture.' The wharfie stated the obvious, hoping that I could solve his problem. A problem that he and his union mates had created. They had just finished a three-day strike. The strike had closed down Darwin Port with military zeal. Nothing had come into or out of the port at Australia's 'Top End' during that time. No one who wasn't a card-carrying union member could get past the picket line.

For three days, I'd driven by multiple times each day only to witness the strikers having a great time. They'd set up their picket right outside the port gates. A marquee provided them shade, essential this time of year. A couple of camp beds were pushed towards the rear, behind a small table and a row of deck chairs. Men in maroon t-shirts stood out front, poking at steaks on a barbeque. At other times the casually uniformed union members stood at either side of the gate, doing their best to look like sentries. There was nothing to report back to the station. The strike was playing out to a familiar script.

The unions made it clear who ran the ports. On paper, it might have looked like the companies were in charge; they paid the wages and they determined the docking schedule. But nothing came through any Australian port without union approval, and the union decided everything that the wharfies did. The union had called their strike two weeks before Christmas. They hadn't had a strike at Easter, so a strike at Christmas was always on the cards. They knew when their action would have the greatest impact. As soon as the strike was called, massive cranes and forklifts dropped the containers exactly where they were. Nothing was permitted into or out of the port.

As soon as the industrial action ended, the deckchairs and barbeque were packed away, no doubt to be used again. Three days wasn't a huge interruption, but the yard looked a mess, quickly taking on the look of a poor tenant's garden. Machinery had been shut down and left where it was. Things quickly looked unkempt.

After the days of inactivity, the ships jostled to unload their cargo. It was chaos. Things started moving again, as everyone knew they would. Containers were shuffled across the yard, and a sense of normality began to emerge from the disarray. Giant forklifts and gantry cranes sorted through things methodically. The wharfies had a list of priority containers. Perishables and those containers where companies had paid a premium to jump the queue came first. The containers, colour-coded by company; blue, white, red and yellow, made it easier. Added to this, each container's identifying number was listed on the Port's manifest list. The days of the wharfies manually moving things from ships had long gone. Cargo was either in a sea container or on a conveyor belt.

'So, what do you want me to do?'

'Well, sergeant, technically, I need customs or the consigning company's approval before I can cut the seal. Customs have told me that they won't be able to get to this one for another two or three days. I've tried getting hold of the consignee, but I get no answer. I hoped that seeing that you're here, you could witness me opening the container and make sure I don't get in any strife. The boys on the forklifts would like to get this one moved out of here.'

'Why so long for customs?'

'I figure they're pissed off with us calling a strike, and now they have to get through a backlog. I guess this container's just not a priority for them. I explained that it looks like there's something rotten in there, but they're refusing to budge from their schedule.'

'So, who is the consignee?'

The wharfie pulled a grubby form from his shirt pocket and read aloud, 'Mr Roland Redman. Darwin Imports. I've tried to call him a dozen times already, but I get no answer. Not even an answering machine.' He then passed me the form, as if by doing so I could decipher anything more from the scant information it contained.

I knew Redman. He was a southerner who had moved to Darwin years ago. His unexplained wealth put him on our 'keep an eye on' list, but he'd never really come to police attention. Not even a traffic infringement. In spite of that, I didn't like him.

I can still remember the first time I encountered him. It was late one afternoon at The Criterion. He was holding court at the end of the bar. I didn't know him by name at that stage, but I knew his type. He enjoyed being the centre of attention amongst three or four barflies, including two I knew through the job. They were not notable criminals but always teetering along the razor's edge of legality. Redman seemed a bit too sure of himself amongst this little group.

Even back then, before anything official, I'd made a mental note to keep an eye on him.

I didn't like his moustache. It wasn't that I disliked all moustaches; I just disliked his. It looked like what you'd expect to see an amateur actor twiddle as he tied a damsel to railway tracks in the path of an approaching train. His shirt was too loud, too tight and too fashionable, particularly for Darwin. He even wore ostentatious jewellery, a chunky gold watch and a pinkie ring. I wouldn't have been surprised if the watch was a genuine Rolex, not one of those more commonplace Bali knock-offs.

He might have passed for fashionable in Sydney's Kings Cross or Melbourne's Chapel Street, but this was Darwin. Up here, the uniform for blokes was shorts, a t-shirt and thongs. If you wore a shirt with a collar, it was considered formal. Why would anyone want to wear any more than they had to? At least he wasn't wearing a tie. In the Territory, only politicians and Mormons wore ties. Politicians' ties were wide and loud and Mormon's were thin and black so you didn't get them mixed up. Though, as neither were liked, it didn't matter much if you did.

Roland Redman, as I later came to know him, just didn't seem authentic. I initially chastised myself for judging him too quickly by his appearance. Maybe I was too cynical, but it is an occupational hazard for a copper. It made me think he was trying to hide something or be someone he wasn't. Deliberately trying to throw you off the scent, distracting you with showy accoutrements, like the exaggerated flourish of a magician's hand, so he could pass something more sinister under the radar without detection. But what was Redman trying to distract everyone from. What was he hiding under his obvious facade?

At that stage, I thought he was just another 'refugee' from down south who had relocated to Darwin to escape. Escape from what? There was plenty about him that set off my primary policing senses. So much about him made me edgy. I was sure the enormous red and white ute parked in front of the pub was his. It fitted the image. One of those ridiculously oversized American things, a Ford F250 with a thumping V8 and every accessory. I'd seen it around town, towing an equally ostentatious boat in matching red and white. It was a twin-hulled thing with some fancy name scrawled down the side in elaborate script. It should have been moored in a pen, not being towed around town like a dingy. I figured Redman chose to haul it through the streets of Darwin so everyone would see him. It all seemed to fit the profile of him that I had initially assembled.

Usually, I'd try to turn these observations off when I wasn't on duty. But a cop's life in Darwin means that you're never really off duty. It was easier when I wore plain clothes, but the job demanded that I do time in uniform too. It was impossible to ever feel totally like a civilian.

At that time, I didn't assume Redman was anything other than a bit of a gaudy prat. He wasn't someone who I thought would ever be a hardened criminal. Sure, he was loud, and he dressed like a ladies' man or someone that fancied himself as a ladies' man but I never imagined he would give me too much of a problem. I put him in the category of someone who got a few beers under his belt and told tall stories. Some blokes were calm when they were sober but became aggressive when they had too much to drink. Redman wouldn't be one of those. The worst thing he would do after too many beers was talk even louder and spout even more bullshit stories to those who were too gullible or bored to listen. Booze and an audience reaction appeared to be the catalysts for his outlandish stories and being creative with the truth.

That first time I saw him, he was entertaining his little group of acolytes with an outlandish story. Looking back on that occasion, I couldn't believe the balls of the guy, and the story he told. I was sure I'd heard his story before.

I watched him tell his tale via The Criterion's stained-glass altar, the mirror behind the barman, through the multicoloured glass of the spirits shelf. I tried to appear as if I were miles away, as I listened from the far end of the bar.

'I'd been floating out there for days,' Roland said, taking a swig as he pointed to the attentive little crowd with his middle finger, while he gripped his beer glass. 'I hadn't had one bite, but I was too bloody good a fisherman to give in without landing something substantial. After all, I'd driven all the way to Glyde Point towing Durendal.'

'Who were you towing?' one of the barflies asked.

'Not who, you idiot. Durendal is the name of my boat. I know it's a long way to go fishing, but I'd heard some big stuff was on the go up there. Towing her was a bit of a job, but the F250 made easy work of it,' he said, confirming that he owned the enormous ute parked out the front.

'Did ya' end up doing orright?' asked a weedy redhead with fluffy stubble on his chin, as he devoured Roland's story.

'Yes, and no. I ended up getting into a school of scaly mackerel,' Roland continued and took another swig of his beer.

'Was that all? Shit, you could have saved yourself the trouble. You'd have done better around here.' said the redhead guy.

'Or the fish shop down the road from Kamahli's place,' said another.

At the mention of Kamahli, Roland froze, eyeballed the guy, seemed to contemplate a response and then resumed, as if the mention of Kamahli hadn't happened..

'Nah, but that wasn't the end of the fishing. The scaly mackerel gave me a lead onto something though,' Roland paused to allow his little group of acolytes to build anticipation before continuing. 'I used a nice, fresh scaly as live bait. I put a hook in him and tossed him over the side while he was still squirming. Ten minutes later I hooked up a sailfish.' Roland said, daring the small crowd at the bar to contradict his tale.

They didn't. The barflies were lapping it all up. They couldn't wait for Roland to tell them what came next.

'So, what happened? I bet she was a beauty. I've heard they get a few up that way,' nodded the redhead guy.

'Not like this one,' Roland said, paused, took another drink and put his empty glass on the bar. He nodded to the barman 'My shout for all the boys, thanks, Jock'. He pinned a fifty dollar note with the clutch of coins that had accumulated in front of him, before turning to his mates, 'I've gotta take a piss.'

'Aw, come on, Roland, what happened with the sailfish?' the redhead guy asked, but

Roland was already on his way to the gents.

While he was gone, the barflies discussed Roland's fishing story. The little crowd was split, some claiming that a sailfish was unlikely, and others who claimed that similar fish had been caught off Glyde Point in years past. None of them thought to question how Roland had launched his boat without a boat ramp, even *if* the big F250 could have towed it there. Some of Redman's little crowd argued that they had heard stories of big fish being caught off Glyde Point before. With the beer they'd consumed, I'm sure they would struggle to remember if it was five minutes ago, or five years ago.

Roland returned, and the small group parted to let him re-take his place at the bar. His freshly poured beer had gathered a ring of condensation at its base.

'So, I fought with this fish for hours and hours. I couldn't tell just how big she was at first. As I say, I'd been on the water for days, and I was already pretty stuffed by that stage. She sure didn't want to get caught. She put up a huge fight. But I reckon she hadn't expected to come up against a fisherman like me, though. I wasn't going to be a pushover. None of this bloody tag and release bullshit either.'

Roland was feeding off being the centre of attention. He was talking up the story to make himself seem larger than life, stretching the truth with the apparent intention of making himself seem like a bigger man, and those around him were lapping it up. It was as if the more outlandish his story, the more they valued his companionship. Roland was on a roll.

'I thought I had her beat early on. I'd let her have a fair bit of line and was slowly hauling her back in. She'd have a bit of a run, maybe fifty metres or so, but for every fifty metres, I pulled back sixty or seventy. Eventually, I could see her big, dark eye every time she lurched out of the water. She'd dance on her tail, trying to flick the hook from her mouth, but I wasn't going to let her go anywhere. I finally got her alongside the boat. She was an incredible size, a deep chest and fantastic blues, silver and iridescent greens. Durendal is thirty foot, or nine point seven metres in the the new language, and I reckon she was more than half the length of the boat.'

'Shit, five metres of sailfish is alright!' said the redhead guy, demonstrating a mathematical ability that was apparently superior to his mates at the bar.

'I leaned down to grab hold of the leader, but as soon as she saw me looking her in the eye, she was off again. Could have sliced me hand right through. I reckon if I hadn't had the sense to wear a leather glove, it would've cut through to the bone.'

'Shit!' the little group exclaimed in chorus.

'So, after another hour or more, I finally wore her down and brought her alongside. But what was I going to do? I was out there all by myself. I couldn't get her into the boat. She was too heavy.'

'So, did you have to let her go?' asked the redhead.

'Bugger that. I'd fought too hard to cave in so easily. She was such a fantastic fish I was sure she'd break records if I could get her back to Darwin. I knew I could haul her out of the water with the winch on the boat trailer back at the shore. So, I hit her on the noggin with the gaff and lashed her to the side of the boat. I tied her up good and tight. I'd have to take it slow back to shore, but I wasn't about to release this beauty.'

'Brilliant. So, was she a new record?'

'I'm sure she would have been, but no sooner had I finished tying her down than the bloody sharks set in. First, a big tiger took a bite out of her guts and then once blood was in the water, it was on for one and all. Every other shark and little shitbag fish within a mile's radius hoed into her like a smorgasbord. It looked like one of those documentaries on piranhas. The water boiled red for a good couple of minutes. I clobbered a few of the sharks with the gaff, but I was just pissing into the wind. They were having a feast, and there was no way I was going to stop them. They'd only finish when there was nothing left. The sharks even ended up biting through the rope I'd lashed her down with. All I could do was watch her nearly stripped carcass sink to the bottom, with a plume of feasting fish chasing her to the depths.'

I couldn't believe Roland's little crowd continued to lap this up. They looked at him with sympathy. Was it the booze, or the way he told the story? Was it the way that he crafted it into their vernacular so they'd feel as if they were a part of the story themselves? He seemed to know exactly how far he could play them before they'd call him out? He held the crowd in the palm of his hand. I didn't like him, but he sure could tell a story.

His story just didn't sit right with me. I knew I'd heard a similar story before; I just couldn't, at that time, remember where or from who. It wasn't until I was on my way home that I remembered. I'm sure it was Roland's retelling of Hemingway's 'Old Man and the Sea'. Set it in the Northern Territory, cast Roland as Santiago and, you've got Roland's pub story. Was I the only one that realised he'd stolen a story from a literary giant, cast himself in the lead role and retold it as his own? I expect none of his pub mates had read Hemingway. I reckon some of them would struggle to read anything other than the Fanny Bay Racing Guide. I couldn't be the only one that thought it all sounded a bit too much.

I turned to the wharfie as he eagerly waited on my permission to open the problematic sea container.

'Okay, I'll vouch for you. Get something to cut her open. Let's see what's inside.'

2

Yates

'Do you know Mr Redman?' I asked the wharfie, as he took a pair of snips off his belt in readiness to cut the security tab on the container.

'Sure, he's a regular customer. He has a furniture import business here in Darwin. I hear he's got a few other things going on too. He doesn't give us a lot of business, but he's a regular, a container every couple of months or so. He is a bloke from somewhere down south, Sydney or Melbourne, I think. He sends me a bottle of Chivas every Christmas. I got a bottle from him just last week. I've never met him in person, but he's a real gentleman. Always Chivas, none of that cheap stuff, though.'

'Do many of your clients send you Scotch?'

'Not really. A few send the boys a carton of beer every now and then. To have after their shift, of course, as you'd know. But as I say, Mr Redman, he's alright by me.'

I looked at the manifest again. 'Contents: Imported wooden furniture. Departure Jakarta, Indonesia. Destination Darwin, Australia.

Consignee: Mr Roland Redman.' I folded the document and put it into my pocket.

'Okay, open it up.'

He cut the security seal with the snips and turned to me, 'I'm gonna need the bolt cutters for the padlock.'

He retrieved bolt cutters from his vehicle. With handles that were almost a metre long, the bolt cutters looked like they would make short work of the toughest padlock or bolt. He applied the cutters to the padlock that secured the container doors, gave a dramatic heave, and levered the handles towards each other. The padlock clattered against the doors before splashing into the offensive puddle, finally dislodging the flies from their feast. He propped the bolt cutters against the wall of the container and cracked the lever on the doors. As soon as he did, he stepped back as if he'd been slapped. He half-opened the door, then put his hand over his face. From where I stood, several meters away, the smell was still a noxious contagion that permeated everything it encountered.

The wharfie took his hand away from his face almost as quickly as he put it there. He turned and vomited. His convulsive retches continued one after the other until he couldn't possibly have anything left in his stomach. It seemed that he was ejecting everything he had eaten and was starting on stomach juices and bile. His convulsion repeated, his back arched as his body heaved, but nothing more was ejected. Before he stopped, he turned to me with pleading, watery eyes. He sucked in air. I placed my hand on his back to convey unspoken sympathy. I couldn't say I wouldn't have done the same if I'd been the first to catch that odour. He regained his composure, stood, turned his head and spat out a bolus of detritus. The chunk-riddled expectorate landed near my foot.

I knew that the best way to avoid being overcome by the smell was to breathe through my mouth. It seemed counterintuitive, but it worked. Just avoid assaulting your sense of smell by not using your nose. The smell was putrid. What the hell was it? Surely someone wasn't silly enough to try to get fresh food from Indonesia past Customs. The wharfie's chest heaved as his stomach contorted again. A thin stream of drool dribbled from the corner of his mouth. He wiped his mouth on the cuff of his shirt and tried to regain his composure. He flung open the door fully. Whatever was in there needed air.

The scene that opened up before us was something that haunted me. If I were a Christian, I couldn't have imagined a more convincing vision of Hell. Out of the darkness of the container, squinting against the sudden sunlight, gaunt, black faces emerged with outreached hands. A token of cheap furniture that had been stacked against the doors, now lay in pieces, providing a final obstacle to their exit.

A woman sobbed, *'Tayaukurntu enakku utavi ceyyavum . . .'*

More faces appeared blinking at the light, moaning unintelligibly. I had no idea what language the woman was using, but it was clearly her desperate cry for assistance. They were in trouble. How many were in there? The scene was like something out of the belly of a slave trader's ship. Too many people in too small a space. The bodies, smeared with shit and vomit across their faces and clothes, seemed everywhere. Several continued to move towards the light, stumbling out of their hell.

Looking further in, I could see some were beyond moving. The container was full of people. They'd been stacked on wooden platforms, three layers high, as far as I could see into the darkness of the container.

'Tayaukurntu enakku utavi ceyyavum, tayavu ceytu. Karunakara mata udav, anne....'

An emaciated body stumbled towards me. These were people who were clearly in trouble. Later, I was ashamed that my first reaction wasn't to rush in to help these people. I should have given these people the help they so clearly needed, but the stench was so overpowering. The smell continued to overwhelm me, clouding any logical process. I couldn't help but be repulsed. What was I witnessing? My first reaction should have at least been pity. The first living corpse to emerge from the container was a young, bearded man. He pushed past the woman the wharfie had first heard and reached a hand out towards the wharfie's shoulder, but he stumbled and slipped on the recently deposited vomit and fell onto the blue metal hardstand. His shoulder and then his head took the weight of his fall. His head made a sickening sound as it bounced on the hard surface. He lay motionless. The pitiful sound of sobbing coming from the container snapped me back to grim reality.

How long had these people been in the sea container? How many are in there? No light, food or water. Even air was limited. Imprisoned in there for days in the Darwin heat, all they could do was wait for the container to finally be opened.

The wharfie grabbed the two-way radio from his belt, spat into the dirt again and called the guardhouse. 'Gaz, Joe here. Mate, get the ambos down here immediately. I've just cracked open that unmarked sea container, and it's bloody full of people. Reffos I reckon. Better get Immigration too.'

'People? Shit. How many? Where are they from?' I heard the crackling reply.

'Fuck knows. Manifest says Indonesia. Who knows where they're really from? Looks like lots of the buggers, more than fifty, I'd say, but I'm sure as hell not going in there to count them. Leave that job to the coppers, or immigration. I'm guessing they won't have their passports handy. Just get me some help for these poor bastards.' Joe clicked off the radio and waited, as more living corpses stumbled out into the light.

We sorted the refugees into two as they came out of the container. A group of men and boys, and a group of women and children.

The women sat to one side, several with whimpering, clinging children. One clenched a lifeless child tightly to her chest.

The men looked across the yard from the other side. Some of them didn't look too much older than children themselves. Their top lips had a trace of fluff, a sure indication that they had yet to have their first shave. The older men all had dark faces and sunken eyes rimmed by dark beards. They sat quietly, staring at the ground. The men appeared unified by their predicament, but their clothes suggested a mix of ethnicities. Some of the clothes looked western; others wore what looked like calico pyjamas. All were stained with vomit, shit and despair.

One of the wharfies who had appeared after Joe's radio call came up to me, 'You in charge here?'

'Not really, mate, but I suppose I'm the closest we've got at the moment. Ambos and Immigration will be here any minute.'

'Looks like you got things under control as best as you can under the circumstances. Twenty-three people in this container in Darwin was never going to be easy.'

'These are just the ones who could walk out. We've helped a few others out but you need to stick your head in there if you want a full count. There are plenty of the poor bastards that won't be coming out under their own steam anytime soon.' he flicked his head towards the container. 'I reckon this will be the final destination for a few of them too. How bad would it have to be from where they've come to put themselves and their kids through this?'

I walked over to the container. I was aware of the multiple soulful eyes that tracked my uniform. The container was the primary source of the stench, but it had followed some of the container's recent inhabitants too. I took the torch from my belt, took a breath and stepped into the container. The beam illuminated a wider vision of a hell than my first horrifying glance had prepared me for. The stench inside the container thickened, became viscous and displaced almost all the air. I swallowed reflexively. I can still remember the smell today, in spite of how hard I've tried hard to forget it over the years. It was something my worst nightmares could not have imagined. The sight of so many bodies crammed into such a confined space haunts me to this day.

The container was fitted with wooden shelves, like bunk beds, running down each side, with a narrow aisle just wide enough for a person to pass through. As I shone my torch towards the end of the container, I could see two plastic barrels sat at the far end. I turned the torch beam to the platform. Fuck, there was still people alive in here, so many bodies.

It wasn't just blood, vomit and shit that was responsible for the stench. Darwin's heat and humidity, amplified inside a sealed container, accelerated the decomposition of the dead. The beam of my torch focused on a bloated face, static staring eyes open but clouded, sunken cheeks and a grossly distended belly.

Fluids from decomposition seeped from the higher platforms onto the corpses below. Twenty-three outside, at least as many still inside. I wasn't going any further. I scanned the torch down the line of shelves. There were two layers, floor to ceiling, three to a platform, four times down each side. I struggled to do the math in my head, two times three, times four, times two. Fuck, that's about fifty people, not allowing for if they had packed multiple kids into the same space as an adult. With twenty-three outside, that could mean at least as many still in here. Ambulances were on the way, but it was body bags that would be needed.

As I struggled to re-check the maths I was interrupted by a hand stretching towards my face from the third level platform.

'Tayaukurntu enakku utavi ceyyavum'

I had no idea what she was saying. She rolled onto her shoulder, trying desperately to reach me. I flinched and recoiled, turned and headed out of the container as quickly as possible. The ambos could deal with this.

'We've got others in there that need help now.' I was suddenly embarrassed by how high-pitched my plea sounded. Every face, including those sitting on the tarmac, turned towards me.

The wharfie who had been waiting for me to emerge, said 'Okay, mate. I can imagine what it's like in there. We've got these buggers out. Our hands are pretty full just at the moment. Take a breath. We'll get to everyone as soon as we can.'

'Yeah, sorry, mate.' I struggled to regain composure, aware that this wharfie was giving me the spiel that I should have been giving him. 'It doesn't look too good in there. I lost it for a bit.'

'You wouldn't be human if this didn't rattle you.'

In the distance, I could hear the wailing of an ambulance, growing louder as it sped closer. The siren stopped abruptly and minutes later it came to a halt in front of me.

The ambulance guys went into the container with torches. The first came straight back out and did the same as Joe, adding to the pool of vomit already congealing near the door. Only the Darwin flies seemed to appreciate the fresh supply. The older of the two ambos came out of the container looking ashen.

He went to speak but paused, then swallowed, preventing whatever was on its way up, from emerging. 'What the fuck has been going on here?' He glared at Joe, 'Didn't any of you bastards hear these people?'

'Don't blame me, mate. We've been bloody chockers getting things back in order after the strike. You know how tough it's been. Could've been another week before we got to this one. It isn't on the list of paperwork. Even when we cut the padlock, there was not a sound coming out of there. They're bloody lucky I opened this one when I did.'

'Fuck, don't go calling any of these poor bastards lucky. There's got to be nearly twenty dead in there and others that are so fucking close they probably wish they were. Give us a hand, and we'll get the ones that are still alive to the hospital. There's no rush for those that are already dead. They're not going anywhere. Jesus, there's going to be too many for the morgue. We are going to have to make other arrangements.' He motioned to me. 'You blokes can sort out the poor buggers inside when you've done what you need to with this lot.'

I pulled the manifest from my pocket. Mr Redman and I needed to have a chat.

3

Yates

Shortly thereafter, two police cars entered the compound with lights flashing but sirens silent. This was serious; the station boss had prised himself away from his air-conditioned office with which he was so infatuated.

'Yates, what can you tell us.'

'Boss, I never thought I'd be so glad to see you. I really need some help here.' I said without realising how patronising I sounded.

'I'm after a brief on the situation Yates, not a fucking kiss on the cheek. Do your job.'

'Yes, sorry, Sir,' I said, recovering, lowering the tone from the whine I had just used, 'We appear to have a container full of refugees, sorry asylum-seekers. There are twenty- three mobile outside who we've put into two groups, women with children, and men.' I said, pointing to the two sorry looking clusters. 'More are still inside, some alive but immobile. We have multiple causalities.'

'Thank you, Sergeant. How many do you estimate are inside?'

'Maybe as many as thirty, up to forty, including those deceased.'

'I'll inform the Federal Police. This looks like a nasty situation. See if you can get a statement from one of the first on the scene. I'll take it from here.'

'Yes, Sir. I've done that. I'd like to see if I can contact the person the container was consigned to, if that's okay?'

'Yes, but be bloody careful, Yates. The Feds will be all over this. We can't afford to fuck it up. Call back to the station and see if you can take a few of the uniforms with you.'

'Thank you, Sir.'

I scanned the scene. The ambos had started to attend to those sitting outside. They were preparing a couple to send off in the first ambulance already. One of the Immigration staff crouched in front of one of the men. Another Immigration official was scanning the scene with a video camera. I straightened as the camera panned towards me. This was going to be on record. I was glad they hadn't filmed my whiny exchange with the boss. I know I'd been told it was understandable in the context, but this would attract a Federal review. I didn't want one of those armchair critics in Canberra to be critical of a reaction that could only be made by being here. The video wasn't going to capture the cries of desperation and the hideous stench of the dead and dying.

I tried to collect my thoughts as I drove back to the station, through the streets of Darwin that would soon be buzzing with the news of this tragedy. I knew that news of the container would be all over town in record time, so I decided to go straight to the address that I had for Mr Redman. No need to delay things by collecting more uniforms. I could handle someone like Mr Redman myself.

Darwin is a country town trying hard to be a city. It sits at the northern edge of the Australian continent, seemingly waiting for the ancient land bridge that once connected it to Asia to reform. Darwin is closer to several southeast Asian capitals than any Australian city. For millennia, Indigenous Australians traded with Malay mariners from the north, until Europeans moved in. Even today, if the weather is kind, it is possible for a competent boatman to set off from Darwin and sail north past Melville Island and onto Timor-Leste, New Guinea or Indonesia.

Perhaps its location, isolated at the extremity of the continent, has shaped Darwin's inhabitants more than they have shaped the location. Darwin is a melting pot of Europeans, Malays, Chinese, Vietnamese and first Australian Peoples, like the Larrakia. Just like a fine stew, the melange of cultures is an exotic combination of all ingredients. Take any component out of the mix, and the whole becomes significantly less. Generations of harmony and hybridisation have meant that most people get on with their own business and stay out of other's. The same can't be said for the lives of many down south. That said, Darwin collects more than its fair share of odd-bods, misfits and no-hopers. Those that have shunned, or been shunned by, the cities to the south to seek solace with kindred spirits among those that the major cities have eschewed. As a copper, the odd bods can be a problem, but most get on with each other unless someone riles them up. There are plenty that choose Darwin to escape. For some, Darwin was just another frontier town, yet for others, it was different enough that you could convince yourself it was somewhere more exotic.

Darwin's proximity to Asia, makes it an obvious entry point for contraband to enter or leave Australia. The security of the busier ports in the southern capitals is more sophisticated. With its many bays and mangroves, the coastline around Darwin offers smugglers plenty of options.

There was scant legitimate passenger trade between Darwin and ports to the north; however freight was constantly going backwards and forwards. Many container ships scooted past Darwin and disgorged cargo to ports further south. But there was plenty of regular shipping traffic of manufactured goods and foodstuffs heading between Darwin and Kuala Lumpur, Singapore, Jakarta and beyond. Beef on the hoof, from stations across the Northern Territory.

Minerals from as far away as Queensland and the Kimberley were shipped out of Darwin. The round trip, Darwin to Jakarta, was less than a week. Just prior to arriving in Darwin, it was relatively easy to drop a dingy off the side of one of these merchant vessels, before officially coming into port, as they passed along the coastline. It was easy money waiting to be made. A vessel could make more profit from contraband; drugs, guns or tobacco, than any legitimate cargo. People were seen as the most lucrative cargo.

Darwin was also an entry point for illegal immigrants. During the 1970s, people fleeing the war in Vietnam fled south as Ho Chi Minh's armies overran the combined forces of the American, Australian and South Vietnamese armies. The civilians fled further and further south until they reached the coast and could flee no more. The war left those fleeing with no option but to risk their lives, deal with unscrupulous people-traders, and pay a fortune for a place on an overcrowded, and barely sea-worthy boat. As the Viet-Cong came closer and closer they were left with little choice but to brave the oceans.

Many lost their lives to the depths or to modern-day pirates, but more than eighty-thousand Vietnamese people survived their journey and reached Australia. Australian politicians should have made them welcome. Australia had contributed to their plight. Australia had lost a war they fought on their soil. The South Vietnamese were Australia's allies, and when the war was over, they knew that the new rulers of a united Vietnam would not treat them kindly. Whether out of losers' guilt, or finally just deciding to do the right thing, the Australian government, led by idealist Prime Minister Whitlam, finally revoked the White Australia policy that had tried to keep Australia 'vanilla' and offered the Vietnamese refuge.

In the years following, it wasn't the Vietnamese or even others from Cambodia and Laos, who's society had been destroyed by the war in Asia that braved an illegal boat journey to Australia. Unrest elsewhere, and a dream of a better life kept the boats coming. Wars in Afghanistan, the Middle East and Sri Lanka forced people to risk thousands of miles of hostile seas to seek a better life.

As far as Australian society was concerned Darwin was a long way from most other cities. But tragedy wasn't unknown in Darwin. Cyclone Tracy had wiped Darwin off the map on Christmas Day, 1974. Since then, every season when a low-pressure system formed off the coast, the population wondered if another Tracy was coming. Disasters like this weren't supposed to happen in Australia. Cyclones were things that happened in countries with huts of grass, bamboo and mud. But when Tracy destroyed Darwin and sixty-five people lost their lives, the rest of Australia took notice. The cyclone destroyed seventy per cent of Darwin's houses, giving a good part of the population reason to uproot and relocate to somewhere south of the 'cyclone belt'. It seemed that even today, Darwin was still on the road to recovery. A road rutted and littered with bumps and potholes, forcing a slow journey.

Although the monsoon weather cycle was a reoccurring pattern that had been in place for millennia, it always caught Darwin's more recent arrivals by surprise. No one carried an umbrella or a raincoat, although everyone knew that the dry was about to break and everything would be drenched. Immediately prior to the break of the season, 'crazy time' caused tempers to fray and behaviours that would normally be consciously hidden behind closed doors came into the open.

Pregnant, grey clouds loomed on the horizon. Rain was coming. Not the rain welcomed by gardeners, but thunderously heavy, torrential, season-breaking rain. Rain that was more likely to wash away your garden, than replenish it. The clouds grew vertically, becoming darker and darker before they finally toppled, disgorging their contents on the arid landscape below. At first, a few fat drops spattered onto the red dust, forming a pattern of dark dots, where the desiccated earth inhaled the water, leaving a damp crater. A Papunya dot painting quickly formed in the dirt. The pattern of dots grew denser and denser until it destroyed itself and the once dusty, red dirt transformed into burgundy mud. Earth that had once been starved of water throughout the dry season now clung onto it greedily. In turn, the mud clung to everything, feet, shoes and tyres. Eventually, what was previously impregnated with red dust became heavily caked with burgundy mud.

With the same abruptness that it had started, the rain stopped. Then the humidity set in. For those that had not been caught out in the rain, a soaking was still inevitable. No one could escape the humidity. Evaporative air conditioners, strapped to the roofs of every building, offered no relief. Shirts, whose owners had kept dry during the rain, became soaked in tropical sweat. Sweat that started at the armpits worked its way across the body until the whole front and back of the shirt was soaked. Fashion victims in the latest polyester were the worst off. The less fashionable, but practical locals in blue singlets, seemed less impacted until you looked into their ruddy faces. Sweat that had begun at the temples, resulted in tacky side-burns that joined in the shadow of their jowls, and dripped from their chins.

Such unrelenting humidity brought with it a malaise producing tiredness that was felt before you'd done anything. To southerners, this made the locals appear lazy. The locals knew to get their physically demanding work done before ten in the morning, sleep at midday and start again after four. Those that had experienced such humidity knew how energy-draining it could be. The body desperately tried to keep itself cool, leaving no energy to spend on anything else. It helped to drink fluid, lots of fluid, to maintain an equilibrium. Liquid in, and sweat out.

4

Yates

The poor bastards from the container said nothing. I doubt that most of them could have strung together a sentence in English, even if they'd wanted to. I suppose most of them were so shit-scared of being sent back to where they had come from, that they wouldn't have said anything, even if they could.

These people didn't appear to be all from the same place. Their complexion and dress, even though unified by a veneer of filth, suggested different origins. I guessed they had been thrown together from multiple places and sent on their way from some staging point. If I had to guess, I'd figure that some were Indian and others were Middle Eastern.

I'd heard reports of people smugglers who operated out of Indonesia. The scum promised refugees an easy passage. They took whatever money they had, and then stuck them on a leaky boat pointing towards some remote speck of Australian territory. The smugglers were not concerned if they reached there or not. They'd had their payment.

Finding a sea container full of refugees on the wharf at Darwin was a cruel, new twist in this sordid business.

Redman's address on the manifest from the container was a unit in Fannie Bay, Ultimo Apartments, about as grandiose as you could get and still be in Darwin. Unit one, on the eleventh level was the penthouse that took up an entire floor. It didn't surprise me at all. From what I'd seen, he liked to flaunt his wealth. Now I was beginning to understand from where his wealth had come.

I knocked on the door, waited, and knocked again. It was hardly surprising that he wasn't there, but I wanted to resolve this mess as quickly as possible.

I drove back into town and disturbed a district judge; the grumpy old bugger was not happy to have me interrupt his day with an urgent request but was mindful of his duty when I explained the situation. I needed a signature on the warrant to search Redman's apartment and his would carry the necessary weight. I needed to begin the investigation before the Federal Police arrived, muddied the scene and took the credit.

I collected two uniformed officers from the station on the way through and headed back to the Fannie Bay penthouse with the warrant. I arrived and knocked on the door, and struck it a second time. Best to follow the prescribed protocols. I re-read the warrant to make sure that everything was correct, to leave no room for some smart-arse lawyer to get wiggle room later. I wasn't going to let any bastard orchestrating this mess, to get off on some technicality. I turned to the larger of the uniforms.

'Kick it in.'

The uniform took a step back and then put his steel capped boot through the door. The door crumpled away from the frame. Doors are made so cheaply these days. It was supposed to be a flash place, but they'd still used cheap materials. The uniform untangled his boot from the cardboard lattice that had been inside the door. Doors shouldn't be made with cardboard.

The three of us entered the apartment. Nice. From this floor, the view looked over the mangroves towards Mindil Beach. The Tiwi Islands were eighty kilometres away, and only a line of clouds on the distant horizon signalled their presence. Beyond that it was open ocean until Timor Leste and further again to Indonesia. It was only eleven floors up, high for Darwin after the stricter building codes following Cyclone Tracy. Indigenous art adorned every wall.

'Don't touch anything!'

The uniforms glanced at each other and rolled their eyes, acknowledging the obvious.

'Looks like our Mr Redman has left a bit hastily.'

The drawers in the bedroom were half-open, and most of the contents had been emptied. The kitchen looked untouched. The bathroom looked similar to the bedroom, with open, half-emptied cupboards. A yellow Post-It note was stuck on the bathroom mirror.

The scrawl read, 'Collect Paul QF1624 16:00 Sunday'.

I left the uniforms at the property, to tape off the door to make sure no one went in or out. They were quite capable of bagging a few things to send to forensics if needed. Even a flat foot couldn't get this wrong. I headed back to the station and put out an APB for Redman and his vehicle, over the radio on the way. His ute would stick out like a sore thumb around here. Sure, four-wheel drives were common, but I wasn't aware of anyone else driving such a tosser's 4WD like the big red and white Ford registered to Redman.

There was no sense chasing Redman until I had some idea where to look. He'd turn up, eventually. There wasn't far he could go without someone seeing him, or his ostentatious vehicle. He might even turn up to collect 'Paul' from the airport.

5

Kamahli

In the meantime an alternative line of enquiry was required. What could I find out about Redman while I waited? I drove back to the station and searched the Police databases for anything on Redman or his business interests. It revealed that Redman's furniture import business was a Darwin registered company that he now owned outright. Until fairly recently, it had been joint ownership, between a Mr R. Redman and a Ms K. Krishnamurthy. If Redman had disappeared, perhaps Ms Krishnamurthy could shed some light on what was going on.

Krishnamurthy's business address was listed as a residential area in Malak Park. I knew the area; I'd visited it many times. It couldn't have been a bigger contrast to Ultimo Apartments. It wasn't a flash part of Darwin. It seemed an unlikely place for a registered company director, in partnership with Redman, to be living.

I pulled up at the address. The bottle shop was half a block down the road. It wasn't a bottle shop where you'd go to find a cheeky chardonnay or a bottle of Grange. The likely hot sellers were flagons of VO Invalid Port and casks of Moselle. Grease-stained paper and betting slips, discarded along with any hope they may have once had placed in them, littered the curb in a symbol of junk food and dreams consumed and abandoned. Maybe the business of furniture importing hadn't been good for Ms Krishnamurthy. That might explain Redman's apparent move into people smuggling. It wouldn't be the first time a reputable business had resorted to crime to provide the cash flow to stop them from going under. Greed and the stigma of a failing business had proved to be an incentive behind many companies heading down a criminal track. I wouldn't be surprised if that wasn't the case here.

I struck the door three times and waited. Nothing. I raised my hand, pointed my knuckles at the door and was about to knock again when the door opened. A young woman, perhaps Indian as the name suggested, looked up at me with big dark eyes. She wore a midnight blue blouse, patterned with large, yellow roses, a thin gold chain at her neck, black pleated trousers and heels that worked to make her appear taller. I thought she looked like a woman that could be heading to a boardroom, or a courtroom. She didn't fit the profile I'd expect to find in Malak Park.

'Ms Krishnamurthy?'

'Yes. May I ask who's asking?'

'I am Sergeant Bill Yates from the Northern Territory Police Force. May I come in and ask you a few questions?'

'Do you have some identification?'

I fumbled the police warrant card off my belt and passed it to her. She handed me back my ID after looking over it meticulously, even turning it over in her hand to see if she'd missed anything on the back. I felt unusually vigilant. No one reads police identification in such detail.

'Thank you, Sergeant Yates. How can I help you?' she said as she waved me inside.

I entered and paused to briefly look around. The place was spartanly furnished, neat but tasteful. The only thing on the walls was a poster of a lighthouse flanked by palm trees.

'I see you like my artwork, Sergeant. It is the Galle Fort Lighthouse. It was the last thing I saw when I left Sri Lanka many years ago.'

'Yes,' I said, trying not to sound too interested in the poster, or her, at this stage. So, she was Sri Lankan, not Indian. My guess was pretty close, I suppose. I knew where Sri Lanka was, but where was Galle? 'I'm sorry, I had assumed you were Indian. I didn't appreciate you were Sri Lankan.'

'You're still mistaken Sergeant; I am Australian. I have a certificate to prove it. I doubt that you could say the same. So, are you here to ask me questions about my citizenship? I can tell you the answers regarding Don Bradman's batting average and many of the other silly questions. I've already passed that test.' She smirked and then withdrew the look and resumed her expressionless visage.

'Ms Krishnamurthy,' I started awkwardly, saying it slowly to make sure I pronounced it correctly.

'Sergeant, please call me Kamahli,' she interrupted. 'You know, like the Australian singer, but with an 'e' sound at the end. Everyone calls me Kamahli.'

'Thank you. Kamahli, are you aware there has been some trouble at the docks?'

'Of course, Sergeant. I've heard the news. The workers have been striking again and all the cargo has been delayed. I understand this happens quite regularly. A former business colleague of mine has been waiting on a shipment of furniture that has been caught up in this action.'

'I wasn't referring to the strike. That business seems to have been sorted out, at least for now. However, there have been some other, more serious matters down at the port. Are you aware of these?'

'I'm not sure what you are referring to, Sergeant. I presume you will enlighten me?'

Kamahli looked straight into my eyes; she was either ignorant of the situation at the port or she was a very practised liar. 'Ms Krishnamurthy, sorry, I mean, Ms Kamahli...'

'Just Kamahli,' she interrupted.

'I'm sorry, Kamahli, it appears people have been shipped to Darwin inside a sea container and many are injured. Are you aware of this?'

Her appearance, which had been so stoic to this point, appeared to momentarily crumple. Her brow furrowed and her shoulders dropped almost imperceptibly, as she sucked in a deep breath. With regained composure, she said, 'I'm so sorry. This is truly terrible news. Are they going to be alright?'

'I am afraid some of the people from the container have passed away and others may yet pass. Several have been taken to Darwin Hospital. Some are in intensive care. Their status is unknown at this stage. Those that have survived are very shaken up, as you can well imagine. They are being processed by Immigration and all of them will be transferred to Immigration Detention as soon as possible.'

I paused to let the information sink in. I believed she wasn't fully aware of the situation, but I didn't know how deeply she might be involved. She moved to the small couch, sat, and gestured for me to do the same on the matching armchair. I sat and took a small notebook and pen from my shirt pocket.

'The container used in this incident contained some furniture and was addressed to your former business partner, Mr Roland Redman. We believe the people in the container are, or were, illegal immigrants.'

'I'm sure Roland had nothing to do with any of this. Are you here to accuse me of involvement in this tragic business, Sergeant? I presume you know that I, myself, was once a refugee? Nowadays, as I have said, I am a legitimate Australian citizen. Of course, Roland and I were once very close. He gave me a job in his café when I needed to find work. He was very good to me.' She glanced at my notebook. 'Should I be getting a lawyer?'

'Kamahli, there is no need for a lawyer. I haven't accused you of anything. I'm just trying to assemble the facts. Can you tell me about your dealings with Mr Redman?'

'As I said, I worked for Roland for a time. When Roland bought the café, he sent all of the former owner's staff on leave while he refurbished it. When the refresh was done, he kept all of them on, and he employed me too. He knew that I had arrived in Australia as a refugee. Though I already had my immigration details in process by that stage, having a steady job obviously helped the process. I started washing up in the café, but progressed to waiting tables and then to managing front-of-house under Roland's guidance. Roland and I became very close at one stage.'

'Do you mean you and Mr Redman were in a relationship?

'Yes. I suppose that's what you'd call it. Roland and I were briefly lovers. Roland was very good to me over several years, so we grew close, and were together in the way that you are asking for a short time. I love Roland, and I am sure Roland loved me at that time too, but he wasn't about to be pinned down by me, or anyone else. I think he had been hurt in the past, and I know he has had other relationships since then too. It was on my suggestion that Roland entered the furniture business. I understand he had come into some money down south and was interested in establishing a few new businesses in Darwin. I guess he wanted to make a statement about arriving in Darwin and making a contribution to things around here. He loaned me the money to start the furniture import business on the provision he was a full partner and shared the profits. I paid back my share and then Roland convinced me to sell him my half, at a small profit.'

'I am aware you and he were in the furniture importation business together. Are you and Mr Redman still involved in any businesses together?'

'That was it really. I suppose I had outgrown working for him at the café, and there seemed to be money to be made importing furniture from Indonesia, through Jakarta. Australians love Bali. I figured the more they could make their house look and feel like Bali, the more they'd feel like they were still on holiday when they got home. I made good money with Roland in the furniture business. It started to drop off, so I took him up on his offer when Roland offered to buy me out. Now I have a little soft furnishing store just off the Mall. I do alright, and Roland is still one of my main suppliers. I buy a few small pieces from his furniture import business. I believe Roland has several interests involving the local Indigenous people. Paintings, carvings and some beautiful woven baskets too. Roland is a good guy, Sergeant. Do you know he started a program in Indigenous literacy? He has some arrangement with the proprietor of a bookshop in The Mall. He strongly believes that education and respect for where you've come from, provides a way forward for most people. He also has a partnership centred on Indigenous food. I understand that in each of his businesses he takes on partners, initially at least. He expects people to stand on their own feet. Sometimes he buys them out. I was a partner in the furniture business, but I am not privy to all of his enterprises. He may have other businesses that I am not aware of too.'

I thought she was laying it on just a bit thick. She made it sound like Redman was a saint. 'Do you know where Mr Redman might be at the moment?'

'I can tell you his address, if that's what you're asking me, but I expect you already know that.'

'Yes, that's correct. I have been to Mr Redman's apartment and he is not there. I hope you're not offended by me saying that his address seems more upmarket than yours, considering you were both partners in the same business.'

Kamahli stiffened and then seemed to make an effort to relax, as if she didn't want to appear ruffled. 'As I say, Roland had made money in businesses down south. He and I have very different backgrounds and obligations. Just because we were once partners in a business, it doesn't mean we share everything. I like living here. I'm sure Roland likes where he lives too.'

'So, do you know where I might find Mr Redman or where he might be?'

'I'm sorry, Sergeant. I was once Roland's business partner. I was never his keeper. I have no idea where you might find him. Have you asked at the café?'

'Kamahli, my investigation into this situation has just begun. The Federal Police will be involved pretty soon too. It would be to everyone's advantage if Mr Redman came to the station and made a statement before the Federal Police are involved.'

'If I see him or hear from him, I'll pass on your message, Sergeant.'

'Kamahli. Let me be clear. This isn't a game; if Mr Redman contacts you, you need to let me know. There are dead people on the docks, many dead people. We need to sort this out.'

'Of course, if I hear from him, I'll let you know. Will that be all?' She made a point of looking towards the door.

I knew that I had exhausted my welcome, but I pushed on regardless. 'Thank you for your time, Kamahli. I am sorry to have to ask this of you, but please let me know if you intend to leave town. I may need to speak to you again. I'd certainly like to speak to you after I've spoken to Mr Redman and I may also need your help as a translator if some people on the docks turn out to be Sri Lankan.' I wasn't sure if Kamahli assisting me was a good idea, or even legal if she was involved, but I wanted her to know that some of these poor people may have had a similar history to her own. If it turned out that there were Sri Lankans among the survivors, I'm sure a Sri Lankan translator would be needed. In Darwin, they would be thin on the ground and I wondered, too, if seeing them would make her more helpful about other matters.

'Of course, Sergeant. I'd be happy to assist you in any way I can,' she said, in a tone that conveyed exactly the opposite.

6

Yates

With Redman unable to be located, at least for now, I focused on getting details from the refugees. Immigration had done its job. By the following day, a number of the survivors had been processed by the Royal Darwin Hospital. Those that had survived their ordeal, with physical scars that could heal, were quickly sent onto Immigration Detention, ironically near the airport. Those that didn't survive were also processed. Eleven were taken directly to the State morgue, filling it to capacity, with the locals that were already there. The rest, thirteen, including the children, were unceremoniously tagged, bagged and bundled into a refrigerated shipping container on the wharf. An undignified end to their journey, but none of them were about to complain.

I wasn't optimistic about getting valuable information out of any of the survivors. They were unlikely to tell me anything, even if they knew. From what I'd seen in the media of other asylum seekers, I knew they'd be fearful of being sent back if they spoke out. Given what they must have fled from, they were unlikely to talk to anyone in authority. Even those who were already in Immigration Detention, waiting for their fate to be determined by some Canberra bureaucrat three thousand kilometres away, become so frustrated that they sewed their lips together. The new arrivals from the container might be just as reluctant to speak.

I drove to Immigration Detention and passed through security. The recent arrivals were held in separate units within the same block. They were effectively in solitary confinement. This was the official protocol to ensure 'contagion containment'. It was apparent that it was also more a way to exert authority with the 'new inmates', to prevent corroboration before questioning. I had called ahead and requested a brief conversation with one of the healthier looking male refugees. Immigration told me none of the refugees were saying much. Those on the way to the morgue, or in the less dignified temporary cold storage on the wharf, were saying even less.

When I arrived, they escorted me to an austere visiting room. The facility wasn't a prison by name, but it looked, felt and functioned like one. There were four small stainless steel tables and chairs in the room, each separated from the other by an unnatural distance. The table and chairs were each bolted to the floor. Waiting for me at one table was a wiry man with a thick black beard. He had been cleaned up and was now wearing ill-fitting grey overalls. A security guard hovered, a long black truncheon hung from his belt and a canister of tear gas, prominent in bright yellow, was attached to his chest by a Velcro strap. I glanced at the security guard's name badge.

'Thank you, Nathan, I'd like to have a brief chat with this gentleman if you don't mind.'

'Not sure if you'll get much sense out of this one. You know I can't leave the room, Sergeant.'

'I understand, but if you could give us a bit of space, please,' I appealed to the security guard. I wasn't confident he was used to following instructions in an automated fashion.

'I'll be over here. Let me know when you're done.' He stared at the new inmate and said, 'Don't you be any trouble, mate, or you'll regret it.' I'm sure the comment to the inmate was more for my benefit. The refugee gave no indication he had understood a word of the discourse between guard and me.

I sat down in front of the inmate and tried to pull in the chair before remembering that it was bolted to the floor. 'I am Sergeant Bill Yates of the Northern Territory Police Force. I need to ask you a couple of questions.'

'*Nan ankilam pecamatten.*' The inmate shook his head in the universal sign for no. I later found that he was speaking Tamil. Even at that time I could have guessed the intent of what he'd said even if the language was foreign to me.

I pressed on. 'I understand you have been through a great deal. I am very sorry that several of your fellow travellers have not survived. We must bring the people who put you through this to justice.'

'*Nan ankilam pecamatten,*' he repeated.

'I am surprised you don't speak any English. You look like an intelligent man. My name is Bill,' I said, tapping my hand to my chest. 'Bill.' I then pointed to him.

'*En peyar Murugan. Murugan.*' He tapped on his chest 'Murugan.'

'Your name is Murugan?' I asked, pointing at him.

'*En peyar Murugan,*' he repeated, pointing at his chest. Then he pointed at me and awkwardly said, 'Bill.'

'Okay, Murugan, let's talk about how you got here.'

'*Nan ankilam pecamatten.*'

Back to that again. It was reminiscent of a World War Two prisoner of war movie; name, rank and serial number, except with even less information. I wasn't making any progress. I could try the same with another of the refugees, but I expect the chances would be that I'd get the same result. It would be months before any useful information would come from this lot with this tactic, and I didn't have months. I needed to make some headway. I had forty-eight hours before the Federal Police arrived. I couldn't believe that none of these people spoke English.

I rose from the chair and waved at the security guard to come over. As he approached, I turned my back on Murugan, winked at the guard, and then sat back down, staring directly at Murugan. The guard hovered at my shoulder.

'Well, Nathan, Mr Murugan is unable to help me with my questions. Perhaps we need to take him for waterboarding,' I lied. It was a cruel thing to do, but the look on Murugan's face left no doubt that he knew exactly what I was saying.

'It would be my pleasure, Sergeant Yates.'

It sounded like Nathan would have enjoyed it too.

'Murugan, it is clear to me you understand more than you are letting on. There is no waterboarding here. It was an unkind lie to establish that you understood English. You have indicated that my little ruse worked. Can we resume our discussion in English?'

Murugan swallowed and the fear drained from his face.

'*Nan ankilam pecamatten*.'

'Okay. We'll be speaking to you again soon, Murugan. That will be all, Nathan. Please take Mr Murugan back to his cell.'

7

Yates

I'd never claim to be a zoologist or a student of human behaviour. I'm just a flat-footed copper, a law enforcement officer who has made it to sergeant after a rocky start. If I were a zoologist, a psychologist or an anthropologist, perhaps I'd have understood. But it has always seemed to me that nature is unnecessarily cruel. Maybe cruel is a way of looking at it that is too emotional. Perhaps nature is just indifferent, nature just couldn't give a shit. Who lives, who dies. Nature doesn't care. The strong survive. The weak perish, or more often than not, the weak become a meal for the strong.

Why is it necessary for one individual to show that it is stronger than another of its own kind? Hyenas eat the weakest pup in the litter. Bears leave their weaker cub to die. Even chickens, those fluffy ultra-domesticated animals, determine which is the weakest in the flock and incessantly peck at it until it dies. Then they start on the next weakest, and so on. The sanguine pattern repeats on an endless loop.

It isn't always the youngest or weakest member of the group; the oldest, the injured, the malformed, the orphaned, or physically different, are all hounded to death. In nature, there is no room for emotion, only cold-hearted indifference. The nature of evolution demands that the superior leaves the inferior in Darwin's wake.

Only the fittest survive. This enables the species to evolve, to become stronger, fitter, more perfectly adapted to the environment in which they live. Of course, hyenas, bears and chickens aren't unique in their relentless evolution. Every species evolves. If a species doesn't evolve quickly enough, it is pushed to extinction. It is rarely pretty and more often than not, it is cruel. It is especially cruel amongst the animals that claim to be the most evolved, those that have an inherently violent disposition to others, especially their own kind – humans. As well as picking on the young, the old, or the weak, humans add many other layers on which to base their cruelty—religion, colour, income, politics, gender, race and more.

I wonder if Darwin's theory of evolution would ever result in our species becoming more mindful, caring, or tolerant of differences? To date, there has been no evidence that any animal, especially humans, could evolve to something that extends beyond primal competitive survival.

8

Kamahli

The ceiling fan in the police station was spinning at full speed, a feeble token against the heat. The best that the fan could do was mix the body odour and ego that permeated the open plan office. Sitting directly under the wash provided no respite. If the proverbial shit were to hit this fan, its blades would struggle to cast a splatter to the nearest wall. The fan's centre described a drunken orbit, wobbling like a tyre just before it takes off on a journey independent of the vehicle. Each blade had a cadence of its own; four scythes ready to maim anyone unlucky enough to be in their path when they inevitably took flight. At any speed, the fan was an injury waiting to happen. At high speed, it was dangerous.

I must be getting soft. Down south, it wasn't until the mercury pushed towards forty degrees that it started to feel uncomfortable. In Darwin, it was five degrees cooler and yet it was unbearable. Humidity was the killer. It was over eighty-five percent and had been for a month. Everyone in the city had just had a gut full of it.

Humidity is the enemy that defies the body's evaporative cooling system. The body senses heat and pumps out sweat to evaporate and cool the body. When the air has reached saturation point, sweat can't evaporate. But the sweat keeps on flowing as the body tries to cool itself, pumping out more and more sweat. As quickly as fluids can be replaced, they are futilely expelled. Everybody becomes lethargic and irritable.

The incessant squeal of the fan was mocking me. The boss's office had a little refrigerative air conditioner that rattled away in his window. Its cooling effect wasn't a slave to evaporation. The little unit shuddered to a halt, paused for a minute and wheezed back into action at the direction of the thermostat. It was cutting in and out every quarter-hour like clockwork, with regularity that was laughing at me. You'd think the least the boss could do was open his door and share some cool air with the rest of us, but the selfish bastard kept it all to himself. He sat in there doing next to nothing other than sucking in sweet, cool, dry air. I'd had enough. I heard the unit kick in again so I knocked on the door and pushed it open without waiting for a response.

'Close that bloody door.' I stepped in and deliberately only half closed the door behind me and took a pace to the left to ensure that I took full advantage of the plume of cool air as it swirled turbulently past the bulk of the boss as he sat in his chair.

'What is it Yates?'

'Sorry to bother you, Sir, I thought you'd like to know I'm going back to have a chat with that Kamahli woman.'

'I thought you were going to wait until that Paul guy arrives on Sunday.'

'Yes, I know, Sir, but I've been looking into her background a bit, and I think there might be more to her story.'

'Let me know when you've got something to go on. Just get on with it and close that bloody door behind you as you leave.'

I didn't need to tell him where I was off to. I reckon he was too dumb to know I was intentionally bothering him just to steal some of his cool air before I ventured into the heat again.

I couldn't help but believe that it wasn't just a coincidence that we had dead refugees arriving in a sea container and that Kamahli had been a refugee herself. Sure, she and Roland Redman appeared to have parted ways as business, and perhaps other, partners some time ago, but I sensed she had more she could tell me about this situation.

I returned to her apartment and knocked on the door.

'Hello sergeant, I've been expecting you.'

'Really, why?'

'You seem like a competent investigator. I'm sure you've had an opportunity to look into my background. I figured you'd have more questions for me. Please come in. Can I assume this is a more official visit than that previously?'

She ushered me into the same sparse room where I had spoken to her the other day.

'Kamahli. You are correct in assuming that I have looked into you and Mr Redman more closely. I would really like to speak with Mr Redman, but we do not seem able to locate him at the moment. I don't suppose you've heard from him since we last spoke?'

'Sergeant, I said that I'd call you if I heard from him. As I haven't called you, you are correct in assuming that I have not heard from him.'

The conversation progressed in a very business-like manner, but I could sense that we were getting somewhere. Kamahli was cooperative with details related to recent times in Darwin—getting her to open up about her life before that was more difficult. From the records at the station, cross-referenced with Immigration, I knew the standard details. Ms Kamahli Krishnamurthy, Sri Lankan born Tamil, Jaffna, 4 February 1967 were the details that would have appeared on her passport—if she had one. The official records showed she had arrived as an illegal immigrant. She was later granted political asylum in times that appeared less cruel than those that exist today.

Clearly, the events in her past had been traumatic. She had experienced the cruelty that was applied on a national scale. She had lived the realities of that cruelty and seen it inflicted on her own family. She had seen prejudice that wasn't just evil but endemic and written into law. At first, she didn't disclose much of her past. I could only imagine she had endured more than she wished to remember, but the ordeal had given her an unshakeable will to survive at all costs.

I wanted to understand Kamahli's former life and the Sri Lanka that she had left. Why had she come to Darwin? How had she and Roland Redman come to be in business together, and why were their lives so intertwined? Eventually, Kamahli acquiesced to my questioning. Once she opened up, it seemed she was eager to unburden her story.

* * *

Sri Lanka is a small island nation, with a size less than Tasmania, but with a population similar to Australia. It is a country with a population density made even denser by the sparsely populated, mountainous region in the centre. Most Sri Lankans are Sinhalese Buddhists, with an ethnic minority of Hindus of Tamil origin concentrated towards the north. Historically the Tamils were migrants from the south of the Indian subcontinent. There had been racial and religious tensions between the two groups for generations. These tensions erupted in 1956 when the Sri Lankan government passed the 'Sinhala Only Act'. This decreed Sinhala to be the only official language permitted in Sri Lanka. This was a cruel blow to the minority Tamil-speaking Sri Lankans. It was like Australia's White Australia Policy, directed not towards foreigners, but towards its own people. A government gone mad.

The Sri Lankan legislation was dressed up as legitimate, nationalist pride. It meant that only those fluent in Sinhala could be employed in the public service. It also meant that Tamil speakers were relegated to menial jobs only. The discrimination quickly spread to Tamils in other avenues of life too. It was sophisticated and systematic ethnic cleansing. It was evidence of that process whereby a stronger group picks off a weaker group. It was government induced evolution, that sparked a revolution and a Civil War. On a national scale, it impacted more than a million people. At least three hundred thousand Tamils were deported to India during the war. Life for the remaining seven hundred thousand Sri Lankan Tamils became increasingly difficult.

Things became progressively worse. In the late 1960s, there was a call to action amongst the Tamils—they'd had enough. A breakaway Tamil state was proposed in the north. It was financially supported by wealthy Tamils from around the globe. A dark side effect of this largely peaceful, political discussion was the formation of the Tamil Tigers. In 1981, the Jaffna library in the north of Sri Lanka was burnt to the ground. It was commonly believed the Sinhala-dominated Jaffna police assisted the politically motivated arsonists with their crime. The fire destroyed nearly one-hundred thousand books, including historical texts that had been hand-written centuries earlier.

The burning of books has been a symbol of impending doom throughout history. The burning of books by the Nazis in Opera Square in Berlin in 1933 heralded the start of World War Two. A hundred years earlier, German poet Heinrich Heine warned that 'wherever books are burned, human beings are destined to be burned too'. Heine's words proved to be prophetic in Europe, and in also Sri Lanka, years later.

The Tamils were not passive victims of this genocide. The Tamil Tigers carried out violent guerrilla reprisals throughout the country. With a heavy police presence and barricades, roadblocks and bollards everywhere, even the capital, Colombo, was not safe. Once the wrath of the Tigers had been unleased, they refused to be pacified. By 1983, it was universally recognised that Sri Lanka was in the grip of a full-blown civil war.

Kamahli was fourteen when the library was torched. She loved books. Her father loved books too. He had considered himself 'a man of letters'. He loved the spoken word, and words on the page. As a journalist he was fluent in both Tamil and English. He also had passable Sinhala. As early as she could recall, Kamahli's father took her to the public library and read to her every Saturday morning. As a young girl she particularly liked books by Enid Blyton. Several of the Blyton books had been printed in Chennai and were translated into Tamil to assist Indian children with their lessons. Kamahli loved imagining going on adventures with *Noddy and Big Ears* and travelling on *The Wishing Chair*. By the age of ten she had taught herself English, so she could read her beloved author's books in their original language without waiting for the Tamil translations. As Kamahli grew, she shared adventures to magical and exotic places with the *Famous Five* and *The Secret Seven* and later romances with Jane Austin and the Bronte sisters. Soon her English was more grammatically correct than most native English speakers. Her accent was more Cambridge than Colombo.

Kamahli's father had cried when he told her about the burning of the Jaffna library. She had never seen her father cry before. As he told her and the tears ran down his cheeks, she cried too. She cried for her father and for the books. She cried for her mother as she tried to console them both and she cried for her country, because she knew that from this moment, her life would never be the same.

The next day, her father called her into his office. 'Kamahli, you know that your mother and I love you very much, don't you?'

'Of course, *Appa*.' She stood in silent compliance, unsure what would come next.

'You know things are tough here now for Tamils. However, as tough as you think it is now, it is going to get tougher.' Her father told her sternly. 'We have to leave here.'

'How, *Appa*?'

'I don't know how yet. But I know we can't stay here.'

9

Kamahli

Kamahli's family packed everything they owned and moved south by the end of the next month. The years her father had so tirelessly worked, amounted to one small truckload of possessions. The truck delivered the possessions and the family to the train that travelled southwards. The route was eight hours to Colombo and then two to Galle. It was a long trip, and Kamahli finally fell into a fitful sleep only to be woken when the white noise of the tracks switched to silence as the train stopped at Colombo. A hiss as the air brakes were applied made her sit upright.

'*Appa*, where are we?' Kamahli mumbled, rubbing her eyes.

'We have reached Colombo Fort Station. We need to change trains here, and then it won't be much longer.'

'What time is it? I'm hungry.'

'It is five thirty. Come, let us find some breakfast.'

They gathered the bags that they had taken with them on the train and disembarked to the chaos of the station. So many people. Everyone rushed to somewhere.

Colombo Fort Rail Station was built when Sri Lanka was still British Colonial Ceylon and the trains had run on steam not diesel. Today more than two-hundred thousand passengers pass through every day.

The trio made their way hesitantly through the crowd, through the diesel haze. Kamahli's father left her and her mother with his bag near an empty baggage trolley, much to Kamahli's concern. However, he quickly returned with a package wrapped in brown paper and three plastic cups of tea swinging precariously in a plastic sling, just as two porters came and collected the empty trolley.

'Here, drink, we can eat on the next train. We don't have much time.'

Kamahli took the milky sweet tea, clasping her hands around the plastic cup to warm them. 'Thank you, *Appa*. Did you get us breakfast too?'

'I bought samosas. We need to make sure we do not miss our Galle train. Drink, we must find the platform.'

They found the platform. The train was less crowded than their previous and they found their seats easily. In minutes they were headed south out of the bustling city, against the direction of most commuters pouring into Colombo to work.

I couldn't understand why Kamahli remembered the details of her flight from Jaffna with such clarity when she had obviously worked so hard to block out so many other memories. Perhaps it was the last time her life resembled something normal. Maybe they were the last memories she had before her life took such a momentous turn for the worse. She fascinated me.

The train hugged the coast as it headed south, often passing within metres of the waters of the sparkling Indian Ocean. At other times, it was if the train was passing through people's yards, colourful saris were strung in long lines to dry on the wind made by the passing train.

The train grunted to a halt, signalling that it had reached its final destination, Galle, their new adopted home.

Galle was not typical of much of Sri Lanka. The city was a fourteenth century Portuguese colonial outpost, before becoming overrun by the Dutch. For centuries it had been a city that defied its Sri Lankan location. Hundreds of years after the colonial invaders left, the architecture remained essentially unchanged. Centuries of once, brightly coloured paint on the buildings, paint that today had been re-coated so many times that it sloughed off in broad patches, helped along by salt air and tropical humidity. The buildings had been repainted so many times that the older ones were probably held together more by the paint than the crumbling mortar below.

Kamahli felt as if she was a foreigner in her own country. Her mother and father were the only people she knew in this strange place.

Galle was a city contained within sturdy ramparts. High walls had been built on both the sea and land sides. They were originally intended to defend against aggressors coming across the sea. Then later they were added to, so as to prevent Sri Lankans from attacking the colonialists. These days the walls served to corral the tourists.

Today, the Sri Lanka contained within Galle's rampart walls is quaint. The colonial past is maintained to amuse visitors, nostalgic for a past long gone. Tourists feel more comfortable among the shops selling 'authentic' souvenirs, that are more likely to be made in the sweatshops of China than Galle, and eating in Galle's restaurants that produce food with fewer chillies to appease Western palates. Tourists can easily fool themselves into believing they are still in the time of the Raj. They can sip G&Ts on wide verandas, served by constantly kowtowing locals in colonial uniforms complete with humidity defying starched collars.

Few tourists venture outside the ramparts, other than the cricket tragics who come to see their teams compete with Sri Lanka at the famous Galle International Cricket Club ground, just outside the old fort. Even these tourists scamper back behind the ramparts as soon as the day's play finishes. Many sit under temporary shelters built directly on top of the ramparts, conveniently looking directly down on the cricket ground. The ramparts offer good views, and enterprising locals can make a good business from hiring deck chairs, umbrellas (of both the sun and rain variety) to the pink-faced tourists. Young children serve as drink waiters, running up and down the walls ferrying an endless supply of beer and soft drink. The local beer, Lion Lager, is very good. Yet many tourists pay considerably more for beers with labels they recognise, ignorant that Carlsberg, Tiger and even Guinness, are all made locally in the same factory as the local brew, Lion.

Outside the ramparts, Galle reverts to Sri Lanka—busy, frenetic and colourful. A distinctive fragrance that only the subcontinent seemed capable of producing, a mix of coconut, jasmine and human sweat, amplified by the unrelenting humidity. Galle adds its own twist to the subcontinent's trademark fragrance: fish. Galle is an active fishing port. Local fishermen sell their morning's catch along the main street outside the Sun Gate between Old Matara Road and the port. The variety of the catch is astonishing. Tuna that would not look out of place in the best Tokyo sushi restaurant, flying fish, barracuda, leather jackets, cuttlefish, squid, all kinds of snapper, trevally and transparent little fish that look too fragile to eat. The more expensive fish receive a token of ice scattered over them; however, most of the seafood is displayed on trestle tables under the shade of a rudimentary canvas awning. If you don't get there early in the day, the fish will have started to turn in the heat, providing an incentive to shop early that obfuscates the need for refrigerants. It also made it easy for a discerning shopper to determine what might have been caught yesterday. Any catch that didn't sell was on-sold to the fish driers, who would gut and scale the day-old fish and dry them on vast hessian mats spread on the sand along the beach. The dried versions of the fish were then sold in their own section of the market.

Also on display, deliberately intended to produce a sensory overload, every conceivable spice with which to cook or preserve the seafood was on offer. Conical piles of ground spices were mounded into wicker baskets. Sticks of cinnamon, cloves and nutmeg overflowed from hessian sacks. Chillies of all sizes and colours, both whole and ground, cumin, cardamom, fenugreek, mustard seeds and turmeric. Peppercorns of black, white, green and pink and each of their ground equivalents contributed to the kaleidoscope of colours. The tumbling spices of red, orange, pink, green, brown and bright yellow, contributed patches to the tapestry. In front of each spice stall was a merchant eager to make a sale.

Kamahli came to tolerate Galle. She laughed at the philosophical tuk-tuk drivers who emblazoned their little three wheeled vehicles with a profusion of lights, chrome and quotes from their chosen philosophers. Words of wisdom from Seneca, Gandhi and Bob Marley were scrawled across the rear of their little cabs, trying to convince potential passengers that the drivers were men of thought, not the crazy, reckless drivers that they were more likely to be. To Kamahli, Galle never felt like her original home. Though the family were never as comfortable as they had been in Jaffna, the family began to settle gain. Unfortunately, the peace didn't last.

Kamahli's father found that work was almost impossible to get in Galle. Prospective employers were suspicious of anyone coming from the war torn north. After weeks that drifted into months, he felt blessed when a friend of a friend offered him a job. It was a low paying role writing articles for a small Galle newspaper, *The Kesari Express*. It was a job far below what he had left behind in Jaffna, but he was grateful to be providing for his wife and child. Had he known the fate of so many fellow journalists in those days, he would have tried his hand at another profession.

* * *

Why do cliché, American films always have abductors driving sinister, shiny black vans with blacked-out windows? The van that took Kamahli's father wasn't shiny or black. It was a white mini-van, underpowered from new, and now clapped-out and so gutless that any significant incline would be too much for it. It was dirty enough to suggest it hadn't been serviced or washed since it was dropped on the dock in Colombo. In Australia, you might have guessed it belonged to a lazy tradie, perhaps a bum-crack-flashing plumber that only the desperate would employ. But the van didn't have any tradie signs on the side advertising the usual nonsense like 'free quote, quality guaranteed, friendly service,' as might be expected of a tradesman advertising his wares. In fact, it didn't stick out in any way, and that was the intention. In Galle, the van was bland enough not to attract too much suspicion amongst so many other vehicles on the road. If anyone did notice they deliberately forgot it as soon as they saw what was going down.

Later, Kamahli described the two men in the front of the van to her mother, and later to the authorities who barely covered their disinterest. The thugs had tried to look tough in open-necked shirts and mirrored sunglasses. One chewed on a match, the red end bobbing around like the baton of some hysterical conductor. Kamahli and her father had been waiting at the bus stop on Negombo Road, just outside of the old city walls, when the white van slowed down next to them. The whole incident took less than a full minute but it seemed to last forever, as if her memories of the event had stretched time and pushed everything into slow motion.

The side door slid open before the van came to an abrupt stop in front of them, as two men jumped from the van. Kamahli's father tugged at her hand as he turned to flee. Before he could get his second stride away, the bigger of the two thugs grabbed him, while the other slipped a black hood over his head from behind. The efficiency of the operation suggested they had done this job many times before. Her father uselessly flayed at his abductors, but he didn't stand a chance because he couldn't see where to hit. He wouldn't have had a chance even without the hood. He was a journalist, a man of letters, not a fighter.

Kamahli tried to scream but couldn't suck enough air into her lungs. She lunged at the closest thug, and he flicked her away, as if she was a bothersome insect that had dared to land on his leg. She fell in an untidy heap at his feet before she scrambled to regain some dignity and prepared to relaunch herself at him. Before she could do this, the van door slammed shut, the driver crunched the gears, the van lurched and the van was gone, disappearing into the chaotic traffic.

That was when Kamahli screamed. She screamed in Sinhala. She screamed in Tamil and she screamed in English, but it was too late. She screamed until she could scream no more. Then she collapsed as she realised what had occurred. She collapsed metres from where the van had been just moments before. She curled on the ground, whimpering. The tears then filling her eyes made seeing anything around her impossible. Time was suspended. She had become invisible to those around her. People on the once busy street had dispersed as soon as the van screeched to a halt. No one ever admitted seeing what happened. It was if the whole incident had occurred within a parallel dimension. People admitted to seeing them waiting at the bus stop and Kamahli wailing, but nothing in between. No one admitted to seeing the white van. People were afraid of being subjected to the same terror that they had witnessed, if they admitted to witnessing the abduction. Many had genuinely erased the incident from their memories. It was safer to convince themselves the abduction never happened, than to admit the truth and find themselves the next victim.

The next time Kamahli opened her eyes, she was in her bedroom with her mother in a chair beside her. Her mother held her hand as she rocked back and forth, softly muttering her husband's name over and over. As soon as her mother saw that her eyes open, she stopped and composed herself. She stroked her forehead and caressed her cheek as if she was five, not a young woman on her journey to adulthood. Her mother told her that a tuk-tuk driver they knew from the market had seen her on the road and brought her home.

They had lost the family's patriarch, had no means of income and little hope. In those times so many journalists, politicians and teachers disappeared. It wasn't just the Tamils, anyone who expressed thoughts that didn't align with the government were at risk. If recent incidents were anything to go by, Kamahli's father would never be seen again. Her mother refused to acknowledge this, but Kamahli knew in her heart he wasn't coming back. Their hearts had been pierced the day her father was taken, inflicting an injury that would never heal. The months following this time were horrible. Although the politicians in Sri Lanka and abroad refused to acknowledge it, they lived in a war zone. How would they survive?

10

Kamahli

The light was beginning to dim. Soon it would be dark outside. The transition from dusk to darkness progresses rapidly in the tropics, but I wasn't about to let her stop. Kamahli continued, at times pausing to regain composure and at other times staring into her hands as if seeking strength from an unknown source. At other times in her story, she looked me directly in the eye, daring me to challenge her retelling of the events as if they lacked accuracy, or perhaps taunting me to express platitudes of sympathy. With restraint, I remained impartial. The detail with which she recalled events was incredible. She had an almost photographic eye for some details, yet appeared to have totally erased other events that she must have experienced. Despite Roland Redman being the primary focus of this investigation, I found Kamahli's world, or worlds, intriguing.

* * *

'Wake up, Kamahli. Wake up! We must go at once.'

It took Kamahli's mother a bit of shaking before her words penetrated her daughter's slumber.

'*Amma*, I've just got to sleep.' Kamahli tried to open her eyes, but she didn't want to wake up.

Her mother continued to shake her, more vigorously than at first. 'Kamahli, the time has come. We've got to go. Now!'

Kamahli heard the urgency and fear in her mother's voice, and it frightened her. She was fully awake now and sat upright. '*Amma*, what is it?'

'We need to go. I'll explain on the way. Get dressed. I've packed your bag.'

'Where are we going? Why do we have to leave in the middle of the night?'

'Quiet, darling.'

A more familiar undertone of love and caring had returned to her mother's voice. She was worried about going anywhere at this time of night, but she obediently dressed. Her mother hurried her along as she watched on from the doorway.

'Quickly we must go now. We have to hurry.'

Kamahli wanted to ask what was going on, but her mother's index finger, placed on her lips, left no doubt quiet servitude was required. Kamahli's mother took her hand and led her towards the front door that was already slightly ajar. A sturdy canvas duffle bag stuffed to capacity and a three-tier stainless steel tiffin box sat at the door. Kamahli recognised the tiffin box as her father's. A patina from years of use was usually apparent, but now the box had a high shine. Her mother took the tiffin box and clutched it against her chest, holding it tightly, as if trying to draw upon her husband's strength. She thrust the duffle bag into Kamahli's arms, grabbed her forearm and steered her out of the front door to a waiting taxi.

A man stood silently near the driver's door. The taxi's lights were off, the new moon hadn't yet peeked above the horizon. Kamahli struggled to recognise the driver's face by the starlight, but from what she could discern he looked worried. The driver inhaled heavily on a cigarette and Kamahli could smell the cloves that diluted his tobacco. She wondered if he knew where they were going. As Kamahli and her mother approached the taxi, he inhaled again and withdrew the thin dhurrie from his mouth and threw it to the ground, stubbing it out with his sandalled toe before running to open a door for them. Kamahli's mother pushed her into the open door and followed her in, causing Kamahli to shuffle quickly across the seat. She kept the duffle bag on her lap. Her mother continued to cling to the tiffin box.

'Let's go,' Kamahli's mother said to the driver, sternly but barely above a whisper.

'Yes, madam,' replied the driver in Tamil.

Kamahli was getting annoyed. Why did the driver know where they were going, but her mother refused to tell her? Why was there such a need for a clandestine departure? '*Amma*?' Kamahli looked at her mother with questioning eyes, the question in her voice apparent to her mother.

'You have to leave. Tonight.'

'Where to . . . how . . . where are we going?'

'Not us, just you.'

'*Amma*, please, you're frightening me.'

'Kamahli, your father and I spoke of this. It is not safe here. You've got to get away while it is still possible.'

'Please, *Amma*, I don't understand what you are saying. Of what did you and father speak? What is going on?'

'Kamahli, it is for the best. Your father and I love you.'

Kamahli was saddened that her mother continued to refer to her father as if he was still present, oblivious to his fate. 'We have arranged for your passage to Australia. The war is going to destroy our beloved country. It is particularly unsafe for Tamils.'

Kamahli had so many questions churning in her mind, but she couldn't think how to express them or put them in any order that would seem logical. She struggled to form a sensible sentence. '*Amma* . . . Australia! What are you talking about? We don't know anyone in Australia. I thought we'd come to Galle to get away from the war. The war is a northern thing. I won't go anywhere without you. We are not Tamils; we are Sri Lankans—even *Tatta* was born in Sri Lanka. How will I get there? Why aren't you coming too? You're frightening me.'

Kamahli's mother took her daughter's head and hugged it to her chest. All she could say was *anpe*, dear one, *anpe*, repeating it over and over before her voice croaked, and warm tears rained onto Kamahli's neck.

Kamahli's many questions hung unanswered. She sensed her mother's heart was breaking. She had lost her husband, and now she was sending her only child away. Kamahli lifted her head. Her mother blotted the tears from her eyes and dabbed at Kamahli's neck with the end of her sari. Kamahli peered through the taxi window, out into the darkness, as they moved swiftly along the nearly empty streets. The sign for Wakwella Road came into view as they turned into it. They were headed towards Old Galle. Where was her mother taking her? They approached the International Cricket Stadium, and she could see the darker ramparts of the old town silhouetted against the meagre light of the sky. Instead of continuing into Old Galle, they turned south before the city gates onto Matara Road. They were heading for the port.

They had only progressed down the road a minute when she saw an armed roadblock ahead. Once these had only been seen in the north, now they were common in Colombo and increasingly more frequent in the south. She had heard rumours of Tamil Tiger activity around Galle. It seemed nowhere was beyond the reach of the separatists. The roadblock was immediately before a little bridge that crossed the stream leading to the harbour before the navy precinct. She could see the soldiers slowly rising from their chairs as if they had been woken by the approaching vehicle.

Their state of readiness for action contrasted with the appearance of the vehicle they stood next to. The Unicorn, the Sri Lankan military's armoured 'blast protection vehicle' was its response to the Tamil Tiger's use of roadside explosive devices. The brutal design of the vehicle, topped with twin seven millimetre cannons, diffused many arguments.

The guard's uniforms were the standard starched blue and grey navy camouflage pattern. Crossed muskets replaced the regular navy crest and the white gaiters worn above their black boots indicated they were navy military police. The navy's motto was 'the golden fence around the country'. Leaving Sri Lanka was not going to be easy.

The taxi slowed to a crawl and stopped ten metres in front of the Unicorn. Both military police were fully alert now; their American supplied M16s pointed directly at the driver through the windscreen.

'Amma, let's go home. I'm frightened.'

'Hush, child!' Kamahli's mother said sharply, using English to emphasise her demand. Her mother leaned forward and said something directly into the driver's ear and then roughly pushed him on the shoulder. He nervously exited the vehicle, hands open and level with his shoulders.

As soon as the MPs saw the driver, they seemed to recognise him and relaxed slightly, lowering their weapons, slinging them over their shoulders as they greeted him. The driver shook their hands, taking each of the reluctantly reciprocated hands of the MPs and shaking it vigorously with both hands. The MP on the right offered the driver a cigarette which he took with hands that, even from the distance could be seen to be shaking less noticeably now. A deep draw on the tobacco, undoubtedly more refined than what he had stubbed out only minutes ago, seemed to calm him. The conversation seemed friendly; it was too far away for Kamahli to hear everything, but their body language made it clear that they knew each other. Now that they had identified each other, their behaviour seemed more casual than business-like. Minutes later the driver turned and pointed to the taxi. Kamahli felt her mother tense. One of the MPs walked over to the car, followed by the driver, who continued to talk quickly at the approaching MP's back. As the pair got closer, Kamahli caught snippets of what was being said. In Sinhala the driver pleaded; 'As we discussed. Fair price . . . Just the girl, not the old woman . . . Yes, I know it is dangerous . . . no guarantees . . .'

Kamahli thought she would faint when her mother leapt out of the vehicle. The front MP stepped back and unslung his M16 and pointed it directly at her in a single motion. The other MP joined his partner with his weapon at the ready, followed by the driver, who looked even more worried.

'*Amma!*'

The MPs were closer now and Kamahli could see that even though they had appeared so menacing in the distance, they were boys, barely older than her. The night shift at a roadblock wasn't a glamorous posting and these two youngsters had probably drawn the short straw. Kamahli's mother told the MP to stop trying to act so tough. Kamahli couldn't believe what she was hearing. Her mother barely had the assertiveness to bargain with the sellers at the fish market and now she was staring down the barrel of an M16, with a tired, young, angry MP at the other end.

'Just who do you think you are calling an old woman?' her mother said loudly, in Sinhala with a heavy Tamil accent, staring directly at the end of the rifle. 'Do you speak to your mother in such a way?'

The MP was taken aback. Perhaps he did speak to his mother in such a way, but before he could answer, Kamahli's mother continued.

'I am not asking you for any special favours. All you have to do is look the other way for a few minutes. This girl,' she said, pointing behind her to Kamahli, 'is hardly a threat to national security. Just let her pass. We've agreed on a price already.'

She turned to the driver, who nodded and produced two envelopes from inside his shirt to offer to the MPs. The MPs re-shouldered their weapons and opened the envelopes, taking out a wad of green currency Kamahli later understood to be US dollars. She had no idea of the amount or how her mother had come by it. Unbeknownst to Kamahli at the time, her mother had paid more money to others too.

The first MP's stern face softened a little and then, perhaps not wanting to let go of his tough guy image, became stern again. The driver returned with a large brown paper bag. Kamahli's mother nodded to the driver who took two bottles of Johnnie Walker Black Label out of the bag and gave one to each MP. The MPs nodded, took their cash and their whisky and headed back to their chairs in front of the Unicorn.

'Kamahli, quickly, gather your things.'

Kamahli slung the duffle bag's strap over her shoulder and grasped the tiffin box, almost as tightly as her mother had done. She took her mother's hand, and they walked quickly past the Unicorn, the MPs already passing one of the now opened bottles between them. Kamahli thought they were going over the bridge but just as they were about to step onto it her mother tugged her to a small path near the side and took her down to the water's edge just near the first of the bridge pylons. A small boat, barely big enough for two, was quietly waiting. An ancient-looking fisherman was ready at the single oar at the stern of the craft. Kamahli was too frightened to speak as her mother enveloped her in a hug and kissed her before pushing her towards the little boat.

'Go, child. This is for the best. We will join you as soon as we can. We love you,' Kamahli's mother said, her chin pointing defiantly seaward and continuing to suggest that her father would also be part of their reunited family in Australia.

Kamahli's mother refused to admit her husband wasn't coming back, and now this was likely to be the last time she would see her daughter. Even these years later, as Kamahli told me this story her stoic resolve crumbled and she wept uncontrollably. Some say that parents always love their children more than a child loves their parent—in this case, it was hard to believe that the love wasn't equitably reciprocated.

Kamahli's mother watched her drift away in the tiny boat and scrambled back up the bank. The boatman wasted no time, his sinewy arms working on the broad oar at the rear of the little craft. He muttered something and pointed to the floor, where Kamahli found a battered lifejacket, bleached from its once bright orange, looking the worse for wear. As she put it over her head, she heard the taxi leaving. She pulled the long tapes of the life jacket down around her, but they became tangled in the duffle bag still draped over her shoulder. The lack of moonlight didn't help. She couldn't remember any other night being so dark. Before she could get her bearings and put the life vest on properly, they had bumped alongside a waiting vessel just outside of the exclusion zone encircling the naval facility. The arc produced by the Galle lighthouse was further out, beyond the harbour exit. Arms reached down and grabbed at her and her things. Strong hands gripped her lifejacket and dragged her up and over the side of the vessel and dumped her onto the deck, like a prized fish.

It was as if she had entered another world. There were instantly dozens of similarly life jacket-clad people on the dhow's deck. Looks that expressed fear, excitement and numbness confronted her as she scanned the faces. No one said a thing. Then the motor in the dhow's rear started, noisily revving so no one could hear anything even if they spoke.

Kamahli couldn't believe that less than an hour ago, she had been sleeping in her bed. Her emotions were so confused. She wanted her *Amma*. She wanted her father back and for her family to be whole again. Why hadn't her mother come too? How could she possibly travel all the way to Australia in this vessel? She sat on her duffle bag, held her father's tiffin box, hugged her knees and put her face in her hands while she silently sobbed.

* * *

Kamahli paused, her shoulders slumped 'I'm sorry Sergeant. I don't usually get that emotional. It has been a long time since I have related my story to anyone. As I have told you, I initially worked for Roland in his Café. The rest you now know.'

Try as I might, I couldn't prise any details from her about how she traversed the seas and arrived in Australia. What had happened between leaving Sri Lanka and her life now in Darwin? I couldn't tell if she was afraid of the authorities changing their minds and sending her back, that telling her story would close a loophole for others to exploit as she had done or that it was just so traumatic that she had erased it from her memory.

11

Yates

I was clearly going to get no further with Kamahli, at least for now. I had thought that we might have had a sighting of Redman by now. If he was still driving that oversized ute around town, someone had to have seen him. I arrived at the station, planning to head out to the detention centre to question another refugee before heading out to collect 'Paul' from the airport at four in the afternoon. On arrival, I was told to head out to a traffic fatality. Someone had run off the road on the Stuart Highway just before Humpty Doo. A truckie heading south had called it in. Probably a tired driver fallen asleep at the wheel or some drunk. No trees for miles and the silly bastard runs into a traffic sign. You'd have to be dumb or damn unlucky.

Humpty Doo, half an hour outside of Darwin, is almost a suburb of Darwin these days. I could do what I had to do at this one and still make the flight. As I drove the half-hour out to Humpty Doo I thought about making a little sign with 'Paul' written in big letters. In my civvies, I'd look like I was just some average Joe sent there to pick him up. I also thought about what a lowlife someone would have to be to put desperate people into a container and leave them there. Strike or no strike, being locked in an almost airless, lightless box for days was not easy. Darwin's heat and the delays in getting the container open meant it was never going to end well. Whoever was responsible for this would be made to pay.

As I crested the rise, with five kilometres still to go to where the incident had been reported I saw the smoke. They'd told me the vehicle was on fire, but I thought it would have burnt itself out by now. I kept driving, watching a tendril of black smoke pencil into the sky. As I rounded the sweeping curve of the highway, I slowed. The vehicle was almost totally burnt out, but the rear tyres were smouldering. The burning rubber was responsible for the black smoke. The smoke rose high into the sky, with barely a murmur of breeze to disperse it.

The smell always got to me at these incidents. Despite all the post-trauma counselling I've gone to over the years, it is impossible to erase the memory of a smell from your mind. I could block out the bloody gore of traffic accidents, where the fragility of bodies are transformed to mangled pieces of meat. The job made me immune to the atrocity of domestic violence, where the frustration of poverty and ignorance battles hopelessly against brutality and cruelty. But the smell of human frailty always stays with me.

Just like the smell back on the docks, the odour at the crash scene continues to haunt me. An all-pervading smell of burning rubber, ignited by diesel combined with the stench of charred flesh, resulting in a macabre blend of burnt bacon and overflowing ashtray. It hit me as I stepped out of the door of the car. I rubbed at my nose, knowing it was futile but just wishing the smell would go away. I swallowed hard. I would not allow myself to chunder.

I walked around the scene, snapping off photos, taking it all in. Forensics would want to assess things from every angle. It looked as though the driver had just driven straight on and failed to take the slow bend in the road. He must have been pissed or have fallen asleep at the wheel. I looked back down the road. No tire marks on the bitumen or the gravel shoulder to suggest a last-minute skid to arrest the vehicle. At least the driver would have died quickly. They'd driven directly head-on into the sign that indicated the highway turnoff. The vehicle had taken out one side of the sign post and then continued down the embankment, rolling and ending up on its roof. The fire had taken care of the rest. It would have been merciful if the impact had killed the driver. I couldn't think of anything worse than being conscious, stuck in a wrecked car and being burnt alive. That's when the realisation came to me. The vehicle was a big ute like the one Redman drove. There couldn't be too many like it. I checked out the number plate, set into the rear chrome bumper. It was blackened but still recognisable. It was Redman's vehicle alright. No wonder no one had reported him driving around town. If he was the charred corpse at the wheel, he was not going to be telling me much about what had happened on the docks. The deceased's body hung oddly, fused to the carbonised plastic of the car seat in the overturned vehicle, the hands, or what was left of them were fused to the steering wheel. Startlingly white teeth, contrasting against the blackened face, snarled at me through lips that had all but been scorched away.

There were no bodily features remaining that I could discern. On one wrist, I could see what had once been a nice watch, a gold Rolex, it now had a cracked and burnt face. The other wrist had a chunky gold bracelet. Geez, it was one of those ID bracelets inscribed with a name. I could never fathom it. Was it narcissism that you wore your own name around on wrist, or was it that you were too stupid to remember how to spell it? In this instance it was pretty handy though. I spat on my thumb and rubbed it over the surface of the bracelet to reveal the name. 'Roland' appeared in cursive script. Shit! Mr Redman was not going to be answering any of my questions.

12

Yates

I reported the details of the accident to the station and waited for the Coroner's vehicle to arrive. At that time, I had no idea how 'Paul' would fit into Roland's story, but I had little else think about until I could pass the scene on to the Coroner and the boys from road fatality. There was precious little information to follow at that stage, and although this accident may have very well led to a dead end, I had few other options to follow, other than to go to the airport to meet 'Paul'.

The flight was on time and full. Passengers spilled out of the arrivals gate, some with parcels wrapped in Christmas paper under their arms, others wheeled overstuffed suitcases as they struggled with hand luggage that was obviously heavier than the allowance. The bulk of the people in the terminal were mineworkers, uniformly in high-vis shirts and navy trousers slashed with reflective fabric at the knee, rotating off shifts in mines across the state, the Kimberley, Pilbara and further afield. The mines were unlikely to give workers any time off for Christmas. There was money to be made digging holes in the ground, and in the Territory, money and mining trumps every other religion.

Paul stood out like a priest in a brothel. Even if he didn't walk straight up to the 'Paul' sign I was holding, his suit would have been a giveaway. Why was he wearing a suit? At least he wasn't wearing a tie. Though, given the contrast of his red face and the pale triangle of skin peeking through his unbuttoned collar, he probably had been until recently. I made sure he saw my little sign and said, 'Paul?' as I extended my hand.

'Yes. That's me. Did Roland arrange for you to pick me up?' he replied, shaking my hand and looking over my shoulder towards the luggage cart.

'Not exactly. I'm Sergeant Bill Yates of the Northern Territory Police,' I said flipping open my police ID. 'I'm afraid Mr Redman's whereabouts are currently unknown.' There was nothing to be gained from telling Paul about the death of his friend at this stage. I avoided telling him about that aspect of the investigation. I hoped to uncover information, anything that might have not otherwise come to light.

'Oh no. Is there a problem?'

'I'm afraid there is a problem. We'd like to discuss a few things with Mr Redman. We believe he could assist us with our enquiries. We thought you might be able to help us find him.'

'Bullshit. This one of Roland's jokes isn't it? Are you filming this or something?' He looked around the arrival hall, trying to find where a candid camera might be concealed.

'I am afraid I am deadly serious, Paul. Mr Redman hasn't been seen for a while now. There have been some concerns in the period leading up to Mr Redman's disappearance. Would you mind accompanying me to the station?'

'What do you mean concerns? Concerns about what? Why do I need to come with you? What's going on?' Paul looked as if he had been slapped.

'Mr Redman was helping us with some police enquiries before his disappearance,' I exaggerated. 'All I'm asking is for you to help us with those enquiries. It would be beneficial if you could tell us a little about what you knew about Mr Redman and his business dealings.'

'Roland and I were mates back in high school. I haven't seen him for almost seven years. He offered me a job if I came to Darwin. I am currently between jobs, so I thought his offer sounded good. What enquiries are you referring to? Are you arresting me?'

'Paul, or should I call you Mister ...?' I left the question hanging to allow hit to confirm his surname.

'It's Mister Winter, but call me Paul.'

'Look,' I said, taking a mental note of his full name, Paul Winter, 'I know this must come as a great shock to you, and I appreciate you and Mr Redman have been friends for a long time. I am certainly not arresting you and you are not charged with any offence. But it would be constructive if you could come to the station with me for a brief time just to clear up a few things for us.'

'What if I don't want to come with you?'

'Paul, you're under no obligation to come with me. As I say you aren't under arrest. All I'm asking is for your help with a few things up about Mr Redman. If Mr Redman was around, I'm sure he'd be happy to help.' I continued to stretch the truth. 'At the very least, I can give you a lift into town.'

'Look, mate, I've just flown for nearly four hours from Perth and really would like to just collect my bag and be out of here.'

'I understand. How about we collect your luggage and have a chat on the way into town? I can drop you at your hotel or wherever you like after that.'

'I'm sure I'll have nothing of interest to your enquiries, but I expect I have little choice,' Paul said nervously. 'Let me get my bag. I can see it on the luggage cart.'

We walked over to the cart, and Paul pointed out his small, old brown suitcase, the kind that your grandfather might have used, cardboard tarted up to give the appearance of leather. I thought it was odd that he had no hand luggage. I made a seemingly friendly gesture of getting the case from the carousel and handing it to him, in the process confirming his name on the luggage tag, 'Paul Winter'.

The drive into town was quick, but the conversation was pedestrian. I drove under the speed limit to extend the time a little and to try to connect with Paul somehow. I didn't push Paul for any real information on the short drive to the station. The best I could hope for at this stage was to find a connection. I tried to keep him talking because I didn't want to give him too much opportunity to come up with some story to defend his mate. It was apparent he was still reeling from the news about Roland's disappearance. I convinced him to stop in at the station and then gave him a moment to catch up with the information that must have been spinning through his head.

'So, Mr Winter, sorry, Paul,' I started, confirming that I'd got the name right and trying to put him at ease as we sat down in the interview room. We had signed him in at the front desk as Paul Winter, Perth WA, tourist and left his suitcase with the duty officer.

'Sure. What do I call you?'

'Paul, while we're in the station, or if I'm in uniform, I'd prefer if you'd refer to me as Sergeant Yates. If I'm dressed in my civvies, like now, you can call me Bill. Can we start at the beginning? How do you and Mr Redman know each other?'

'We were mates in school.'

13

Paul

I explained to Paul that I would like him to go back to when he and Roland first met. No detail was insignificant and that even the smallest detail might prove to be useful. It was a tactic that I had successfully used in the past. Try to put the witness at ease, take them back to long before the area of interest, to where the details were obviously unrelated to the current investigation, but in doing so getting them into a better mindset for when the relevant time frame comes to be discussed.

Paul and Roland had met on Paul's first day at St Philip's High School. Paul knew no one and was miles away from home. Roland had two older brothers at the school so he had already traversed the school's corridors many times on school award ceremonies, not that Roland was ever likely to be the recipient of any awards. Paul described the day they first met with a melancholic sigh, reminiscing about a time when things were so much simpler and the outcomes of actions less likely to end in grief. It was amazing that the bond, a result of a chance encounter on the first day of school, had stood the test of time.

Paul was running late on his first day at St Philip's. He hated to be late. Everything seemed so unfamiliar to him. He should have paid more attention on the orientation tour, but there had been so much to take in. By the time he found the class that he was meant to be in, the students had already gone in and the door was closed. He had so wanted to make a good first impression, but now he was going to look foolish. He put his ear to the door and heard a loud voice inside.

'Sit,' the voice on the other side of the door said emphatically.

'Yes, sir,' responded the class in a sing-song followed by the scrapping of chairs.

Paul took a breath and knocked on the door.

'Come!' the voice boomed from within.

Paul slowly pushed open the door and entered the room. Every eye in the class was on him. He felt as if he was about to get blasted.

'Well, boy, what is it?' the teacher asked. He seemed so tall, old and bald. The teacher had such an odd physique. Thin but with a pot belly as if all the fat in his body resided in the region directly above his belt buckle, leaving the rest of his body in an emaciated state.

'I, I, I think I'm in this class,' Paul stammered.

'What class do you think you're in, boy?' The teacher removed his bifocals to get a better look at him.

Paul felt like a rabbit in the headlights now. There were a few snickers from the class. He held his books to his chest with one hand as he dug a piece of crumpled paper out of his pocket with the other. With some relief he read off the timetable he had, 'Year 11 English Literature, Mr 'Ball-sack'.'

The class instantly fell silent.

'What did you say, boy?' The teacher was red in the face and increased the volume of his already booming voice.

'English Literature, Mr Ball-sack.'

'The name is Balzac, with a hard 'z', not an 's'', he boomed. 'Haven't you heard of the great nineteenth century French writer Honoré de Balzac?'

'No, sir. I'm here for the *English* literature,' Paul replied, emphasising the word 'English'. He hadn't meant it to sound like a smart-arse comment, but as it came out of his mouth the class that had previously been silent class erupted into laughter.

The teacher looked as if he was about to explode. He turned to the class and bellowed through yellow teeth, 'Silence! This waste of space seems to be no more cultured than the rest of you cretins.' Balzac walked towards him and came to within a foot of Paul's face, leaning downwards for greater effect. White spit had collected in the corners of his mouth with a glob that was snapping elastically between his lips. 'As you ignorant little morons are incapable of pronouncing my name correctly, you will refer to me as 'sir'. Do you understand? Sit!' He took the last word to a new level of volume and expelled the elastic gob of foaming white spit onto Paul's cheek with the 't'.

'Yes, sir,' Paul said as he wiped the sticky gob with the back of his hand and transferred it to his trousers. He looked around, but all the chairs seemed to be taken, except for one right at the back. Paul started to make his way to the vacant seat at the back of the class.

'No, not there. Here.' Balzac pointed to the already occupied chair in front of him. 'You, boy,' he said to the bespectacled occupant, 'Move. You, (pointing to Paul) sit here. 'You,' pointing at the student who had been ejected from his seat, 'can move up to the back row. There's no need to be the brown-nose in every class.' He pointed at Paul, 'I'm going to be keeping an eye on you boy.'

'Sorry, sir. I didn't mean any offence. I've never heard of Honoré de Balzac. I will look him up and—'

'Enough. I'll let you know when you need to speak. Just sit there.' Balzac screeched.

Paul sat down next to the boy he would later come to know as Roland Redman.

Roland leaned towards Paul and whispered, 'You really made an entrance with that one.'

'What did you say, Mr Redman?' Balzac asked, not happy Redman was weighing into the discussion.

'I was just telling our new classmate that '*a flow of words is a sure sign of duplicity*', Sir.'

'Don't go quoting Balzac to me, Redman. I'm sure there are enough smart alecks in this school without you becoming another one.

That was Paul's first encounter with Roland and the first time he experienced his savant-like ability to pull quotes from books he'd read out of thin air. He had an uncanny ability to remember whole passages of texts, even after only reading it once.

Paul and Roland endured the first English Literature class Mr Balzac provided without further incident. At the end of class, as they headed to geography, Roland made a point of catching up with Paul.

'You really got up old Scrote's nose,' Roland said.

'What? Who?' Paul said, turning to see Roland behind him as he left the class.

'You know, old Balzac, Ball-sack, Scrotum, Scrote,' Roland replied, giving him an abridged derivation of the schoolyard nomenclature that had started at Balzac. 'He really hates it when he gets called Ball-sack. You doing it with the first words you used, in the first class of the first term was gold. I loved it. I'm sure everyone else did too. I'm Roland, Roland Redman. Seems like we're going to see each other now Scrote has put us together under his nose—right in the spit zone.'

'Paul. Paul Winter. Yeah, I know. I made a blunder getting on the wrong side of him first up.'

'He's all piss and wind, really. Just tell him you love literature like I did, and he'll give you an easier time of it. Drop in a Balzac quote and he'll forgive you almost anything. I heard someone got '*humanity is passion; without passion, religion, history, novels, art would be ineffectual*' into an assignment last year and he got one hundred percent. I don't think he even read any of the assignment after the Balzac quote. So, I reckon if you put the odd lit quote into an assignment, he will think you're tolerable.'

'Did that work? Do you really 'love literature'? Is that why you're up the front?'

'I love a good story. I'm thinking about journalism as a career. I've read all the books on the Top One Hundred list at Dymocks. I do love bookshops and could spend whole afternoons in them. But the reason I'm up the front is Christina Brown.'

'Who?' replied Paul

'Christina. You must have noticed her. Don't tell me your nuts didn't tighten the moment you saw her. She's the most beautiful girl the school's ever seen. She's right opposite you on the other side of the aisle. I try to sit where I can see her in every class.' Roland didn't mince his words. It was more like they'd known each other for years, rather than minutes.

'Can't say I've noticed. But I'll keep an eye out for her.'

Paul and Roland were placed together on that first day and then every school day for the next two years. It wasn't just in Balzac's class where they were made to sit together. Teachers had a good network of who was who, and a strategy of putting those they considered potential troublemakers together, so they could keep an eye on both of them at the same time. As a result, Paul and Roland found themselves front and centre in Ms William's geography class too.

Roland didn't particularly mind as long as Christina Brown was in line of sight.

Christina was a fresh-faced girl with skin that glowed like Renaissance marble and shoulder length hair that caught the light and was always swishing at just the right time to highlight her high cheekbones. She even made her school uniform into a fashion statement. The pleated skirt was within a millimetre of what the nuns would permit. Her school blouse, that had probably been purchased when she first started high school was now tight in places where Roland couldn't help but direct his gaze. Roland couldn't unglue his eyes from Christina most of the time that he was in class. When he wasn't in class, all Roland could talk about to Paul (or anyone else who would tolerate his monologue) was how beautiful Christina was. Roland couldn't wait to get to his geography or English literature classes.

Paul was less lucky. Across the aisle from him in geography was Bradley Armstrong, commonly known as 'Arm-pong.' The guy's body odour was legendary. Even from across the aisle it was toxic. It must have been hell for Mary Cocci to sit next to him, but she was too shy to say anything. 'Arm-pong' must have had some medical condition. He really stank. All the time. The odour was all-pervading and sometimes it was all Paul could do to get through the class without gagging.

'Paul, what is the matter with your neck?' asked Ms Williams seeing Paul rubbing the back of his neck in an exaggerated fashion.

'Nothing, Ms Williams, just some whiff-lash,' Paul replied.

'Pray tell me how did you get whiplash, have you been in a car accident or some other tragedy, Mr Winter?' Williams replied, her tone acknowledging she knew a less-than-credible story was about to commence.

'Not whip-lash, Ms, whiff-lash. I just copped a nose full of 'Arm-pong'.'

The class erupted into laughter much to the embarrassment of poor Bradley Armstrong.

'Mr Winter! I can't believe your insensitivity regarding Mr Armstrong,' Ms Williams said and in doing so confirmed she too thought of Bradley Armstrong as 'Arm-pong'. The bell for recess saved any further discussion as Paul and the rest of the students rushed into the fresh air.

* * *

That was how Paul described meeting Roland on his first day of school. From that point on the boys were inseparable, at least for the next few years, anyway.

Despite saying he had little to say once I got Paul talking, he didn't want to stop. I hoped that amongst the many details he would inadvertently reveal something relevant to the case or provide some detail of Roland's background that would prove useful.

Any outside observer might have wondered why Paul and Roland were such good mates. Superficially, neither seemed to be interested in the same things, didn't move in the same circles or indeed have any obvious common ground. But in truth, each secretly wished they were the other. Roland had admired Paul's measured approach to life, his stable family and that he knew how far to push a risk before it became a problem. On the other hand, Paul admired that Roland was more carefree, had the 'gift of the gab', an extensive circle of friends and was always ready to push his luck. Everyone seemed to want to be Roland's mate. Paul even admired that Roland was admired. It wasn't a case of attraction between opposites, but it wasn't far off.

'Look, Sergeant, I've answered a lot of your questions. I could really use a coffee.'

'Yeah, sorry, Paul I should have offered you one before. Instant okay? That's all we've got.'

'Sure, white and none, but before I go on, I want to know why Roland is attracting this level of interest from the police. I'm not sure how any of this could interest you. You've told me bugger all.'

'Yeah, back in a minute.' I left the room and made Paul's government issue coffee. A teaspoon of Pablo chiselled from the tin, into a ceramic mug that had an indelible tarnish of coffee stains from years of careless cleaning. The coffee clumped onto the damp spoon. I sniffed the carton of milk before pouring it into the cup and quickly decided against risking it. The milk smelled decidedly off and had started to look more like cottage cheese. I put it back in the fridge.

I put Paul's coffee in front of him. I know you're supposed to get used to certain things after a while, but try as I might, after all these years, government issue coffee still tasted like it was something that had been brewed in a bedpan.

'I hope you don't mind it black. The milk was smelling a bit risky.' I didn't wait for an answer and proceeded.

'Mr Winter, sorry, Paul, I need to tell you some bad news. I've just been informed by one of my colleagues that there has been a single vehicle incident outside of town and we suspect that the deceased was your friend Mr Redman.'

'What. That's bullshit. First, you're telling me you have no idea where Roland is and now all of a sudden you tell me he's dead. What sort of game are you playing?'

Paul looked genuinely deflated. I'd held off telling him to judge his reaction, but there was nothing in how he responded that indicated anything that I wouldn't expect, when hearing your lifelong friend had passed away. 'I'm very sorry for your loss, Paul. As I've told you, Mr Redman was involved in a single vehicle incident in the early hours of this morning and is believed to be deceased.'

'Yes, but the way you're telling me I suspect there's more to it.'

'We are not really a hundred percent certain what happened at this stage. It would appear Mr Redman went off the road and collided with a sign post. The vehicle then caught alight. The road was fine. It was on a slow bend, but road conditions do not appear to have been a factor. It is uncertain what caused Mr Redman to have the accident. He may have been drinking, fallen asleep, swerved to avoid hitting something on the road, a roo or livestock. We are also investigating the possibility that Mr Redman may have deliberately driven into the post.'

The whites of Paul's eyes dominated his face. 'I'm sure you can tell all of those things these days, but I'll tell you right now, there's no way Roland would top himself.'

'Circumstances are unclear at this time. We have no reason to believe the deceased, Mr Redman, had been drinking, but we estimate the collision on the road leading out of Darwin towards Katherine occurred early this morning. There isn't a lot of traffic on the road at that time and we haven't found any witnesses to what happened. It is possible he may have fallen asleep at the wheel. It would appear though, that Mr Redman was planning a long drive. Had a large quantity of fuel cans in the rear of his vehicle. The resulting fire has made it difficult to determine exactly what went on. Mr Redman was barely identifiable.'

'So, there's still a possibility it might have been someone else?'

'It is definitely Mr Redman's vehicle. His vehicle was quite distinctive. We've checked the plates and the VIN of course. It's his vehicle. We've also recovered some personal effects known to be Mr Redman's such as his watch and jewellery. Did you know he wore a gold bracelet with his name on it?'

'No, as I say we hadn't been in regular contact for some time.'

'I am sorry to say that at this stage there is little doubt the deceased is Mr Redman. Of course, we could send some things to forensics in Perth, but there's not much for them to go on. The fire that followed the crash destroyed almost everything.'

'So, what is this case you're investigating? If my friend's dead, why can't you let him rest?'

'There seems to be more to your Mr Redman than there might first appear. He has several business interests that we are interested in knowing more about. I hoped you might tell us more about Mr Redman.'

'Don't expect me to do your job for you sergeant. You're the copper, I'm not the bloody detective. You're going to have to sort out this one yourself.'

'Don't be a smart arse with me. I can hold you in the cells with the drunks for forty-eight hours while I look into things if you'd prefer. You might want to think about being less sassy.'

'As I've said before, I haven't seen Roland for some time. I didn't even know he was in Darwin until a few weeks ago. Last I'd heard from him he was some bigwig in Sydney. He was making a fortune in insurance.'

'Okay. Let's assume I believe that.'

'Look mate, I mean, Sergeant, there's nothing I'd rather do than pack up and go home now. I've no idea what Roland's been up to. I really don't think there's much I can do to help you with your enquiries.'

'I want you to tell me everything you can about Roland Redman. Tell me about Roland's family.'

'I'm not sure if that will be of any help to you. Are you thinking of writing his life story or something? Maybe you can do the eulogy.'

'Careful. I'm just trying to understand if it is possible that Mr Redman's background can shed some light on the current situation.'

'What is the current situation, Sergeant?'

'The current situation is that we have a fucking shit-fest on the docks.'

'Surely Roland can't be involved with the unions striking.'

'If that was just it, I wouldn't be having this conversation with you. The strike is over. This is far more serious than that.'

'So, what is it then? You want me to tell you what I know about Roland from way back when, but you're telling me next to nothing. What's going on?'

I rubbed my chin as I tried to figure out if telling Winter more was a good idea at this stage. It would be all over the papers tomorrow. I knew the *NT Times* would jump on it.

The *NT Times* is such a satirical paper. It's niche is sensational stories – the more sensational the better. Whenever it couldn't report the news it just made up a sensational headline to grab the reader's attention. Headlines of aliens abducting a Territorian, someone being eaten by a crocodile or some NT politician on the take, occurred regularly in an almost scheduled fashion. Only the politician story was likely to have any semblance of truth to it. Having a real story of national or international interest like the lives lost on the docks would be manna from heaven for the journos at the *NT Times*.

'We are looking into your Mr Redman as a result of an incident on the docks where people have died,' I said, continuing to ration the information.

'You're going to have to do much more than that. You've told me nothing.' Winter wasn't about to continue while it was so obvious that I knew more.

'Okay. This is part of an ongoing investigation and therefore confidential. But I expect you'll probably read about it in the paper soon, anyway.' I took a breath and continued in police-speak. 'It is apparent someone in Darwin has facilitated the arrival of approximately sixty people in a shipping container. Said persons have been in that container for almost a week, no doubt delayed by the strike, and as a result many are deceased. The manifest on the container indicated that it was intended for Mr Redman. We were hoping to speak to Mr Redman so he could assist us with our enquiries. Of course, now that is impossible. So, we are left with talking to you.'

'Other than a name on a manifest, what makes you think Roland has anything to do with this? He told me he was in insurance.'

'As you've said it has been a few years since you and Mr Redman have spoken. I am sure a lot could have transpired since then. I think Mr Redman ceased working directly in the insurance industry several years ago, around the time he came to Darwin. His current business interests, that we have been able to determine include owning a café, patron of Indigenous art, and an importer of Indonesian furniture.'

'Are you sure you've got the same guy? A patron of Indigenous art? Doesn't sound like the Roland I knew. And I don't think the Roland I knew would be dumb enough to put his own name on a container if he was up to no good. I think you're barking up the wrong tree. Sounds to me like someone's tried to stitch him up. Have you considered that?'

'People change, Mr Winter. It would appear that Mr Redman made a great deal of money down south and despite his business interests here he is independently wealthy. Some accounts suggest Mr Redman still receives an income from business dealings in Sydney. Furthermore, the haste with which he left Sydney might also suggest some of those businesses might be dubious. We have reason to suspect that part of Mr Redman's current wealth is derived from people smuggling.'

'Bullshit.'

'I know this must be difficult, Mr Winter but the more you can tell me about Mr Redman the better. It must be hard to reconcile Mr Redman with people smuggling. Perhaps I'm wrong. The more you can tell me, the better picture I can put together about Mr Redman. Perhaps I'm on the wrong track altogether. The information you give me, however old or irrelevant it seems, allows me to build up a profile. What you tell me might be the information that puts Roland out of the picture.'

'Alright. I'll fill you in on what I know. I can't really tell you anything about his time in Darwin and even what I know about his time in Sydney is second or third hand. As I've said I know Roland from years ago. Roland was one of three boys. His dad died when he was fifteen. He and I both got a job at an insurance company, ANP. It wasn't my cup of tea, but Roland took to it from the start. He had the 'gift of the gab' and could sell anything. He got a promotion and moved to Sydney with the same company. I heard he did pretty well. Then he called me out of the blue and said he needed a hand in bloody Darwin of all places. I thought he was still in Sydney. I was feeling shithouse, so when he called, I thought time away from Perth would do me good.'

'What, right before Christmas?'

'Too right; Christmas gives me the shits.'

'That's an odd attitude, isn't it? I thought everyone loved

Christmas.'

Paul didn't exactly recall when he had first started to hate Christmas. He said it wasn't so much the religious dogma that had been drummed into him over the years at school, but the commercialisation and the saccharine-sweet goodwill to all. It had seemed okay to him when he was a kid; the presents, staying up late, too much food and drink and catching up with the cousins. Perhaps it was when the food and drink became excessive. Too much drink inevitably led to arguments, frayed tempers, a few punch-ups and sore heads. Even the presents eventually led to bitterness as the balance between expectations and gratitude irreconcilably tipped towards resentment. Pretty soon a real dread of Christmas set in. It was exacerbated by the commercial onslaught when shops began to roll out their commercial Christmas Juggernaut before the end of September.

He wondered who in their right mind would contemplate buying those little foil wrapped chocolates in Santa shapes or snow-capped Christmas trees in September? You could almost guarantee the chocolate was recycled from unsold Easter eggs, from earlier in the year. Even as a kid he remembered the chocolate being a horrible waxy stuff that almost refused to melt in your mouth. What place did snow-capped Christmas trees have in an Australian Christmas, anyway?

He couldn't understand the whole Christmas thing. Paul had been taught at school that it was meant to be a celebration. But when you look at it with older eyes, it is a commemoration of some kid being born under dubious circumstances more than 2,000 years ago. Where did that kid feature in today's Christmas? Where did it say in the Bible that it was necessary to max out the credit card in the run up to the end of each year, and then spend the rest of the year paying it off, only to repeat the cycle the following year? How did the birth of Christ relate to giving excessive gifts to unworthy people that you didn't like and rarely saw?

It was bad enough for him to deal with this crap with his family. Dealing with it at work was unbearable. But he bore it, at least to a point. He had attended many work Christmas functions over the years and he couldn't think of one that he'd enjoyed. Invariably someone would think that ten beers as an entrée to telling the boss how she should be running the business was a wise career move. Or some young, half-pissed clerk would think shagging one of the not-so-young secretaries, and then telling everyone about it, was a good idea. Sure, it made the young bloke feel good as he experienced the classic Aussie second coming—the first euphoria during the act, and the second when describing the conquest to his mates. It was always going to end in tears. The tears were invariably the young bloke's after he was told his contract would not be renewed or he'd been reassigned duties to some remote country location when the not-so-young secretary wielded her unsanctioned power and influence to her office-political advantage. There was always someone who had a chunder, or got caught pissing in a pot plant in the corridor instead of walking the extra twenty steps to the loo. Hadn't any of these people heard of security cameras?

Whoever thought that Secret Santa, the Americanised habit of secretly allocating colleagues someone to buy a present for, was fun? It was bad enough buying expensive crap for your own family, but to have to do it for a relative stranger really cheesed Paul off. He had been coerced into doing this stupid thing at work for too long. From his 'lofty' position as Call Centre Manager at Perth Water, it was just plain painful. If the minions thought it was fun, let them do it. He craved to opt out. He didn't want a present from someone he didn't know. He was sure the crap he'd buy for others he'd been allocated wasn't truly 'just what they'd wanted'.

It seemed to have become, even to the least cynical participant, a way of re-gifting crap from the same stupid exercise the previous year. So much so that Paul was sure Dawn from accounts recognised the lavender drawer liners he'd received last year when she got them this year. It may have been Dawn that gave them to him last year.

Paul had received some classic gifts in the past; an *'I'm with Stupid'* t-shirt, a pair of souvenir shot glasses from the *'Hot Tuna Bar, Pattaya'* and his personal least favourite the Brut 33 stick deodorant. He was sure the deodorant had been used previously, judging by the conspicuous lack of packaging and the short curly hair embedded in the tip of the claggy emulsion.

Paul particularly hated the Christmas cards that Perth Water sent out. They may have once been an acceptable way of letting that person you'd avoided all year that you really thought well of them. The department's line was that it was an important marketing tool senior staff had to carry out. Why there was a need for marketing at Perth Water at all was beyond him. Perth Water was a monopoly in the region. It was not as though anyone in Perth could get their water from anywhere else, anyway. Paul couldn't fathom how much time and money marketing the department drained from the organisation. Was it really necessary to market to a captive audience?

14

Yates

So many things concerned me about this case. The refugees in Darwin hospital or those already incarcerated at Immigration Detention. The bodies, too many bodies. So many that Darwin's morgue at the hospital was quickly filled beyond capacity. While it was seemingly disrespectful, a practical solution to the number of bodies they had to accommodate, was found meters from where they'd been discovered. Those that couldn't be housed in the morgue were conveniently put into temporary storage right there on the docks in a refrigerated sea container.

I was also worried that the Feds would arrive any day, brush us locals away like an inconvenience, and then claim to have solved the case. I'm not sure if it was fair to compare my annoyance of Roland and Paul to the rest. Roland and Paul annoyed me for what it appeared they had done but also how closely their backgrounds resembled my own. I struggled to understand how our similar environment had produced such different outcomes. Each of us appeared to be only a sliding door away from disparate outcomes.

I wasn't about to publicly divulge my background, least of all to Paul. My colleagues at the station knew I was originally from Perth and had been in the Western Australian Police Force before working for the Northern Territory Police. I expect the recruiters had done a thorough background check on me too. A few unofficial phone calls to the powers that be down south would have also been on the cards. But I had nothing that would have caused too much concern. I could explain any issue from my departure from the WA force by being a few years older and more world-hardened. The NT force was always after to recruits.

What I heard of Roland from Paul was chillingly similar to my own story. I was a few years older than them, but I was a product of the same Perth that Paul described. A few years earlier, but it was much the same.

Roland and Paul had grown up in the northern suburbs, and I was from the south, with the Swan River dividing our respective territories. The Swan is not a majestic river like the Mississippi, Nile or even the Murray-Darling but the Swan in those days was a hard border, forming a barrier that separated parochial communities. Maybe the Swan seemed more significant due to the desiccated environment that it meandered across. The contrast made it appear grander than it would have in a more verdant environment.

I have always hated to be lied to, but for a copper it is an occupational hazard. There are many examples from my Police career, both in the West and the Northern Territory, where the truth was a tough admission. It often becomes less painful to reveal the truth than to have it discovered sometime later. Over my time I have developed a sense that tells me when someone lies to me. I imagine it as having a wise sage sitting on my shoulder who poses questions about what I'm being told. The sage was posing a torrent of questions during my recent conversation with Kamahli, but the sage was strangely quiet when I spoke with Paul. Was Paul a pawn in a cruel business, or had he managed to convince himself and the sage on my shoulder that he was telling the truth?

After years of calling Darwin home, locals still refer to me as a southerner. Yet whenever I travelled to Perth, people refer to me as a Territorian. Without leaving Australia, I felt, as I am sure most immigrants do, caught between two cultures, and fitting comfortably into neither.

My police career didn't start well. Looking back, the thread that led to its unravelling commenced within weeks of starting the job.

'Yates, when you get the lunches today, I want you to do a little errand for me.'

'Sure, Sergeant Connor, no problem.'

I had joined the Western Australian Police Force as a young recruit. At the bottom of the pecking order I copped all of the menial tasks. Collecting the lunches for six or eight coppers from The Re Store in Lake Street was one of those tasks. It was a ten-minute drive from where I was stationed in Adelaide Terrace, but worth it for the fresh continental rolls overflowing with fresh salad, salami and cheese. It sure beat the options of a days-old, lukewarm pie, a curly crust sandwich or a reheated greasy curry from the Police canteen. I remembered the conversation with my first boss like it was yesterday.

'I want you to call in on a Mrs Rosa-Lea Bray in Roe Street on the way back from getting the lunches. She has a little package for me.'

'What number Roe Street, Sarge?'

'That's the tricky bit Yates, but you're a bright, young lad. Mrs Bray's address is two-twenty-two Roe Street, but you need to enter the property from James Street through the service station. Walk through the front of the service station and out the back door. The rear laneway connects Roe and James Streets. Knock on the door and tell Mrs Bray that Sergeant Connor sent you. She'll know what it's about; she'll have a package that I need you to bring back to me. Don't open it, and don't call in anywhere on the way back. Get the lunches first, not the other way around, and get the package back here.' Sergeant Connor winked as he gave me his final instruction and slapped the keys into my open palm along with a fifty dollar note. 'Here's a few bucks for the boys' lunches – keep the change.'

I was concerned about what he was getting me to do, especially with the wink and the overly generous amount for the twenty dollars of lunches. We'd just taken delivery of latest Kingswood into the carpool, so driving for the lunches was something that I would have volunteered for anyway. Even if I had wanted to, there wasn't any way that I could get out of doing the Sergeant's little errands.

Roe Street marked the southern edge of Northbridge just north of the business district. The fruit and vegetable market to the west and the Sunday Times and Michelides Tobacco Factory to the east marked the other boundaries.

Northbridge was dull during normal business hours. The markets buzzed before sunrise when farmers would drive from their market gardens and orchards that fringed the city, to disgorge their wares. Then the fruit and vegetables would be on their way to shops all over as the sun came up. Then there was a period of relative quiet before night fall.

Most of Northbridge's shops in those days catered to immigrants: Greeks, Italians and Chinese. A couple of barbers were hidden behind advertisements for Brylcream and tobacco. I suspect that the obscured windows, advertising Benson and Hedges or Marlborough, also provided cover for the non-barbershop activities that went on inside.

The barbers were known to make more as SP bookies than from their legitimate businesses. A few boarding houses had once been accommodation for young single men returning from War. Now they were the refuge for drunks, druggies and no-hopers, whose only other option would have been sleeping on the street.

Roe Street's biggest claim to fame was that it was the epicentre of prostitution in Perth. The laws governing the brothels were covered as part of a unit we did at the academy.

Judge Finlay, recently retired and therefore ancient, presented the law lectures at the academy to us. I thought he was always more likely to fall asleep during one of his lectures than those of us who had to suffer through them. He explained that a policy of containment of had started years ago in Kalgoorlie, where the services provided by the girls to the cashed-up miners, were supposed to keep women not 'on the game' safe. The policy seemed to work in Kalgoorlie, so it was adopted across the state.

In reality, it meant that the politicians couldn't get laws applied to the brothels sorted out. It was never going to be an industry with a lack of demand, so it became a police responsibility. The police contained the brothels to specific areas to prevent freelancers from selling their wares across the suburbs. An undisclosed consequence of this was the police were frequently on the take from the brothels.

Pubs and clubs were Northbridge's second most profitable business segment. They kept similar hours to the brothels and I suspect there was a fair bit of cross-trade of clientele between the two. Hannibal's, Gobbles and Beethoven's were icons of Northbridge in those days. Interiors of red, purple, black or mirrors and meters upon metres of shag pile carpet. Carpet that was permanently sticky from the volumes of spilt, diluted beer and overpriced sugary cocktails. Hannibal's scored a coup over its contemporaries with an illuminated dance floor – challenging its rivals to a higher level of neon tackiness.

The nightclubs were the breeding ground of many unsavoury types, but they also supported Perth's thriving live music scene. Perth punched well above its weight musically in those days. Northbridge was the birthplace of The Hoodoo Gurus, The Numbats, and even INXS, who went onto to international fame. I never saw INXS when they played Northbridge as the Farriss Brothers, but I saw Silver Hills, The Triffids, and Dave Warner. Dave Warner sang the biography of my life with '*Suburban Boy*' - I can still recall every word in the song from memory.

It was said that the complaints of noise marked the end of the heady days of live music in clubs of Northbridge. I think it was more likely to have been the clubs' owners squeezing more profit by paying a DJ instead of a four or five-piece band playing real music. I suppose when most of your patrons are pissed, as long as the music was loud, it didn't matter.

I was a suburban boy that mirrored the character in Warner's song. I'd done okay at school and could have gone into a trade, but I suspect I was influenced by Homicide and Matlock Police on the TV than I would have given credit to. Mum and Dad thought getting into the police would be a promising, steady career, a bit less dead-ended than Dad's career.

Dad had worked for almost twenty years at Coventry's at that time, selling car parts and spares. He never complained, but it must have bored him stupid. He had left school at 14 and had a job working in a foundry for the railways. Dad and Mum met when he was twenty, and she was seventeen. I was on the way pretty soon after that. Then Dad had his marble pulled from the conscription barrel that sent him off to Vietnam as a twenty-two-year-old. I was just a baby, and my sister would have to wait for him to return before she was conceived. Mum told me she held me in her arms as we saw him and hundreds of others off, as he boarded a Hercules at Pearce Airbase. I don't have any memory of it, but I remember him and Mum telling me about it. I also remember Dad telling me what a shithouse experience it was coming back. He'd fought for his country, only to be spat upon by 'a mob of doped-out, fucking hippies waving peace signs', as he called the crowd that 'greeted' him on his return.

He'd worked in the Royal Australian Airforce as ground crew for the Canberra bombers. He never talked much about his time there, but he and Mum were grateful for the war service home they scored as a result. A brick veneer, asbestos-roofed, three-bedroom house on a quarter acre block in Willeton. Ill-designed for Perth's summer heat and equally inappropriate and freezing in the winter. But Mum and Dad loved their little kingdom on Woodpecker Avenue. They'd convinced themselves they were in the more prestigious, neighbouring suburb of 'Burrendah Heights'. They were also happy that their kids could walk through the pine plantation to schools in Rossmoyne. They're still there today. I expect they will be there until they are carried out in a box.

Dad once said that his 24 months of 'killing gooks in Vietnam was worth it if he could score this prime property', referring to his Woodpecker Avenue home. He was usually less overt in his racism, not that the same could be said of much of Perth at the time. Still, I suspect he said it when he was a little pissed from one of his ANZAC Day outings.

He wasn't much of a drinker usually. He would take down his RAAF blue slouch hat from the top of the wardrobe. Polish the brass Second Squadron insignia to a brilliant shine and go off to the ANZAC Day Dawn Service in Kings Park each year. He would never wear a uniform or any of his medals, just the hat and insignia. Off to the Dawn Service he'd go and then he'd spend the rest of the day at The Raffle's Hotel in Applecross with other servicemen. He'd get a taxi back and collect his car the following day. He enjoyed it but was never one for marching or any other Returned Service League functions that I can recall.

I only went with him once to a Dawn Service. I would have been almost 15. I don't know why I only went just once. He woke me up at four in the morning, and before five, we were standing at the War Memorial with hundreds of others. We watched the sunrise across the Swan as it crested the scarp. We listened to a speech or two, The Ode and The Last Post and watched politicians and service brass in their starchy uniforms lay wreaths at the base of the obelisk. We lingered as the crowd dispersed and slowly walked back along Fraser Avenue, chatting about the service, before collecting our car where we had left in the shadow of Dumas House.

'There's something I want to do before we head home, son.'

We drove back into Kings Park, where workmen were already removing the barriers set up to contain the crowd that had already dispersed. In another ten minutes, Kings Park would resume looking like it always had, with little evidence other than flowers left at the memorial to signify the morning's service. Dad wound down his window as we drove slowly, even slower than the signed limit. The scent of the majestic lemon-scented gums lining Fraser Avenue was amplified by the stillness of the morning, riding on the wave of the increasing temperature as the sun crested the Scarp. Dad pulled the car onto the side of the road and got out.

He leant into the open window and said, 'Wait here, son. I won't be a minute.'

He crossed the road and stood silently in front of one of the trees, staring at the little plaque at its base. He hung his head, removed his hat and held it over his heart. His demeanour took on a religious appearance. He put his hat back on, straightened and saluted. He then turned and walked as slowly as an arthritis-riddled pensioner, that he was soon to be, back to the car.

'What was that about, Dad?'

'Just paying respect to my old mate, son.'

'Who?'

'Joe Ferazzi.' He started the car, paused, double-checked his mirrors, and we were on our way home. We exited Kings Park and were heading south.

'Dad, who was Joe, Joe Ferazzi? I've never heard you mention him before.'

'Joe and I were mates in Vietnam. We were shared the same birthday and so we were called up in the same draft. We were given pretty much the same job in the RAAF, working on the bombers. We started on the same day and went through basic training together. We shared one or two adventures over there. I came back; Joe didn't.'

'What happened to Joe Dad?

'Joe and I started off working on the same ground crew on the Canberra bombers, but when they bought in fresh recruits, they split us into different shifts. We still saw each other occasionally, but usually, when I was sleeping, he was working and vice versa. We were pretty removed from the fighting in Vietnam, at least initially.

We were ground crew back at the base. Even the pilots didn't see too much action up close. But things started to get worse towards the end of things there.

We were on loan to the US at their base at Bien Hoa just outside of Saigon. The yanks needed a hand with some of the newer ordinances that they had recently received. I've never really figured out why they couldn't have done the bloody job themselves. I suspect our brass was sucking up to the yanks.

It turned out the VC were a bit closer than anyone gave them credit for. They'd penetrated the zone around the base and started lobbing in mortars. The bastards took out nine planes and damaged twenty more before we saw them off. Six personnel were lost too, five yanks and Joe from our team. It could have just as easily been me.'

This was the most I'd ever heard him talk about his days in Vietnam. His hands gripped the steering wheel as he stared intently down the road. I pushed my luck and asked a question I'd often thought about asking.

'Dad, why don't you march on ANZAC day? There seems to be plenty of people that do?'

'I'm just not into that fuss, son. When we came back, people made it pretty clear that they thought we should have never been in Vietnam in the first place. I wasn't about to give them another chance to have a go at me.'

'I thought all of that stuff happened years ago. Haven't things moved on?'

'They might have for some but not for me. Don't get me wrong I don't have anything but respect for anyone who's served. They've put their lives on the line for a bunch of politicians who couldn't have given a shit. If they want to march, good luck to them. But it does make me sad seeing those guys. They are reminiscing over the toughest time of their lives when they were shit-scared and wanted nothing more than to go home. But those who got to go home realised that they were never going to be as close to any other human being as they were to their mates back then. They were in a shithole doing the job that nobody back home supported them to do, and yet for most, it was going to be the pinnacle of their lives.

It was war. No war is glorious. Vietnam was a horrible one. It was sobering to think that you'd given your best years up for a war that you weren't allowed to win.' He swallowed hard and didn't say another word until we pulled up in front of our house.

He dropped me off without coming in, turned the car around, and headed off on his pilgrimage to the Raffle's Hotel.

* * *

I continued to collect the lunches and the little brown packets from Rosa-Lea Bray for the best part of the following year. I'd also experienced more that policing in Perth had to offer. I wasn't about to complain; many of my contemporaries from the academy had been sent out to far-flung outposts, Menzies, Roeborne or Meekatharra. I was stationed in the relative luxury of Police Headquarters. Police Headquarters on Adelaide Terrace was a plum posting. It was even possible to watch the Test Cricket at the WACA from the sixth floor back then.

I'd been given a few roles while I was there, license checks with traffic, foot patrols through the city during the day or Northbridge at night. I'd even a few stints in plain clothes at a few clubs in Fremantle. Through it all, whenever I was there, I collected the lunches and the little brown parcel for Sergeant Connor.

Mrs Bray, or Rosa-Lea as she insisted on me calling her after the first month or so, always came out to give me the parcel herself. I'm sure she could have given it to one of her staff to pass on. She never failed to tease me about something every time. Initially, it was about how young I looked, then the offer of coming back later for a 'freebie'. Lately, it had become teasing me about being Connor's lacky. I shared the joke with her initially, it was all pretty good-natured, but the bit about being a lacky for Connor started to annoy me. I didn't have a choice. Connor knew that he could send me off to one of the far-flung postings if I complained. He knew that plenty of others would jump at a posting in the city, let alone at Headquarters.

I never opened any of the little brown packages, and I didn't need to. I knew what was in them, but I had convinced myself that if I never saw the contents, I couldn't be accused of being party to the mess that I had landed in went it all went sour.

It was about a year after I'd first started collecting the lunches and little brown paper parcel from Rosa-Lea. I walked through the service station, crossed the laneway and knocked on the door every Monday before lunch, as usual. I waited, and waited, and knocked again just as the door slowly opened. Rosa-Lea stood in front of me.

'Good morning, Rosa-Lea. Just here to pick up Sergeant Connor's parcel.'

'Sorry, Bill. No parcel today. Tell that bastard Connor there'll be no more parcels for him from me.' There was foreboding in her tone that unsettled me.

'Okay. I'll let Sergeant Connor know. Should I come back tomorrow?

'No, sweetie. My little arrangement with Sergeant Connor is over. He couldn't keep up his end of the contract, so I won't be providing any parcels from now on.'

'Have you told Sergeant Connor about this?'

'You're a big boy Bill; you can let him know.'

'I'm sure he won't be happy, but I'll pass on your message.'

'You do that Bill, run along now. I doubt we'll be seeing you again.'

I got back to the office and distributed the lunches. I usually gave Sergeant Connor his first, together with the little brown packet. This time I left his until last. I was dreading not having the little packet to hand discretely to him with his lunch.

'Here's your lunch Sarge. Italian cheese, salami and salad, no onion, just like you ordered.'

He snatched the roll out of my hand and glanced into the empty cardboard box I had used to carry the lunches.

'Left me till last today, son?' he didn't wait for an answer to the obvious. 'Where's the packet from Rosa-Lea's?'

I could see the colour in his face rising. 'Sorry, Sarge, but Rosa-Lea, I mean Mrs Bray said to let you know that there wasn't a package today.'

'What the fuck do you mean – there's no package today. What does that mean? Are you sure you haven't just pocketed it yourself, son?'

'Absolutely not, Sarge. I've never even opened any of the packages. Mrs Bray just said to let you know that there wasn't going to be any more packages.'

I could see the veins popping out like extension cords in his neck.

'What the fuck does that mean? Are you running errands for Rosa-Lea Bray now? You work for me, son. Who the hell does she think she is?' He threw his roll at the wall behind his desk, then gathered himself. He must have thought better of it, walked over and picked his lunch off the floor. I suppose he'd realised that he didn't want his little tantrum to do him out of lunch.

'Do you want me to go back tomorrow, Sarge? Maybe she'll have it by Tuesday.'

'No. I'll deal with Rosa-Lea Bray – the piece of shit. Who does she think she is? If she wants to do business on my patch, she knows the rules.'

I left his office as soon as I could and made myself scarce until knock-off time. There was no need to put myself in Sergeant Connor's line of fire. I was glad to go home at the end of the shift.

I fronted up the following day, hoping that the fire and brimstone that Connor had been venting had subsided a little. Like most days, I changed from the civvies that I had worn on the bus from Willeton to the bus terminal next door to Police Headquarters, into my uniform in the change room. I had been pulled off the city walk around to do the day patrol of Northbridge with Rob Clark. Rob had been around for a while. I expect they were keen to pair him up with me. Even after a year in the job, I was still considered the new guy.

'G'day Rob. Ready for a walk around the lovely streets of Northbridge?' I half-jokingly said to him as he came in.

'Sure, young Bill. Northbridge could be interesting today, though. I see your lady friend is in the news.'

Rob took *The West* from under his arm and threw it onto the bench next to me. I finished squeezing into my Doc Martins and unfolded the newspaper. Across the front page in large print was '*Northbridge Identity Bashed*.' An old photo showing Rosa-Lea in a full-length ball gown, diamond earrings sparkling almost resting on her shoulders, matching necklace, accenting the plunging neckline of her dress with a caption that read '*Local Northbridge businesswoman Rosa-Lea Bray*'.

'Shit, I was only speaking to Mrs Bray yesterday. I hope she's okay.'

'I don't think she is going to be okay for a while', Rob muttered as turned the page and continued to read the article.'

'Local businesswoman Mrs Rosa-Lea Bray was viciously bashed by an unknown assailant in the small hours of Tuesday morning. Mrs Bray had been sleeping in her apartment above her business premises on Roe Street. The attacker somehow lured Mrs Bray into the laneway at the rear of her apartment.

Mrs Bray is a well-known Northbridge identity known to support many Western Australian charities. She has supported Perth's Telethon since its start in 1968 and has generously sponsored Sister Kate's Home for many years.

The motive of the attack is unclear. Mrs Bray is well-liked by many in the area and throughout Perth's business community.

Trouble in Northbridge is nothing new, but the escalating level of violence, with this the latest case, is concerning for local businesses and the citizens of Perth. Sir Noel Crompton, Leader of the Opposition and Parliamentary Spokesman on Law and Order, stated:

'This government must be held accountable for this criminal act against one of our outstanding businesswomen. It is a disgrace. This government has gone soft on law and order. If my party were in government, things would be different. While this government postulates change it dawdles on legislative reform. My colleagues are keen to get on with things. The good people of Western Australia

will have the opportunity to put things right when we go to the polls early next year. The forthcoming election will provide every eligible Western Australian with a vote to voice their dissatisfaction with this government and put my party into government. My party will not tolerate these heinous acts of violence.

Perth must purge the rising tide of criminal activities. There is no place in our modern society for those who think that bashing anyone, let alone respectable Northbridge businesswomen outside her own home, will be tolerated. My government, when elected, will ensure these thugs are found, tried and sent to Fremantle Prison for a lengthy stay. I encourage every one of you to join me in expressing outrage at this government by voting them out of office at the very next opportunity.'

Mrs Rosa-Lea Bray is currently recovering in Royal Perth Hospital. It is expected that she will be in there for several weeks before then require a lengthy period of convalescence at Shenton Park Rehabilitation Hospital.

Police have asked for anyone with information on the case to come forward.'

I folded the paper and passed it back to Rob.

'Jesus mate, what happened?'

'Can't exactly say, young matey. But what I can say is you don't want to be asking too many questions. You'd be better off not knowing the answers to some things.'

'You nancyboys finished in there? When are you going to get out and do your bloody job?' Sergeant Connor stuck his head around the men's room door. His hand gripping the door had an Elastoplast over the knuckles, haloed by bruises. He noticed me looking at his hand and snatched it away. 'Come on, you two get a bloody wriggle on. We must show a strong presence in Northbridge today of all days.'

The reality of the situation was staring at me.

'Sorry, Sarge, we're on our way. Did you see what happened to Mrs Bray?' Bob, give Sarge the paper.' Bob looked directly at me, his back still towards Sergeant Connor, and rolled his eyes.

'Sarge, we've got to get going. You're not interested in any of this, are you? *The West* is a bloody rag.'

Sarge snatched the paper from Rob and unfolded it to the front page. He saw the headline and mumbled, 'Fucking whore got what was owing to her,' before walking off with Rob's paper tucked under his arm.

Rob turned to me and said, 'Listen, son, I don't care if you're intent on career suicide, but don't include me in any of it. I've got a family to feed. Like I said, keep your mouth shut if you know what's best for you. You might be Connor's little golden-haired boy at the moment, but don't think he won't turn on you if he thinks it's in his best interest. You'd be wise to think before you next speak.'

When I returned to Headquarters late that afternoon, a brown envelope was placed on top of the folded civvies in my locker. The locker had been locked when I left. More concerning was the bulging envelope. It was the same as those that I had collected from Mrs Bray.

While I didn't consciously have career suicide in mind, I knew that I couldn't continue to be part of this caper. I joined the force to uphold the law, to bring criminals to justice, not to become one myself. I knew what was going on here. I'd known for longer than I'd admitted to myself. I was ashamed that I had stuck it out as long as I had. I knew what was in the little brown package, but I'd convinced myself that it was part of the way Northbridge business was conducted.

I tucked the envelope into the back of my jeans and said nothing. I waited for three weeks and applied for a transfer to traffic. The transfer came through six weeks later. I used the first fatal that I attended as an excuse to get out. I spun the trauma counsellor a yarn that I was having reoccurring nightmares about the mangled bodies in the crash and that it was affecting my ability to do the job. It was all bullshit, but it was a clean exit that was less likely to have people asking questions that I didn't want to answer.

I got a reasonable final salary from the leave that I hadn't taken and headed north. Mum and Dad were disappointed, but they bought my story too. I needed to get out of the city to where I didn't know anyone.

I worked a season on a cray boat out of Shag Island, near Leeman.

It was only three and a half hours drive from Perth, but it was off the main highway, a town that wouldn't have existed but for crayfish. The job was physically demanding and brainless, precisely what I needed back then. The first fortnight I thought I was going to throw up every time the boat slapped the base of a swell, but the money was good, and the sickness subsided after a fortnight or so. I stuck it out until the end of the season.

In those days, it was possible to go on the dole in the off-season. and live off government hand-out and if you hadn't pissed it all away during the season, have a pretty comfortable existence. I couldn't stand the thought of a government hand-out though. It seemed too much like the business that I'd nearly been suckered in to back in the cops. I took the money that I'd ferreted away and kept heading north. I ended up getting another boat job, a deckie on a prawn boat out of Exmouth. I stuck that out for two seasons, working for the Shire grading roads in the off-season.

Grading gravel roads gives you plenty of time to think and what I was thinking for a lot of the time was how it could have been different. I could have made a career in the WA Police Force. I should have played it differently, but I suppose I was too young and wet behind the ears back then. A few years of labouring amongst fishermen had made me wiser and tougher. I maintained a desire to make a difference in society, and I knew I could make a better job of it if I had a chance to live it over. Fate intervened when I stumbled across the recruiting advertisement for Northern Territory Police in the paper. That was about fifteen years and three stripes ago now.

I've been happy with most of my time in the Northern Territory Police. They gave me credit for my time in the force down south and didn't ask why I'd left. I did a six-week stint in their Academy, and I was back on the job. Sure, there were days when the job gave me the shits, but all jobs do, right? Drunks, especially around pension week, and car thieves, made up most of my 'clients'. Things could get a bit messy at times, but mostly it was a doddle compared to bullshit I'd endured down south.

15

Paul

When the final exams were over Paul and Roland heaved a sigh of relief. They felt they had focussed on the work required to get the best results they could manage. They imagined that they had done enough to get where they had wanted to. Roland was going to go into journalism and Paul was keen on commerce. They attended high school graduation parties, and spent their days at the beach, while they waited for their university entrance exam results to come out.

While they waited the boys experienced their first hangovers and vowed never to drink Brandivino again. However, they found the same result could be obtained from Stone's Green Ginger Wine or quantities of Swan Draught.

When the entrance results arrived, their optimistic bravado faded to disappointment. Paul was disappointed for his parents; they had expected more from him. Roland was disappointed that despite good marks in English Literature, he would now have to find a job.

The prospect of three years partying at university while doing an BA in journalism that had so appealed to him failed to materialise.

Several of their school contemporaries went to university: the dux to medicine at the University of Western Australia, runner-up to engineering. Even Arm-pong got into Geology at the WA Institute of Technology or WAIT, as everyone called it. Some were offered positions at universities and colleges to become teachers, arts students (also eventually to end up as teachers), while others went to trade school to become plumbers, chippies and electricians.

Both young men found themselves stuck in the limbo of an undefined future. Poor marks and no job amounted to diminished prospects. They had little idea of what they wanted to do with their lives. An advertisement in *The West* provided a lifeline, '*Young Men Required for Sales and Marketing, Australian National Provident (ANP)*'. The respected Australian insurance company was recruiting. Anyone '*with good people skills and a willingness to learn could earn good money—no qualifications required.*' It sounded like it had been written specifically with Paul and Roland in mind. The reality was less than glorious—selling life insurance policies door to door. It was a paying job, and as their living expenses were minimal, living at home, life didn't turn out too bad.

Roland was a natural at sales. His way with words and charm provided a 'foot in the door' from which he could sell almost anything. Paul was more conflicted. He was the only one among his door-to-door selling colleagues that actually read the policies he tried to sell. To his moral dilemma, most had dodgy exclusion clauses, so the company would rarely pay out anything to those who tried to make a claim on their policy. He particularly disliked their educational annuity policy. This was structured so young parents, hopeful that their child would go on to greater things, paid a weekly fee into a policy that provided a fixed amount for each year their child was at an approved course at university. If they didn't go to university or if one payment was missed over the period of the policy, all of the accumulated funds were forfeited to the insurance company. The clients that the door-to-door salesmen targeted were unlikely to read the legalese that disclosed this deliberately cruel potential trap. Anyway, how many of the kids from the state housing estates that Paul and Roland were assigned to, would break the mould? For many going to university was a far too distant dream. ANP policies like these, and there were many, were a license for the company to print money. They were selling snowflake dreams to delusional fools in the heat of Perth's summer.

Roland soon became the star employee among the local ANP sales crew. Meanwhile, Paul struggled, unconvinced selling something of close to zero value to a person that could neither afford it or needed it, was the right thing for anyone but the bigwigs at the top of the ANP sales pyramid. Roland could see the conflict, but he believed that fundamental principles were at work here.

'Darwin was right. It's the survival of the fittest. If someone is too dumb to know that they are being ripped off, evolution has worked it out. Darwin's theory might have focussed on physical attributes at one time. Sorting out the weak from the strong. Nowadays it says the smart should leave the dumb in their wake. Dumb people should be encouraged to give their money to smart people. It's a better investment. It's how the species improves. If we interfere and pander to the bleeding-heart social activists, the species will just get weaker and dumber. We will all be worse off. All I'm doing is helping evolution along its rightful course,' Roland said. But Paul could see that he was trying to convince himself as much as anyone else.

'So, what you're saying is, if someone rips you off, it's okay as long as they're smarter?'

'No-one is going to rip me off. I'm going somewhere with this company. They're going to give me a promotion. I can just feel it.'

'Yeah, but how can you sleep at night?'

'I sleep really well. Even the poorest person in this country is better off than those in third world countries. This country has it all wrong. Everyone has to keep accumulating more and more, another car, a bigger house, a blonder wife, more and more stuff. Do you think anyone here is happy? I know I'm not, and I can tell you're not. What is being happy, anyway?'

'I just want to do the right thing. I don't want to make poor people poorer. I don't want smart people to rip off dumb people just because they have the power to do so. It's just not fair. All you're doing is making the fat cats at ANP fatter.'

Paul could see this line of argument was getting him nowhere and left it at that. He wasn't getting through to Roland. It wasn't the Roland he had originally met. It wasn't the Roland that had been the Vice-President of the St Vincent de Paul Society at school. The Roland *he* knew had a good heart. Roland's failure to get a university place when so many others had, that he considered less deserving, had made him bitter. He wasn't the same Roland that Paul had once been so fond of, but in his heart, Paul knew that the real Roland would eventually shine through.

Selling insurance was not everyone's cup of tea, but as they had no other job prospects on the horizon, the boys persisted with it. It wasn't exciting. It wasn't glamorous. At that stage, it wasn't even that financially rewarding when you broke it down. If you totalled the hours they spent traipsing around the suburbs doing the job, it was the same hourly rate as the minimum wage, but the rewards seemed huge to the boys. If you'd previously got by with next to no money, suddenly having a little felt exhilarating. Having enough to buy a few of the things they'd always coveted produced a euphoria that was evidenced by a series of adolescent spending.

Roland's first purchases with his newfound wealth were pretty modest: a pair of Levi 501s, a Golden Breed surf shirt covered in hibiscus flowers and a pair of Cuban-healed leather boots, handmade by Bodkins Bootery in the city. It was an odd look, sort of James Dean goes to Hawaii, but Roland thought he looked cool.

Paul's purchases were more sophisticated but not much more. He went in for a chunky Pulsar digital watch and the keys to the car of his modest dreams—a 1970 Holden Brougham. Sure, it wasn't a new car, not even close to new. It wasn't even all that flash, but it was a mechanical status symbol that his peers recognised. Paul, with Roland sitting uncomfortably in the passenger seat, felt as if they were landed gentry. They had received an automotive step up the social ladder. They wouldn't have been happier if they were driving a Rolls Royce. To them, the Brougham was just like a Rolls Royce but with a thumping big Aussie V8. All their mates, at least those in the Holden camp, thought the Brougham was 'real cool'. Only a Holden Statesman would have been better. If you had a Statesman, you were king of the block. A Brougham, the Statesman's immediate subordinate, must have made Paul a prince.

In those days, true young Aussie guys fell into just two camps, where cars were concerned: Holden or Ford. Everything else was just the rest. For a while, Chrysler came close with its Charger, but then it slipped back to mediocrity. The P76 had been an attempt to keep up with the Big Two but was forever remembered as a famous failure. Japanese cars of the era like Corollas and Civics were small, buzzy, little old lady's motorised shopping trolleys. If your preference was something like a Fiat, a Lancia or an Alfa, your mates thought it was almost okay as long as you were from European stock, but why any real Aussie would want one was incomprehensible.

So, the Brougham, affectionately christened as '*The Beast*', resplendent in Burgundy Maroon, was their royal chariot. The exterior paint was dark enough not to make the rust coming through the quarter panels too obvious and the interior was pure bogan-boy luxury. The seats had brand new black velour seat covers, and custom-fitted black shag pile carpets completed the look. '*The Beast*' was the realisation of Paul's mechanical fantasies.

Roland was still stuck on Christina. Not that Paul cared to hear it all the time, but Roland kept reminding him of a dream he had. It centred on Christina in a gossamer blue nightie on a sleepover with other schoolgirls. The dream always involved Christina and her similarly minimally attired friends in a pillow fight.

He couldn't make out details of other girls' faces, but could recount the details of each jiggly breast through the soft focus of his dreams. Christina was the only one who was in clear focus. It was the cliché schoolboy fantasy stuff of skimpy nighties, clouds of feathers from split pillows and bouncing young breasts. It felt odd that Roland told Paul about it. Roland never stopped thinking about Christina. Paul doubted he had seen her in some time, but he clearly hadn't stopped thinking of her. Perhaps it was more than a schoolboy crush.

Roland hadn't thought about where he intended to go in the ANP, but he knew he intended to go somewhere and get a ticket out of the 'burbs. If ANP was the vehicle that let him do that, he was on board. He'd do whatever it took, as long as he got his commission. The people who bought the policies wouldn't even know the limited extent of their coverage until he was long gone. He never envisaged a long-term future working for ANP. He was a good salesman, and he knew it. He could sell pretty much anything he set his mind to. He had a disarming manner so that even when he had his hand in your pocket, all you got was a warm sensation. It didn't bother him what he was selling. That he was working for ANP was immaterial. As long as the money kept rolling in and he didn't have to answer to a boss every five minutes, he was okay. All the while, his bank account was building.

ANP was one of many Australian companies that had sprung up after World War Two. The returning soldiers had counted themselves lucky to return at all when so many of their mates had not. So lucky in fact, they would buy an insurance policy to insure that if, for some unknown reason, they were taken away, their loved ones would continue to be provided for. It was a time ripe for a life insurance company. And if morals could be suspended for a while a profit was made, the time was cherry ripe.

After the war, the period of economic growth and relative prosperity saw ANP grow at a rate that exceeded many other companies. Those at the pinnacle of the company did incredibly well. The war had weeded out those with underlying medical issues, so those left, failing some traumatic accident, would be around for a while. This meant ANP quickly became unbelievably prosperous too. The company invested the funds in its coffers in big, safe, major infrastructure projects. In post-war Australia, where growth was rapid, expansion was unrelenting, and the commodities Australia produced fetched great prices in a world intent on rebuilding.

When Roland and Paul joined the company the post-war glory years had long gone and the company had entered a period of stable respectability previously reserved for governments and banks. In Sydney, their head office even looked like a bank, with sturdy grey granite Corinthian columns that dominated Phillip Street down near the Quay. They even used a stylised version of the building in their company logo. It was a grey building, full of grey-haired, grey-fleshed, men in grey-striped suits. The board was full of stale, pale, male directors with old school ties. Many even had overtly pompous, double-barrelled surnames that dripped of old money. Barton-Smythe, McFadden-Jones and Cullinan-MacKenzie. The directors and the company became fat on lazy profits.

The goings-on at the board level were of no concern to Roland or Paul. They were not only miles away in Perth but miles away from the pinnacle of the company's structure. They also really didn't care what went on in the lofty heights of the company. It was unkind to suggest Roland was motivated solely by his pay cheque, though that might have been true. But the company's lack of strategic awareness, was eventually felt by the Board and even down to Roland and Paul's lowly levels.

ANP was ripe for a takeover. It was cashed up, fat on its customers' premiums, and its board and executive were asleep at the wheel. ANP's share price was low compared to the funds it held. In the summer of

1987, the multinational insurer Britannia Holdings launched a hostile takeover. Over the previous 18 months, Britannia had bought parcels of ANP through a dozen holding companies registered in Singapore, Hong Kong and Macau. By the time the crusty, complacent ANP board members woke up to what was going on, Britannia already held the majority of the company's shares.

An immediate restructure ensued, and the existing pompous directors on the board were dumped. Britannia installed its own board, put in their own chief executive and drew the rest of the directors from the British diaspora, with a sole symbolic Australian director. The Australian director was intended to give the board a more 'local' feel, with most of the other directors instructed to keep a close eye on the local 'maverick'. The Australian director knew he was a token. This only made him more intent on making his mark. The new board launched an aggressive expansion plan that Roland was to profit from.

Roland had been comfortable with ANP before the takeover, and he wasn't keen for too much change; however, when the company offered him a promotion to move to Sydney, he jumped at the chance. Perth had been good for him, but he saw that Sydney could be even better. A bigger city, more policies, more clients and more money. Roland thought he was finally heading somewhere.

16

Paul

Roland's call caught Paul by surprise. If it hadn't been for Paul's life seemingly taking a turn for the worse, it wouldn't have amounted to much, he would have turned down the invitation of a trip to Darwin. But he was so over the festive season, and bored with his life. He was relieved to have an excuse not to hang around for Christmas festivities in Perth.

Paul had received calls from old friends out of the blue before. He'd caught up with a few of them over the years, and a common theme always emerged—they all wanted to sell him something. Or, more correctly, they wanted him to sell something for them. One guy was flogging Amway via a tarted-up Ponzi scheme that would see him alone getting wealthy at the expense of his friends and family. Another was flogging little bottles of plant oils, claiming they cured cancer, Alzheimer's, carbuncles, boils and almost every other ailment imaginable. They'd be 'putting big pharma out of business,' and 'you'd better get in quick, or you'll miss out.' He wasn't sure if his old friends actually believed in the stuff they were flogging. Had they drunk the Kool-Aid or were they just intent on getting to the top of the scheme when they realised they were the worker bees at the bottom of the pyramid? Normally, Paul would have dismissed a call from an old friend as another get-rich-quick scheme, but Roland wasn't just any old friend. Roland's call came on the back of Paul, re-assessing where his life was heading.

'Hello.' Paul picked up the phone reluctantly. He wasn't really in the mood to speak to anyone, but this caller was persistent. The phone had been ringing for a good minute, much more persistent than any of those pain in the arse telemarketers.

'Paul, maaaate. How's it going?'

Paul had an odd sense he recognised the voice, but he couldn't quite place it. 'Who is this?'

'Paul, don't jerk me around. It's Roland, your best mate. How's it going?'

'Roland? Roland Redman? Wow, that's a name I haven't heard in a while. How are you?'

'Yeah, sorry, mate, it's been a while. What's it been, three or four years since we last spoke?'

'Almost seven, I think.'

'Sorry, been distracted. You know how it is.'

Paul was already suspicious. Anyone that referred to themself as your best mate but had not contacted you for seven years was either delusional or after something. Sure, it was common for every Aussie male to call each other mate. It was a fall-back position, and meant you didn't need to waste brain cells remembering someone's name. Roland was already setting off the alarm bells in Paul's head that he was about to offer to get him into some dodgy, get-rich-quick scheme selling essential oils, Amway or any other such thing.

'Roland, it's been a long while. I, I—'

'Yeah, too long, mate. What have you been up to? Geez, it's good to hear your voice,' Roland cut him off before he could continue.

'Roland, I don't want to be rude or anything, but you've caught me at a bad time.'

'Why? What's up, mate?

'Roland, are you trying to sell me something? Whatever it is, I'm not buying.'

'Paul, this couldn't be better timing. I'm in a bind up here. I'm calling to offer you a career opportunity.'

'Up here? Where are you calling from? You're in Sydney, aren't you?'

'I was in Sydney, but it got . . .' Roland paused, '. . . complicated, shall we say. I decided to seek greener pastures. I'm based in Darwin now.'

'Darwin? Why'd you want to move to Darwin? I heard you'd made it big in Sydney.'

'Yeah, yeah. I'd done alright, in Sydney, but it was time to move on. I've found some new things to keep me out of mischief. You know how it is. I've been in Darwin for almost two years now.'

The needle on Paul's 'sixth sense meter' was maxed out at the 'warning, warning, disaster imminent' extreme of the scale. If the meter were real, red lights and a klaxon horn would be going full bore too.

'Roland, I appreciate your call, but, I'm in a transitionary phase, and I need to attend to a few things here. I really couldn't just up and move to Darwin right now, even if there was a great job waiting.'

'Paul, it doesn't need to be forever. I just want someone to sort out my front office for me. I need someone I know I can trust. You know, do the accounts, admin, handle payments, manage the staff. I'm crap at that stuff, but I know you'd be brilliant. It doesn't need to be forever, come up and try it.'

'No, I don't think I'm the person you're after. There must be heaps of people who could do that stuff. I—'

'Look, it doesn't need to be a permanent move to Darwin,' Roland cut in again, heading off Paul from rolling out another reason not to agree with Roland's plans for him. 'Just come up for a month, a few weeks. If you like it, stay. If you don't, consider it a working holiday. You know, no one else is going to be putting on new people until after the New Year now anyway. By that time, you'll know if the job is for you or not. What have you got to lose?' Roland had always known what strings to pull with Paul, and he could sense he was on a winner.

'Roland, you know I appreciate your offer, but how can I just up and leave? I've got commitments that I need to sort out.'

Roland continued. 'Paul now that your between jobs, you've got some time on your hands. Let me sort out a plane ticket. Just come up for a couple of weeks. I'll book you into a hotel—my shout. If you want to stay on, you can rent something longer term. I'm sure your commitments can wait a couple of weeks. I know you'll love it up here.' Despite not contacting Paul for some time, it was apparent Roland had done some homework on Paul's work situation. 'Mate, I'll send you a plane ticket. You'll receive it in the next day or so. Keep an eye out for it in the registered mail.' With that, he hung up.

Paul felt like he was back at school. Roland didn't argue for consensus, he just took the decision out of your hands and you had to play along.

There is no problem travelling around Australia other than the size of the place. The distance from Sydney to Darwin or Perth to Darwin is nearly two-and-a-half-thousand kilometres as the crow flies, roughly the same as London to Moscow. Buses, trains and cars all offer reasonable options. Many Australians think nothing of driving hundreds of kilometres in an afternoon. The distances and the resolve to drive for hours increases as you go further north, where consequences of travelling long distances seems to shorten as you leave the big cities further behind. The vastness of the place encourages air travel. Those that haven't travelled around Australia always underestimate its size. Is it a quirk of Cartesian maps or just that people expect cities and towns to be spaced a day's horse ride apart as they are in the northern hemisphere? You could fit a half dozen European countries into the footprint of Western Australia alone, and still have room to spare. There are cattle stations in northern Australia that are bigger than some countries.

Paul was tempted to avoid the plane trip and travel the four thousand kilometres by road. He had time on his hands and could grab a bus for a fraction of the plane ticket. The cost of the flight was frightening expensive, but Paul was paying. It was possible to fly from Perth to London for less than the cost of the Perth-Darwin fare, a fifth of the distance. Archaic government-imposed monopolies and regulations limited the number of carriers on routes, so the airlines scalped the locals as much as possible. He was glad when he received the air ticket in the mail. He could have used the cash difference between the flight and the bus fare but didn't think it was the right thing to do if Roland had already paid.

Paul flew over the landscape that quickly became parched as the plane set off to the northeast. He flew high above the red dirt that formed most of the trip between Perth and Darwin. He couldn't get over how empty the landscape appeared. Away from the green veneer on the coast, the country was packed to the brim with nothing. An occasional mine site emerged as a grey scar slashed across an ochre background. Salt lakes littered the landscape, appearing as reflective, white snowdrifts across the dry earth. There were scant signs of life. A spiderweb of tracks led out from occasional water holes. Nothing man-made bigger than an occasional roadhouse, connected by the grey lines of highways was to be seen. If aliens landed outside a major city in Australia, they would be tempted to claim *terra nullius* just as fraudulently as the first white colonialists had done.

17

Paul

I let Paul reminisce until I thought I was risking it becoming a therapy session, rather than a police investigation intent on gathering useful information. I wanted details on Roland that could build a profile to provide an insight into his motivations or a lead on his whereabouts. I was receiving a lecture on the world according to Paul. I brought his sermon to a close, and got things back on track.

'So, Paul. You mentioned that Roland's Dad died while Roland was quite young.'

'That's right. And a horrible death it was too. Roland's dad was an electrician by trade, installing air-conditioners and stuff. The years he spent crawling around in roof spaces where they'd used asbestos as insulation on ductwork meant he ended up with mesothelioma. He was diagnosed and died within a year. The way he went made everyone believe he would have like to have gone quicker if he had a choice.'

'What's that supposed to mean?'

'Well, one minute he's this larger-than-life character, drinking with the blokes down the pub and having a kick with his boys in the park, the next, he is reduced to skin and bone and dragging oxygen cylinders around on a little trolley.'

'How'd Roland take this?'

'How do you fuckin' think? He was the youngest of the boys, the only one still at home. He hated seeing his father die in front of his eyes.'

'Did he tell you that?'

'He didn't have to. You could see how he was taking it. The guts had been ripped out of the whole family.'

'So, did he open up to you about it?'

'Not directly. Though there was this once when he just bawled his eyes out. It was probably about a month or six weeks before his dad died. He and I were chatting. You know, just talking rubbish really, and he said he was sorry about a conversation we'd had years ago. He said he wished he'd said nothing and made me promise not to tell anyone he'd cried.'

'What was the conversation about?'

'Doesn't seem right really, after I'd promised Roland not to tell, but I don't suppose it matters now really, him being dead and all. It was about his dad being a tight arse.'

'Is that it? Doesn't sound that significant.'

'Roland told me how stingy his dad was.'

'What, tight with money and stuff?'

'Yeah, but often the level of stinginess seemed unnecessarily so. Roland still had a chip on his shoulder about the present his dad gave him for his twelfth birthday.'

'What five or six years earlier?'

'That's right. It was even before I knew Roland, but we were almost seventeen when we had the conversation. Roland had dropped many hints to his parents he wanted a new bike. Not just a new bike, but one with a banana seat, a sissy bar and a little T-bar, three-speed gear changer. Totally impractical, but that was what every young boy was hankering for at the time, I suppose. Do you know what I mean?'

'Yeah, I do. I'm a product of the '70s too. Couldn't see the sense of a T-bar gear change on a bike myself, but the '70s produced some quirky ideas.'

'Anyhow, Roland's hints didn't seem to be hitting home, so a good month before his birthday Roland told his dad exactly what he wanted, and his dad said if Roland played his cards right, did his chores, was good to his mother and didn't muck up at school, he would see what he could do. So, Roland became the perfect son and student, at least for a while. He reckoned he was set. He reminded his dad a week before his birthday, and Roland's dad said he had it sorted.'

'So, what's the problem with that?'

'Well, the day finally arrived, and Roland couldn't wait. He got up early, but, as no one else was up, so he just had to sit there and wait. Finally, his dad woke up, came out of the bedroom scratching his balls, and said to Roland, 'Your new bike is in the shed out the back, son.' Roland rushed outside, and there was his older brother's bike with a new seat and a sissy bar on it. His dad was pleased with himself 'cause it had a banana seat and a sissy bar just like Roland wanted, but Roland was shitty cause it was not a new bike at all, just his brother's old bike tarted up.'

'Sounds like that could have gone better for young Roland. Was that what he was shitty about?'

'Yes, and no. He was shitty about the bike, but he was mostly over it by then. As I say, a few years had passed. It wasn't even as if a bike of that sort was still cool. He was shitty because he'd told me what a tight arse his dad was. I suppose he felt bad because he recalled that he had said bad things about his dad when he was at death's door.'

'What did he say?'

'He told me that he and his mates were just twelve or thirteen-year-old kids back then, but he could remember most of the conversation.

Roland remembered every word and recited it back to me. It was just like him. He could even quote directly from books he'd read years before. Sometimes they just seemed to flow out of him, and you'd wonder how or why he even remembered that stuff. He never got one word of a quote from a book wrong. I tested him a few times, thinking I'd catch him out, but he was never wrong. It was always word for word. He was like some sort of savant or something with quotes and stuff. He wasn't brilliant with numbers, but any book he'd ever read, he could recite whole passages from. It is almost funny remembering him recall his conversation about his dad with his mates back then. Roland was on about how miserly his dad was, and he and his mates came up with these juvenile expressions, trying to outdo each other.'

'Such as?'

'Roland said his dad was so stingy he saved the fluff from his belly button for years so that he could use it to stuff a cushion. As I say, it was pretty childish stuff, but they just tried to outdo each other. One of his mates said he was so stingy he wouldn't give the sweat rolling down his bum crack on a hot summer's day to a man dying of thirst. Roland said his dad was so stingy he'd sell a dying man one of his lungs and charge him extra for the phlegm. Those words of Roland really cut home because, in his mind, they became weirdly prophetic. When Roland remembered what he had said, he took on some of the blame. It's that conversation that made him teary.

Not long after he'd said it, Roland's dad was in desperate need of a set of lungs. But by the time his Dad realised how bad he was he was too far gone. In those days, there was no hope of a turnaround. Roland blubbered some crap about it being his fault for saying that about his dad and how he'd caused it to happen and that he'd gladly pay the extra for someone's phlegm if he could get his dad even one lung that didn't have asbestos in it. He was blubbering shit, really, but I'd never seen Roland like that before. He was normally so sure of himself. He was pretty embarrassed for bawling in front of me when he told me all about it. He never mentioned it again. His dad was genuinely a tight arse though.'

'So, you'd agree with Roland on that one?'

'Yeah, his old man was a bloody tight arse. Lots of people at that time were tight. I suppose they'd seen their parents come through the times when you went without a fair bit. If you didn't stretch what you had, you went without. Roland's dad brought home the plastic wrap from his lunch so he could use it again. He saved all the little end bits of soap and then squeezed them together to make another bar. You know that sort of shit.'

'Wasn't this odd?'

'I suppose it wasn't odd enough for him to stop doing it. His mates must have thought he was a tight arse too. He always seemed to have a smoke when he was at the pub, but he only ever smoked OP's.'

'OP's?'

'Yeah, 'other people's'. Right up to the mesothelioma diagnosis, he was a regular smoker but had probably never bought a pack in his life. And his mates would tell you he'd always finish up at the pub just before he had to buy his next round of beers. That way, he got away with drinking a skinful on the cheap. Even his best mates would describe him as having short arms and long pockets.'

'Didn't they get pissed off with that after a while?'

'I suppose they did. I know I would have. But Roland's old man was a good bloke at heart and most people liked having him around. He told a good joke and knew a lot of people. Being a tradie, he got around a bit. I expect he did jobs on the cheap for his mates too.'

'What about his dad's business? Did he do alright?'

'I think he did okay. Everybody seemed the same back then. No one was overly flamboyant or on the bones of their bums. Most people back then were just steady. I remember one family at school that was only there because the eldest kid had a scholarship and as a result the siblings got reduced fees. The uniforms were always hand-me-downs from one to the other, and kids were always 'sick' for excursions, because they couldn't scrape together the few extra bucks it cost. But other than that, most people seemed to get by okay. Roland's old man was never stingy where his wife was concerned, though. He always bought her flowers and little presents.'

'What about Roland's mum? It must have been tough for her when Roland's dad passed away.'

'Eileen was a classic. Roland's dad was always Mr Redman, but Roland's mum told us off if any of us called her Mrs Redman. Eileen told us that Mrs Redman was the name of her mother-in-law, and she 'sure as hell didn't want to be mistaken for her'.'

'How'd his mum and dad get on?'

'They were good. From what I saw Mr Redman was totally smitten with Eileen. He wasn't shy of telling anyone he was punching above his weight with her. He said he'd never have got a wife as posh as Eileen if he hadn't got her 'up the duff'. Roland would squirm every time his dad would say that. When we were old enough to do that math, we worked out she was three months gone with Roland's oldest brother Frank when they got married.

'Eileen's family was horrified. And Eileen's mum wasn't shy about saying that Eileen could have done better even in front of Roland's dad. When Mr Redman's mum got wind of this, she tried making life tough for Eileen. You know, the typical stuff: 'he likes his eggs cooked this way, he left nothing on the plate when I cooked', etc. Eileen thought Granny Redman was just an old bitch, and she probably was. But I think it was just trying to even the score with Eileen's side of the family.'

'Sounds like you liked Eileen.'

'Yeah, I suppose I did. All of us did. She was one of a kind. A classic really. She probably had married beneath her status, but she didn't make any bones about it, and she genuinely seemed to love Roland's dad and the boys. I think Roland's parents loved each other even if they were opposites in many ways. Eileen had an endearing way of seeming both posh and rough at the same time.'

'What do you mean by that?'

'Little things. She spoke differently to the rest of us. I expect she went to a posh girl's school. It might have just been a Melbourne accent too, but it was also how she said things.'

'Such as?'

'She'd never talk to us like we were kids. Right from when we were little until we definitely weren't, she always called us 'darling'. Even with her posh accent, she wasn't averse to dropping the odd f-bomb. Or the occasional c-bomb, for that matter. When she said the c-word, it didn't even sound like swearing because her accent made it just sound like an anatomical description or something. She'd walk around until lunchtime in a silk dressing gown she referred to as her 'brunch coat'. We all just thought she was in her pyjamas. She'd always have a cigarette on the go and carried around a little portable ashtray. It was a little thing about the size of an egg, designed to fit in the palm of your hand with a little flip top that popped open when you pushed a button on the side. I never once saw her manage to get any ash into it though. She'd always leave her cigarette dangling from her fingers for so long the ash would fall onto the carpet. Then she'd make it disappear by rubbing it in with the toe of one of her silly shoes. They looked like slippers, but they had a heel and a fluffy pom-pom on the top. She'd seen them on '*Bewitched*' or some other TV show back in the day, and thought they looked sophisticated. Every evening she'd have Mr Redman's dinner on the table at six sharp knowing that nine times out of ten he'd stop off for a few quiet ones with the lads on the way home. Mr Redman must have had more cold-hot dinners than you've had hot dinners.'

'So, did she work or anything?'

'By any measure bringing up three boys and Mr Redman was pretty tough work. She did the books for the business. But by the time Roland left high school, she'd given herself a redundancy.'

'What do you mean by that?'

'She'd probably just had enough. Roland's was the youngest of the three brothers. Roland's dad was pretty hard work, especially when he got crook, and that's when she figured she'd done her bit. Eileen did her best to nurse him before he died. By that stage, the boys could fend for themselves, at least the older two. Roland's dad's illness took the wind out of her sails. She'd just had enough, and she wanted time for herself. Initially, that meant permitting herself a G&T in the afternoons. Over time the amount of gin grew as the amount of tonic shrank. The volume stayed the same, but the potency increased. Eventually she even ditched the ice to fit in more gin. After Roland's dad died, when the insurance money finally came through, she suddenly up and left, moved to Melbourne and lived with her sister. Last I heard, she was still there. She'd be getting on now though.'

18

Paul

There was no need to tell Paul every detail that I knew, at this stage, but I felt for him. He'd just lost his mate. I had already had him at the station for hours, but I also knew I had to press on. I wasn't going to be the one to call a halt while he was on a roll. Tomorrow he might clam up. I decided to take a different tack.

'Does the name Christina Anne Brown mean anything to you?'

Paul looked both surprised and tired. He rested his forehead in one hand and reached for his, now cold, coffee with the other. 'Don't tell me Christina was in the car too?'

'Christina passed away several years ago, Mr Winter. Do you know if Mr Redman had kept in contact with her?'

'Of course, we both knew her. We went to school together, as I told you earlier. I told you Roland had a thing for her.

I'm tired of this bullshit; take me to my hotel. I need to sleep. If you want any more answers, arrest me.'

'Mr Winter, I'm not going to arrest you,' I said, not necessarily believing I wouldn't if I could find a reason to. 'I can take you to your hotel, but I'd like to speak to you tomorrow. Where abouts are you staying?'

'Roland made a booking for me at Hotel Apollo. Do you know it?'

'Yes. I know it well. It's not a fancy place. I thought your loaded mate might have put you somewhere a bit flashier. How about I drop you there, and we catch up tomorrow morning? I appreciate you've had a less than ideal introduction to Darwin, but there are a few more things I'd like to run past you.'

'I'm done for tonight. I need to sleep. I'll stay at the hotel. Drop me there and we can speak again in the morning. If there's nothing to keep me here, I might as well head back to Perth in the next day or so.'

I drove Winter to Hotel Apollo. We'd used it plenty of times to house visiting police from down south, new starters and the occasional informant. It was cheap but clean. I tapped the bell on the front desk to alert the desk clerk, who had heard us arrive but hadn't moved from his chair.

'Hey, Spiros, this guy's just lobbed into Darwin and needs a room.' I'd always struggled to say Spiros' surname correctly. It was something Greek, about 27 letters long ending in 'opolous.

Spiros stubbed his cigarette into the ashtray. It was overflowing with ash, burnt matches and cigarette butts. Old rolly butts reclined on a bed of cigarette ash and burnt matches, tapered cylinders, moist and stained at one end making them look like a pile of miniature sun-bleached turds. He wiped his hands on the front of his singlet that had long forgotten that it had once been white, prised himself off the chair and glanced back at the tiny black and white TV that was playing the theme tune of M*A*S*H in the background.

'Gotta booking?' said Spiros, who made no secret of being pissed off because he hadn't finished watching the end of his program. The end credits rolled, so it wasn't as if he'd missed much.

'I'm not staying here. He is,' I said, pointing at Winter, who was standing near the lift staring at the '*Not Working*' sign written on yellowing paper. He was staring mindlessly at the little sign as if he couldn't figure out how to proceed. Was he waiting for the lift to magically fix itself? If this were the case, he would have to wait a long while.

'So, *he* gotta booking?'

'Sort of; I think you'll have a booking made by a Mr Redman.'

The hotelier muttered something and flipped open the guest ledger. 'It's nearly Christmas, you know. We're pretty full. Lucky Mr Redman made a booking. Made it for his friend Mr Ball-sack. You Ball-sack?' asked the Greek, pointing at Winter.

With that, Winter turned around and said, 'I'm Ball-sack,' with a smirk.

'You, Mr Ball-sack? Got a reservation for a Mr Ball-sack,' said the hotelier. 'Reservation's for the for a whole week, made by Mr Redman.'

Paul chuckled to himself, knowing Roland had deliberately used the name that he had called his old English Literature teacher. It was a typical Roland thing to do. A little in-joke. 'Yes, yes, I'm Mr Balzac, but I'm afraid Mr Redman is dead.'

Up until that point, the hotelier's every word had been delivered with such exaggerated fatigue, as if even speaking was an effort and indicating that we should be eternally grateful for his efforts. Hearing that Redman was dead pierced Spiros like a stiletto. Now, he seemed genuinely saddened.

'I very sorry to hear that, Mr Ball-sack. Mr Redman was a good man, and a good friend to this place too. So sorry to hear about Mr Redman. *Anapafsou en eirini*. May he rest in peace,' Spiros said, punctuating his concern with a sign of the cross.

As he completed the reflexive religious gesture, a couple looking more than a bit tipsy came down the stairs arm in arm, almost missing the last step and stumbling into reception towards Paul. They giggled as they headed for the exit, but not before the man had almost bumped into Paul. The girl turned and gave Paul a second glance, I'm sure not out of polite concern, but more likely assessing him as a potential client.

'Steady on you two, this bloke, he just lost a friend,' said the Greek.

'Well he's gonna find it hard to get a new one with that clobber,' said the girl, referring to Paul's suit that was more of a crumpled mess than it had previously, much to her man's amusement.

'Did you say Mr Redman had made the booking for a week?' asked Winter.

'Yes, paid in advance. He came to see me himself to make the booking. As I say, Mr Redman was a good friend to this place. Even if he only wanted a room for an hour or two, he'd pay for the full day. Not like some stingy bastards,' he spat, pointing at the departing couple with his chin, 'who try to only pay for half an hour. I've still gotta change the sheets most of the time, you know.'

Winter must have been having second thoughts about staying here. If Roland was rolling in dough, surely, he could have put him in a better class of place, but it was late, it had been a hell of a day, and it was paid for. He took the key, picked up his bag and headed off to room 214 on the second floor, via the stairs.

'It's Mr Winter, Paul Winter. Mr Redman was playing a little joke on you,' Winter said, 'and on me too.'

'Spiros, please wake up Mr Winter in the morning. Paul, I want you to meet me tomorrow morning at ten-thirty,' I said, handing him a slip of paper on which I'd written 'little café next door to 'The Bookshop Darwin' in the Mall'. 'I need you to answer a few more questions before you leave town, okay?'

'Sure, café near the bookshop, ten-thirty tomorrow.'

By the time Winter reached his room, his mind had raced through all that had happened since he had left Perth, but he was exhausted, and he couldn't make any sense of it, let alone put it in a sensible order. The emotional rollercoaster had kept him running on empty for a while, but as soon as he saw the bed, all he could do was flop onto it. He instantly fell into comatose slumber.

* * *

'Mr Ball-sack! Mr Ball-sack!'

The bloody Greek was knocking on the door. It seemed like I'd signed in just minutes ago. Surely it hadn't been long, but it was light outside. The bright Darwin sun was shining through the room's threadbare curtains. The sun was up so it had to be at least seven, though when I glanced at the clock on the bedside table, I was surprised to see that it was already eight-thirty. I opened the door and saw the Greek holding a breakfast tray out in front of him.

'Thought you could use a feed. You looked tired when you came in. I didn't think you'd want dinner. Mr Redman paid for bed and breakfast too. Hope you like sausages and beans?'

'Yes, thanks, mate. Beans and snags sound good. It's Mr Winter, Paul Winter, remember. Not Ball-sack.'

'Oh yes, sorry. My name is Spiros, Spiros Petropopolous. I would have changed my name too if it was Ball-sack.'

The Greek noticed I was still wearing what I'd had on the night before, albeit now even more crumpled. He could see that my bed had been slept on, not in. In his hotel, I'm sure this wasn't out of the ordinary.

19

Roland

Roland had assumed he would have the same job in Sydney that he had been doing in Perth. He'd be walking from house to house in new suburbs selling the same, dodgy insurance policies to naive families, just in the bigger market of Sydney. But the freshly restructured insurance company had more aggressive plans. Roland's promotion meant that instead of selling policies, he was buying them.

Roland's job was to find ANP clients with sizable life insurance policies and correlate them against hospital records, not always sourced through official channels, to find policyholders with a terminal illness. Then he bought the policy in return for a cash sum lower than the company would have to pay out when the policyholder died. The policyholder often needed the cash in the hope, however futile, of managing the illness that they were dying from. Experimental drugs, even those for palliative care, were always more expensive than the average person could afford. At least in this way, the final days of the policyholder's existence were made a little more bearable. The cynic might see this scheme as little more than an insurer's twist on the cliché ambulance-chasing lawyer. Still, Roland massaged his conscience enough to make it palatable and very profitable. Profits flowed for both him and the company.

The hospital staff didn't like Roland, the insurance company, or his job. They knew there was nothing illegal about his activities, so they begrudgingly tolerated him. Sure, buying a five hundred thousand dollar policy for fifty thousand didn't seem fair, but in the late eighties, fifty thousand dollars could buy some decent care and a lot of morphine, and five hundred thousand dollars was of no use to a corpse. The closer the patient was to death, the better the deal Roland could squeeze out of them.

Roland couldn't believe his good fortune, even though it was at the expense of others. Pancreatic, liver or bladder cancer, and leukemia were hidden windfalls in full view within the hospital records. It was only a question of when not how these illnesses would take away the patient. These were such virulent ailments that any hope of a cure was so remote that it was dismissed. Cancer is a complex collection of varied conditions that just looking for 'cancer' in the hospital records was never enough.

Cancer isn't a single illness. The public was often asked to put their hands in their pockets to fund a 'cure for cancer'. What few appreciate was that a solitary cure for the monster that is cancer is impossible. Cancer is a Medusa, where cutting the head off one snake leaves many others to grow and flourish. Winning one battle against cancer doesn't guarantee the defeat of any other. Cancer remains the body's confused and misdirected response to a range of conditions. But Roland knew that focusing on the top four or five least treatable cancers would enable him to make money. Lots of money.

Roland's focus on cancer patients provided him with a rapidly growing bank account, but the HIV/AIDS pandemic, a previously unheard-of disease, quickly outnumbered his cancer patients. When the patients had originally taken out their life insurance policies HIV/ AIDS was unknown. Later, the insurers hid an HIV/AIDS exclusion clause in the miasma of the policy's fine print. Roland didn't think about the lives these people had previously lived. He wouldn't let himself be persuaded to give them a better deal. What would they do with more money, anyway? They were dying. Some would hang around for months, a year at most, but many were gone within a few weeks. If he analysed the numbers, he could do exceedingly well. Even if they had morphine for breakfast, lunch and dinner, they'd still have enough left over for a dessert of OxyContin. In some cases, it wasn't the lure of better palliative care that made the patients sign his settlement agreement.

Many of those he approached with his proposal just told him in no uncertain terms to piss off. A few called the nurses and requested that he be blocked from seeing them. That was mainly unnecessary. Roland knew how to approach people and could tell a willing client and those who were not. There were enough willing clients, so he didn't need to harass anyone that wasn't interested. If potential clients wanted to hand their money to a partner or loved one after they passed, it was their choice. He didn't argue with those that wanted to hand over their insurance funds to the Cat Haven, the Catholics, or their own undeserving family.

Over time, Roland eventually charmed many nurses in the palliative care wards and got the orderlies on side with occasional flowers, a bottle of Champagne or Scotch or a carton of cigarettes. The bigger problem was the relatives of the dying. They knew Roland was doing them out of their inheritance. Roland had had to talk his way out of more than a few angry confrontations. The wives, husbands, lovers, sons, daughters, mothers and fathers of the dying had called him all manner of things.

The families didn't mince their words when they were upset, or even when they were not. The angry and upset relatives directed the most colourful insults at him. He quickly developed a thicker skin.

But some of the insults still hit home. Insults that included the usual colourful terms combined with descriptions of him being a vulture or parasite cut him. They stung the most when a wife, a mother or worst of all, a grandmother delivered them. Sure, many insults were pretty blue, but deep-down Roland knew he was profiting from the misery and misfortune fortune of others. Whenever he could avoid the families of his soon to be ex-customers, he would. The dying themselves were always more resigned to their fate than their families.

When he first heard the job proposal, it didn't sound too bad. The company had framed it as giving someone without hope the means to live more comfortably in their final days. It sounded like he was providing a public service. Providing succour to the damned sounded like an honourable thing.

Roland's first foray into the AIDS ward was memorable, but not for good reasons. He couldn't stay long. A fog of despair infused everything. Initially at least, the smell didn't seem worse than a normal hospital ward, but later as patient density increased, the pervasive rancid yeast smell of candida permeated everything. The characteristic odour of the fungus that fed on human flesh eventually became so pervasive that it ingrained itself into his memory. Every patient ended up with an out-of-control fungal infection. At first, powerful drugs kept the fungus in check, but an immune system under constant attack couldn't hold out forever. The body eventually had no strength left to resist.

Roland's desire to make money surpassed his initial reluctance in dealing with AIDS patients. There was plenty of money to be made. Before the 80s, who would have thought an insurance policy for a twenty or thirty year-old would be called upon so soon? Hell, the average Aussie twenty-year-old male never even visited a doctor, let alone a hospital. That was before HIV/AIDS.

'Hey, honey!' the patient said as Roland passed by before lapsing into a coughing fit. 'Come and spend some time with me.'

Roland kept walking; he had a potential client that he wanted to speak with in the ward. He approached the duty nurse, who looked at him with distaste and tiredness. He could sense that if he was going to regularly here, he would have to win the nurses over.

'I'm looking for Mark Ridgeway. Could you point me in his direction, please?'

'Bay twenty seven, third bed on the right,' the duty nurse replied tersely.

'Thanks. You are wearing a lovely perfume. Do you mind if I ask what it is, Nurse Carlyle?' Roland said, reading the nurse's name badge and trying to make a friend at the start.

'*Arpege*. It helps to mask the stench of candida that permeates this place, and it is Sister Carlyle if you must speak to me, though I'd prefer it if you didn't.'

Roland's efforts to make a good first impression had failed. This nurse would be a more challenging assignment than he'd first thought. Roland took it on the chin. He would have to take a different tack next time.

Roland found Mark Ridgeway. He was a slip of a man with sallow cheeks and remnants of orange hair. Clumps of hair lay littered across his white hospital pillow, leaving bald patches scattered across his scalp. An oxygen line led to his nose. He watched Roland approach and smiled revealing bloody holes in his gums where teeth had once been. He wouldn't be around much longer.

'Hello, Mark. My name is Roland Redman. I'm representing ANP Insurance.' He had practised the spiel the night before. He could recite the company's recommended opening lines as well as any of his beloved book quotes. He thought he'd prepared himself for the task ahead, but Mark cut him off before he got into a rhythm.

'I know what you are,' Mark wheezed and paused to let the oxygen line refill his failing lungs. 'I've been expecting you or someone like you. What's *your* story?'

Roland continued with the pitch. 'ANP values you as a client, and your policy has been accumulating—'

'No, no! I don't need to hear your ANP bullshit. What's *your* story? I know what you want. I sign a form, you give me a fraction of what I'm owed now, and you and your company get the rest as soon as I die.'

Mark then lapsed into a coughing fit. He pulled a handkerchief out from under his pillow and held it to his mouth. When he finished, Roland could see it was covered in blood and sputum. Too much blood.

Roland didn't know how to respond. This guy had summed up the process concisely. Get some money now by signing the bulk over to the company, payable on death. Roland swallowed hard; he couldn't bullshit this guy. He was close to meeting his maker. It wouldn't be good if he thought Roland was being an arsehole, even if he was.

'Guilty as charged, I'm afraid,' Roland said, thinking his new career in this was over before it had even started.

'Okay, where do I sign,' replied Mark.

'What? It sounded like you weren't interested.'

'I think your company is pond scum, but what choice do I have? I can wait around and get nothing, or I can take your blood money now and do what I can to make my time left as bearable as possible. God knows I don't have too long to wait; I might as well enjoy a bit of luxury while I can. Mind you; if you weren't such a cutie, I mightn't have been so willing to speak to you. Are you seeing anyone?' Mark certainly wasn't wasting any time.

'I, I, I'm not seeing anyone, but, but I'm straight,' stammered Roland.

'Pity, but I'm only messing with you. My man chasing days are over. You'll do okay with people in here as long as you're upfront with them. Don't bullshit them about the possibility of a cure, what a great company ANP is, doing the right thing by families and stuff and sure as hell don't harp on about God. Everybody in here has heard it all before. The less bullshit you say, the better off everyone will be. Especially these girls,' Mark said, waving a hand towards other men in the ward. 'They know their fate. Just treat them like real people, offer them a conversation not a contract. See if you can give them bit of respect and dignity in their last days, and you and your horrible company will do alright.'

'I can't thank you enough, Mark. I was dreading coming here today,' admitted Roland.

'There you go. That sort of honesty and your natural boyhood charm will get you a long way,' said Mark, winking a watery eye.

Roland blushed. This guy, dying as he was, was still flirting with him. 'Thanks,' said Roland and offered him the form ANP had prepared, effectively giving Mark forty thousand dollars for his four-hundred-thousand-dollar policy. Roland would get twenty thousand dollars for his efforts from ANP. Mark's policy really had been bought for pennies on the dollar. Roland had just made as much in the first few hours in this new job, as he had made in whole of the previous year.

Roland spent the next hour and a half talking with Mark. It wasn't the ANP sanctioned banter. The company was keen to get the signature and move on. Don't get emotionally attached. Don't divulge any personal details. Roland had thrown the ANP rule book out the window on the first day. Roland told Mark about his life in Perth and his recent moved to Sydney. Mark told Roland about moving to Sydney from rural New South Wales, doing commerce at UTS and his career as a grain broker for Elders in the city.

Roland told Mark about his teenage aspirations of being a journalist and his love of books. Mark was well read too and he and Roland spent some time talking about their favourite authors. Mark was impressed with Roland's talent of being able to recite tracts from his favourites from memory. The words of Harper Lee, Alice Munroe, Franz Kafka and Ernest Hemingway ricocheted across the aseptic and hard hospital surfaces. Roland couldn't believe how easy making $20,000 had just been.

'I'm back here Tuesday, tomorrow. Is there anything I can bring you Mark?' Roland asked, feeling uncharacteristically generous after such a windfall.

'I'd kill for a pizza, ham and pineapple. I know, I know, ham and pineapple isn't the classic, but the food in here either tastes like cardboard or shit. If you can get a pizza past the nurses, that'd be great. Here, take twenty bucks.' Mark leaned towards his bedside drawer.

'Mark. I can't take your money.'

'Roland, you just have!' Mark said, making sure Roland understood the irony of what had just transpired.

Mark's request was humbling. Roland wasn't a fan of ham and pineapple pizza. But he wasn't about to deny a dying man what might be his last meal. He'd do what he could.

The following day, Roland dutifully rolled up to the ward with the pizza. He skipped past the duty desk, not wanting to get told he couldn't bring a pizza on to the ward. He knew where to find Mark; bay twenty-seven, third on the right.

Roland stopped dead in his tracks. He looked at the bed Mark had been in the day before, except now it had a different occupant.

A large, Mediterranean-looking guy said, 'A pizza for me? That's lovely. I hope it's pepperoni. I could kill for pepperoni pizza. The food in here is dreadful.'

Roland still couldn't move. His feet felt stuck to the hospital linoleum.

'Don't look disappointed. I'll still eat it if it's not pepperoni.'

'I, I, I was looking for Mark.'

'I'm sorry, love. Mark's checked out.'

'What do you mean checked out?'

'I think you know what I mean; he didn't make it. It'll be a miracle if any of us in here makes it out alive. You know the trip to Ward 17 only goes one way.'

Roland spun on his heels and headed for the exit. He stopped himself, walked back to the new patient's bed and left the pizza on the hospital table, straddling the bed. The reality of the human face of AIDS hit Roland more than he had expected it would. He felt crushed. He'd have to toughen up if he wanted to make the most of this new venture in his career.

20

Roland

When I look back on those days, the widespread lack of compassion shown to patients suffering with HIV/AIDS appals me. It wasn't enough that they had received a death sentence at the hands of a virus, it was the vilification that the media cultured that appalled me.

It was inconceivable to live in Sydney and not know someone who had died from HIV/AIDS in those days. While it was most devastating to the gay community, at least in its early days, it was a disease that didn't discriminate. Gay, straight, black, white, rich or poor, men or women. The disease fed on people, irrespective of their circumstance or orientation.

The killer was rarely the disease itself. The real killer was complications that resulted from a decimated immune system. Some died of organ failure, many died from pneumonia, hepatitis and far too many died at their own hand. Parents commonly advised extended families and friends that their son or daughter had died of pneumonia, cancer or leukemia. Something that elicited a sympathetic response. Almost anything but HIV/AIDS. That so many fit, healthy, attractive young men and women succumbed to pneumonia must have aroused suspicion. Still, the spectre of being gay and dying from HIV/AIDS in the eighties was enough to make people accept an inconceivable death over accepting an unpalatable truth.

The preliminary symptoms of pneumonia, more correctly, *pneumocystis carinii pneumonia* or PCP, were generally the first signs of HIV/AIDS. It would start as a niggling cough or an unexplained shortness of breath that just wouldn't go away. Most would ignore it. 'Its just one of those twenty-four-hour viruses. I'll get better soon', they thought, but they never did. The next step was a trip to a doctor and an x-ray. The truth was too brutal to deny. In an x-ray necrotic tissue was visible even to the untrained eye. Generally, by the time the x-ray was taken, the patient's lung tissue had atrophied. Doctors would prescribe massive amounts of broad-spectrum antibiotics. The doses became progressively so large that the body's natural biota was destroyed, allowing an invasion of yeasts and bacteria. White patches of candida would take up residence in the patient's mouth, and anywhere moist. Eating and drinking became painful and it gave them appalling halitosis.

Fleshy, sarcomas erupted randomly over the patients' bodies. Purple-red blistered growths appeared from candida-breached skin. The progress of the disease meant that patients wasted away. They took on a look that might have been expected from someone unfortunate enough to have been in Auschwitz or Bergen-Belson, not Sydney. Translucent skin hung off bony frames, like a kid dressed in their parents' clothes. Once fine-skinned, beautiful people were reduced to pus-oozing, foul-smelling abominations of their former selves. Few patients asked for compassion, as they found it impossible to look in the mirror and give any compassion to the face they could hardly recognise as their own. By the time Roland came to speak with them about their life insurance policy, they placed little value on their own lives.

Roland considered his move to Sydney to be lucky. It was brilliant timing. After San Francisco, Sydney held the dubious title of HIV/AIDS capital of the world. Sydney was the epicentre of Australia's gay community. The annual Mardi Gras through the streets towards the gay mecca of Kings Cross and its bars, clubs and colourful nightlife were the outward signs of Sydney's vibrant and populous gay community. By proxy, it also meant that Sydney became the capital of HIV/AIDS treatment in Australia. The appallingly ineffective and employment-linked health insurance system in the US meant many Americans travelled to Sydney for treatment. More young American men died from HIV/AIDS than had died in the Vietnam War, yet mainstream society refused to acknowledge the reality of such a confronting statistic.

Royal North Shore Hospital, Sydney, established a whole ward specifically to treat HIV/AIDS patients. Roland had no difficulty finding clients willing to sign over their insurance policies for funds to help ease their pain. Some took the deal as a final act of defiance against a family and society that had shunned them, others took the funds just to pay for their last days in hospital.

Unlike other hospital wards, Ward 17 quickly became surreal. Any compassionate person would have found it impossible to resist being sucked into the vortex of despair in which these fragile souls were drowning. Like a kitten washed into a storm-fed culvert, HIV/AIDS patients bravely struggled against their illness. The kitten fights valiantly against the current as it is swept into a raging storm culvert. It understands the inevitable, it knows that drowning will be the only outcome, but it fights on, determined to defiantly use its last tranche of energy to prolong the journey by moments. But the end looms largely. Just as the kitten makes a stand against the odds, HIV/AIDS patients are proud enough to care about their final days, hours or minutes of their lives that, while knowing their resistance is feeble against the inevitable, they are determined to go with the dignity in defiance of the disease that has engulfed them.

Roland had to become immune to the pain that surrounded him. He had to ignore the requests that he was presented with to accelerate a patient's final journey. He struggled with the pain that was before him every day, but he couldn't take the pain away by assisting them with an early death. Initially, he was horrified anyone could ask him to do such a thing. Despite the macabre business he found himself, and the growing number of pay cheques he cashed, he still believed that life was a sacred gift.

Roland did not believe in a traditional God, but he was spiritual. He struggled with the contradictions and the years of inculcated doctrines of his catholic school education at St Philip's. The nature of his current job and the disgraceful expose of countless church paedophiles gave him a more logical perspective on God and the world. If God existed, Roland believed, He or She wasn't the interventionist God that answered prayers, took sides in wars or made images of Christ appear on slices of toast in some Louisiana Baptist backwater. Roland's god didn't need such nonsense to prove their existence to convert pagans. If they existed, they were more likely to be a super-intelligent, cosmic experimentalist. Though he never voiced this as an opinion, he sometimes lay awake thinking of such things. If it was some sort of cosmic experiment, what was it trying to prove and when would it reach a conclusion? In reality, Roland was much more likely to just say, 'all religion is crap'.

So, Roland steeled himself against becoming emotionally invested. He taught himself to see the dying, not as people but as policy numbers, as commodities that contributed to his booming bank account. Roland convinced himself that his job helped dying people gain comfort towards the end of their life. He didn't think about who these young people were before they were relegated to just being policy numbers on his client list. He didn't acknowledge that just a short while ago, they had been beautiful young men and women, living their lives to the fullest.

Most saw Roland as a parasite, preying on the sick, the weak and the dying. Sucking the remains of life from those who had already had most of their lives sucked away. An emotionless, robotic drone for the big insurance companies, happily taking patients' money. The terms on the policy meant that they, or their beneficiaries, were paid, however, the timing of any such payment and the amount was negotiable until the end.

The insurance industry needed to act quickly. Roland's new job was part of that reaction. AIDS was an out-of-control rollercoaster that threatened to go off the rails. It could swamp the insurers. This new, devastating disease ruthlessly taking out 20-40-year-olds, who the insurers had previously assumed posed the least risk. They could have scarcely imagined at the time that HIV/AIDS would grip the 20-40 year-old demographic in a wave of terror that left the insurers only marginally less scared than the insured. The epidemic would cost many lives and the insurers many, many millions.

The plan was simple. Buy out the policies of the terminally ill, with cents on the dollar, while they are alive, instead of paying out the far greater amount to the patient's estate. It was the same deal that Roland had employed with the cancer patients. All the scheme needed was a patient whose disease had eroded their hope and resilience. HIV/AIDS alienated most friends and relatives, so their deteriorated condition and social isolation made them willing targets.

AIDS hysteria swamped the seemingly tolerant and rational Australian public. Some ignorantly thought that AIDS could be caught by merely speaking to affected patients, as if it was passed through the mystical ethereal miasma like those in the Dark Ages thought occurred with Black Death. Even though there were no known cases of doctors or nurses occupationally contracting the disease, the general population was not easily assured. Some on talkback radio said AIDS was a good thing—the wrath of God on sinners. Compassion is quickly swept aside where fear and ignorance thrive.

Roland's new job was even unpalatable to many of his insurance industry colleagues. The job was perceived to have a greater risk in dealing with the infected; as such, the commission was raised. Roland got a generous amount from every policy he bought for ANP.

Soon Roland could use his rapidly mounting bank account to directly tackle the policyholders from other insurers from his own bankroll. If he was being paid to fleece ANP clients, what harm did it do to fleece ANP's competitors' clients too? He thought of it as doing ANP a favour. Soon Roland had signed most of the competitor's clients over—not to ANP as the beneficiary, but to himself. He had learnt to time it right, so he didn't wait long for his payouts. He even countered his conscience by offering the dying client a better rate than he received from ANP. The other insurance companies eventually cottoned on and weren't at all happy but they were powerless against him.

Despite his newfound wealth, Roland remained naïve with his personal finances. His bank account rapidly passed six figures and was well on the way to seven as it built on the exponential numbers of HIV/AIDS deaths. His purchases included a $15,000 Rolex Yacht-Master watch, a gold and onyx pinkie ring and other baubles, the latest wide shouldered suits and a Jaguar XJS V12. He had too much money and not enough time on his hands to spend it sensibly. All the while he ignored compassion and counted his cash.

21

Roland

Roland compiled his list of clients for his Monday visit to Ward 17, as he had done for the last two years. The staff greeted him with progressively less derision over time. They knew him and tolerated him. He wasn't liked, and the staff certainly didn't like what he was doing, but they acknowledged him as part of the hospital's landscape. He was a hyena in Attenborough's documentary, *Life on the Plains of Africa*. No one liked that the hyenas preyed on the wildebeests. No one wanted to acknowledge the reality that the hyenas had to eat too. No one recognised that the hyenas made the wildebeest's gene pool stronger by taking out the old, the weak and the sick. The pre-destined cruelty was necessary for everyone to survive.

The nurses saw Roland as a hyena; not liked, but a necessary part of the landscape. It was that he was profiting from it that made it so unpalatable. He'd gone from wearing a suit that would have been embarrassed to sit on a rack at Good Sammy's to wearing tailored Zegna suits and too much jewellery. Roland liked to show off his newfound wealth—too ostentatiously for most people's taste. If the nurses knew that he'd gone from arriving at Ward 17 by bus to now arriving in his Jaguar so quickly, could they have despised him even more?

Roland had two clients on his list that morning, Damon Cousins and Chris Smith. Although it was always difficult to predict how long any client would take, two clients for the day wasn't a demanding schedule. He'd usually have to schmooze them anything from ten minutes to two hours before he could walk away with the necessary signature. Roland knew where he had to go on the ward. He winked at the ward nurse as he skipped past. The nurse ignored him.

The discussion with Damon was easy. Damon was determined to inform him that he wasn't 'meant to be in this situation'. Through much coughing and gagging, he advised Roland that he was a haemophiliac, not gay. His illness was given to him through a HIV/AIDS infected blood transfusion. He was sure to point out that his illness was not a result of his sexual behaviour. Either way, HIV/AIDS had decided his days were numbered. Damon found it difficult to speak. As he struggled to get each word out, Roland noticed the thick, white, furry lining of his mouth. He'd seen enough of this to know that the level of thrush Damon was fighting against meant he would not be around much longer. Roland received the necessary signature and moved on to his next case, Chris Smith.

Roland started his introduction before he had properly sighted the patient in the next room. 'Hello, Mr Smith, I'm Roland Redman from the ANP insurance company . . .' He plucked the doctor's notes from the end of the bed, his tactic to imply that he was officially sanctioned and he noticed he'd already made a big mistake. Mr Smith was a Ms Smith. It was a mistake he'd made before. He had promised himself to be more mindful of such a thing. Women were fewer in number among the HIV/AIDS patients at that time, but their cases were on the rise. Initially, it was unusual for wards to have mixed patients, but in Ward 17, HIV/AIDS was the common determinant. He shouldn't have made the error. Chris could have just as easily been Christine as Christopher. Roland was professionally embarrassed. He was about to launch into an apology, but there was something about the patient that caused him to pause.

'Hello, Roland. It's been a long time,' the patient wheezed, sucking oxygen from the line clipped to her nose.

Roland couldn't speak. He recognised something in the patient's face, something in the voice. It was as if being given a few pieces of a jigsaw puzzle. If you were lucky, the pieces gave you an inkling of what the completed picture might be. If you were unlucky, you were none the wiser. Roland had no idea, but he felt he should have recalled who, where or why this person triggered a memory.

'I can't say I blame you for not recognising me. I'm sure I'd have trouble recognising myself these days,' she said before running out of breath. She paused, sucked in several breaths and said again, 'It has been a long time.' She couldn't afford the luxury of repeating herself, but she carried on, hoping Roland's perplexed expression would dissipate if prompted with extra information. 'It looks like you're doing okay.' She paused and wheezed. 'I think we've both come a long way since high school.'

Sudden recollection slapped Roland in the face. Chris was Christina. Christina Brown, the subject of his schoolboy infatuation. 'Christina, how, how, how are you going?' Roland blathered. What a dumb question. As if anyone in Ward 17, was likely to give you a positive answer

'To be honest, Roland, I've had better days,' Chris squeezed out.

'It is so good to see you after all these years,' Roland said, trying to recover from his idiotic opening but still tripping over his tongue. The years and the disease had ravaged the person before him, so far from how he remembered her. 'How, how . . .?' Roland struggled as he tried to reconcile the beauty that he had held in his heart for so many years with the reality of the desiccated shell of a woman in front of him.

'You know how it is, Roland. Wrong crowd. Wrong time. Wrong

man,' Christina said.

'Christina, I'm so sorry. I had no idea. The list said Chris Smith. I never would—'

'No apology necessary,' Christina said, cutting him off before she took three determined draws on the oxygen line that seemed to scare off the wheezing for a while. 'I stopped being Christina after I left school, Roland. I go by Chris now, and you know that a lot of us in here are Smith or Jones.'

The use of Smiths and Jones was, of course, a thinly veiled attempt that the patients made to keep their family names off the record. The hospital admissions staff turned a blind-eye to it, until a death certificate revealed the patient's real name. It made Roland's job a little more difficult to have so many Smiths and Jones on his lists, but HIV/AIDS didn't give a shit who you were. HIV/AIDS didn't care about your name or origin, if you were Czech, Serb, Arab, Jew or just plain Aussie

Early on, it looked like HIV/AIDS would prey exclusively on young, gay men, but that distinction didn't last. It didn't discriminate. It was a cold, heartless disease that eventually touched everyone. The message that confronted every Australian in their lounge rooms via the blunt but effective 'Grim Reaper' TV advertising campaign made sure everyone was aware if the diseases' reach.

Despite the public health campaign, there wasn't a let-up in hospital admissions. The ward was full. There were now four beds in rooms meant for two. The ward mixed men and women—the disease categorised them, not their gender. There didn't seem to be any respite for those that found themselves on Ward 17. Some hung around for months, others only weeks, but their fate was eventually the same. The only way patients left Ward 17 was in a box destined for the crematorium. The paranoia was so high surrounding those in Ward 17 that the discrimination continued even after they died. They weren't even allowed a burial. The grieving families were confronted with laws that were swiftly introduced that demanded their 'burial' by fire. Their exit by cremation was meant to purge all of the 'toxins'. Roland made a ton of money from their deaths, and so did the funeral directors at the crematorium.

'How have you been, Roland?'

'I, I've been mainly good,' Roland said, clearly struggling to string words together while his foot was still in his mouth.

'Relax, Roland. Sit down. I won't hurt you. Please call me Chris. I stopped being Christina years ago. Only my granny still calls me Christina.'

'Okay,' he said unsurely.

'I have to ask, though. What's with the moustache Roland, you look like some sad porn star?'

He laughed, and stroked his moustache, 'I know. The boss told me to grow one when I started working in Sydney. He thought it would make me look older, better for the job. A lot of the clients have moustaches. At least it provides a talking point I suppose. At first, I didn't like it, but I've got used to it now.'

Chris had broken the ice, and soon they were talking, or mostly Roland talked, while Chris listened and nodded. Roland recovered from his initial clumsiness and knew not to ask too much about what had happened since school. They spoke of things from more innocent times.

Looking back, their school days seemed innocent and so much simpler. The traumas of who was dating who, or frictions between groups that had seemed such a big deal at the time, caused them both to chuckle now. In retrospect, Roland and Chris's reminiscences over that time, while surrounded by hospital paraphernalia and the spectre of death, took them to a happier place for a while. They spoke of mutual friends, teachers and what their contemporaries had done and where they had ended up.

'You do know I had a hopeless crush on you in high school,' Roland confessed.

'Roland, the way you carried on and seemed so transfixed on

me in Balzac's class, didn't leave anyone with any doubt,' Chris said, smiling through cracked lips.

'I didn't think you noticed. I thought I was subtle, so I told you. Remember when I had that conversation with you after one of Balzac's classes?'

'How could I forget it? I'm not sure if it was more awkward for you or me. "*You have bewitched me body and soul. You must allow me to tell you how much I ardently admire you.*"' Chris chuckled before coughing again.

'Wow. I didn't think you'd have remembered,' Roland laughed, but cringed too.

'Of course, I remembered. Roland, I even remembered where I'd heard it before. We were in the same class you know. I knew you were claiming Mr Darcy's words as your own. I think every schoolgirl wanted to be swept off her feet by Jane Austen's Mr Darcy.'

'Christina, sorry, Chris, I wanted to tell you I loved you. I just couldn't use the L.O.V.E. word without it seeming dorky.'

'Stealing words from Mr Darcy was way dorkier Roland. But I really appreciated you saying it, though. We were both only sixteen, and we were probably dorky even when we thought we were cool.'

'I used to dream of you, you know.'

'I hope you're not going to get all creepy now,' Chris teased.

'If I had told you in high school, it would have been creepy, but I had this reoccurring dream of you and some other girls having a pillow fight.'

'Really? It sounds like a scene from a *Gidget* movie or something.'

'I suppose it does, really. I know now it all seems a bit cliché. You know a high school sleepover, lots of giggling and pillows eventually splitting and clouds of feathers in the air.' Roland could see Chris was getting tired. He glanced at his watch and her eyes closed and it was clear she had fallen asleep. The conversation had gone full circle, as Roland described how he had ended up being in Sydney with his current job.

Chris considered her fate stoically and knew she couldn't afford to waste her remaining time on self-pity or dream about what might have been. She knew what Roland was here to do. He was supposed to get her signature, sign over the benefit on her insurance policy to ANP, he should just get his commission and leave. He should move on to the next client, forget about her and not return tomorrow. He should have done all he needed to on the first visit. It was bad enough he'd spent most of the day talking to her. Was he still the dopey teenager that had been so much in love with her? Why couldn't he just ask her to sign and leave? He'd done it with no emotion to many clients before Chris. ANP expected him to get on with it. He needed to remember what his mantra was: 'don't get emotional, just get rich'.

He sat quietly by her bed, watching her sleep. She slept for a long while. He thought she was still beautiful, despite her current condition. Cheeks that had been full, a smile that had once made him weak at the knees, eyes that were once attractive that were now so dark and sunken. They were the eyes of an octogenarian, not a twenty-something young woman. Skin that had once looked as smooth as marzipan. Skin that he had dreamt of caressing, was now translucent, grey and paper-thin. Yet, he still loved her. Looking back, he had always loved her. Hormones and immaturity had confounded his adolescent feelings, and yet here he was, years later, sitting by her bedside, waiting for her to wake up.

Roland couldn't believe his feelings for Chris were still so strong after so many intervening years. Why hadn't he tracked her down before all this? It was astonishing that he still couldn't rationalise it to the voice inside his head. He argued with himself. What he had written off as a teenage crush all of those years ago had clearly meant so much more. Even seeing her now, like she was, he realised he had merely suppressed what he had always known. It wouldn't go away, even if he wanted it to. The years and her current situation hadn't extinguished the spark that had been ignited so many years ago.

He looked down at the emaciated figure lying in the bed beside him. Christina had been so beautiful, so full of life's promise. Now she relied on oxygen being piped directly into her nose. She smelled bad, and he knew that she was not long for this world. He checked himself. He had worked so hard to cultivate a tough exterior. He had to steel himself against his better judgment, knowing he was sailing close to the wind. The cute sixteen-year-old he'd known bore little resemblance to the corpse that barely clung to life in front of him. But in the few hours, they'd spent together today, a random phrase or sentence structure reconjured the Christina he had always loved.

It may be an affliction isolated to the teenage years that love can be so polarizing. Love can eclipse everything, so that it deftly and carelessly throws all reason aside. Roland recalled the American writer Henry Miller once saying that, *'The one thing we can never get enough of is love. And the one thing we never give enough of is love.'* Here was a last-ditch chance to redress the ledger. His love for Christina continued to blind him.

That Roland could be thrown into such a state of irrational behaviour by such a chance and fleeting encounter was inexplicable. Neither he nor Christina had looked for each other after Christina suddenly left school. Their lives had taken separate paths, yet they could have found each other if they'd set their minds to it. Still, this encounter with Chris as she had become, in Sydney, seemed determined to change Roland's destiny, perhaps more than even he could have predicted. It was the embryonic cell from which monumental decisions grew. It wasn't wise, it wasn't logical, but it was unavoidable.

Seemingly random occurrences and a Tetris of outcomes combined to form an improbable series of linked events. The power to choose how to react to any set of stimuli is an attribute that lifts humans above other animals. It is possible to be a bystander as life passes by or choose to be an active participant that jumps in and sucks the very marrow from every experience. Roland sucked the marrow out of life, not always deliberately but instinctively reacting to circumstances in such a way that he was determined to make the most out of every situation. On reflection, his decisions even perplexed him at times.

Roland's thoughts were broken by the *Arpege*-perfumed ward nurse.

'You're still here. I'm afraid you're going to have to leave immediately. Give this poor woman some rest.'

'Sorry, Sister, Chris here, is an old friend of mine. I'll be back tomorrow.' Roland left, glancing over his shoulder to steal a glimpse at the still sleeping Chris as he went.

Roland couldn't believe that he had re-found Chris. He was more confused that his feelings for Chris had been so instantly rekindled.

He didn't check in with the office that afternoon and he had no intention of working the following day. He just wanted to be with Chris. He had a sleepless night thinking of how things could have been and what he could do to fix things.

On the following day he passed by the duty nurse, who appeared too exhausted to even acknowledge him.

When he entered Chris' room, he was reminded of the stench of pseudomonas, the flesh-eating yeast was rampant across the ward. When a patient's defences were under attack even the simplest of organisms could bring down evolution's most complex.

Chris was asleep. Her face was haggard but peaceful. He thought about what could have been and how beautiful she still was. Her cheekbones, a feature evident in her youth, had become gaunt. The wasting that accompanied this horrible disease had given her skin a morbid translucency. Now her cheekbones threatened to break through her thin skin. Blistered contusions grew on her skin. Roland's heart ached as he thought about how he had once envisaged a wonderful life with her. It was another schoolboy fantasy that had no link to reality.

'Hello, stranger, I didn't expect to see you again,' Chris rasped as she opened her eyes when Roland sat in the visitor's chair.

'It's a professional courtesy. I wouldn't be back if you weren't my favourite client.' Roland teased and straightened in the chair, as he struggled to keep the conversation light. The talk about their youth the previous day had taken its toll, but he couldn't deny how he felt. Any sane person would have run away from this predicament. Focus on the dollars, this person isn't going to be around for long. She isn't the same girl that you loved in school. Focus Roland, don't let your emotions cloud your better judgement. Remember that you're only doing your job. Don't let this dying woman distract you.

'Do you bring all of your customers flowers or just those you're still trying to get a signature from?' Chris asked.

'No. But I probably should.' He let the comment about the signature pass. 'These are for you. See, they've got those little purple orchids. I know you like them. You had them in your year eleven corsage at the school ball.'

'Roland! How could you even have noticed such a thing or remembered it after all this time? I love them,' as she reached out for the flowers the veins in the back of her hand showed through the tissue-thin skin that once had been so beautiful.

Roland saw the track marks and dark bruises in the crook of her arm, where nurses had struggled find a vein that hadn't already been compromised by too many needles. Her arm graduated from purple to yellow as the bruises transformed over time. Even the back of her hand looked like it had been used as a site to administer pain-numbing drugs.

'I probably notice a lot more than people give me credit for. Did you know I wanted to ask you to that school dance?

'No. Why didn't you?

'I thought you'd never agree to go with me. You were such an A-lister. You were way out of my league. I was such a wannabe.'

'Roland, I've never thought of you as a 'wannabe'. If you had asked me, I would have said yes.'

'Really! I thought you and Wayne were an item back then.'

'Wayne was nice enough.' Chris paused and had another coughing fit. She spat phlegm and blood into a disposable paper cup. 'He was a nice guy, but he and I were never 'an item'. He asked me, and as nobody else had, I said yes.'

'The bastard beat me to it!' Roland joked. 'If only I'd acted sooner. Things might have been different.'

'I'm not sure they would have been any different, Roland. Our lives took very different paths after that. I probably would still be in the predicament I'm in now.'

'Don't say that. You don't deserve to be in here. You don't deserve to have this horrible disease.'

'Roland, no one deserves to have this horrible disease.'

'I know, but I feel such a prick to be making a fortune from it.'

'Roland, you're doing a job. If it wasn't you, it would be someone else.'

Roland wasn't sure he believed her. None of these desolate souls deserved to be here. They were a collection of hopeless cases, marking time in increasingly decrepit bodies, waiting to become corpses. Each time he saw them, he was reminded that his first impression of this ward. It was like stepping into a concentration camp. He had choice. She didn't have a choice, none of these people had a choice.

'I know, but I don't have to do this job. I could retire on what I've made already. You've no idea how much money this shit job has given me. But what use is it when I'm making money off other people's misery? That sure doesn't make me happy. Do you know what I'd like to do? I'd like to open a coffee shop. You know, really good coffee, and good simple, fresh food. People always want good coffee. I could buy one now if I wanted. Cash! I'll buy the coffee shop, and you and me can operate it together. There would be a couple of intense hours in the morning and then a break while until the lunch crowd comes in.

We could close at three o'clock, then go to the beach for a few hours after work if the sea breeze hasn't come in—'

'Roland, you know I'm not leaving here. We talked about this last night. There's only one way out for me now. It's very sweet of you to include me in your plans, but I don't have long left. I wouldn't have been on your list if I did. You know that.' She paused, wheezed and then drew in several breaths before going on. 'Roland, there's only one conclusion for me.'

'Chris,' Roland swallowed, 'I still love you.'

'Roland, don't be silly.' A tear formed in the corner of Chris's eye. 'Look at me. I'm not sixteen, and neither are you. You might be in love with your memory of the sixteen-year-old Christina, but I'm Chris, I'm not that person you think you know. The Christina you knew doesn't exist anymore and you're not the sixteen-year-old you once were either. Things have changed. You've changed, and you can certainly see that I have changed. I've loved reminiscing about our younger lives with you yesterday, but neither of us can turn back the clock. Stop being such a fool.' Chris's winced. 'You know I only have weeks to live. It's cruel to taunt me in such a way.'

'No, no, I, I'm not taunting you. I'm not being cruel. I love you. I would do anything I could for you. Let me see if I can get you moved to a fancier place. Someplace nicer, with a view and better food. And nurses that aren't grumpy all the time. *You know a loving heart is the truest wisdom.*'

'*A loving heart is the truest wisdom.* Is that another one of your Mr Darcy quotes?'

Roland blushed; he'd been caught out. He'd been sprung stealing someone else's words again. 'No. It's Charles Dickens. I can't help using the words of great writers I admire. Don't you love how these guys put words together. They just had a knack. It's genius.'

A nurse interrupted their conversation and asked Roland to leave the room while she attended to Chris. He reluctantly left but waited outside the room, close by the door. He was prepared to wait. The nurse eventually came out of the room carrying a plastic bag of soiled dressings.

'Chris said she'd like to see you again if you are still here. She may be disorientated from the medications for a bit. Be kind to her, Mr Redman; she's had a rough time of it.'

'I certainly will. Thank you, Sister.'

He re-entered the room and saw that Chris had dozed off. He was prepared to wait for as long as it took. The visitor's chair was as functional as you'd expect from hospital furniture. It wasn't the most well-padded or comfortable, but he finally dozed off.

'Hi, stranger. How long have you been there?' Chris rasped, waking him up.

'What, oh, only about five minutes,' Roland glanced at his Rolex and lied. It was closer to five hours than five minutes. A glance out the window confirmed it. It was getting late in the day.

'I thought you'd had enough of me yesterday.'

'Oh, ah, no.' He couldn't believe he was still tripping over his words like a nervous schoolboy. Despite his feelings for this once beautiful young woman, his behaviour defied logic. He told himself to just get her signature and leave. Toughen the hell up. If he had been tougher and just left, a lot might have been different. In retrospect, it would have saved a lot of pain, for him, and others too.

'I suppose you'll want your signature now,' Chris said. She'd known all along what Roland was after. She knew that it meant. She was a terminal case and she wasn't expected to live for more than a few weeks as best. But she hadn't expected to find Roland.

He couldn't lie to her. Despite being able to 'tailor the truth,' to almost everyone he had ever met, he couldn't lie to her. 'I'm so, so sorry, Chris. I'm doing my job, but it's a job I've had a gut full of. It's a job I can't do anymore.'

'Toughen up, mate. What's your problem?'

'Chris, I really don't think I can do this. You and I both know what me coming to see you is about,' Roland whispered.

'I know I'm sick. I know I won't get better. I know what it means. I won't be leaving here. None of us on Ward 17 make it out. They tell us we're coming here for treatment, but we all know its only palliative care. I don't have long. You have already comforted me by coming to see me. I loved reminiscing with you yesterday. I have to admit your story about the pillow fight had me worried. I thought it was weird to begin with, but I know it was just a schoolboy fantasy. In fact, I'm touched by how frank you've been with me. I'd like you to think I've been frank with you too but there are some things in the more recent past that I'd rather not think about at this time. I didn't expect that you'd be back today. I'd even thought I wouldn't be here today. Seeing you again is a bonus.'

'Chris, they're doing lots of research. They could find a cure tomorrow,' Roland interrupted. He couldn't believe what he was saying himself.

'Roland, don't bullshit me now. I know you're a good bullshitter, and you've always been a good bullshitter, but it's me you're talking to. I knew you when you were still in school. Pass me that piece of paper.'

Roland reached over and passed Chris the paper that had been sitting on the bedside cabinet. Chris unfolded it and read, '*Hope is a bad thing. It means that you are not what you want to be. It means that part of you is dead, if not all of you. It means that you entertain illusions.*'

'What? Who said that?' he asked.

'Don't you recognise the words? They're Henry Miller's. You like to use the words of others, don't you? I thought I'd try the same. Don't you think they fit?'

Despite himself, Roland blushed.

'Roland,' Chris wheezed. 'Let me speak.' Chris continued as Roland started to interrupt again. She tried to get as much oxygen through the nasal tube as she could. 'I, I'll give you your signature, gladly, but you've got to do something for me too.'

'Chris, you know I'll do whatever I can for you. I'll try to give you whatever you want.'

The way he said it, she believed he truly would. 'Roland. I'll give you your signature, but you got to help me end this,' Chris said sternly; her wet eyes looked deeply into Roland's.

'What! Chris, what are you asking me to do?'

'Roland, I want you to help me check out, now, with what little dignity I have left.' Chris's voice went from a wheeze to a rasp. Her coughing wouldn't stop. Roland passed her a tissue from the bedside table. She coughed for a full minute. To Roland, it seemed like an hour. When she took the tissue away, it was wet, stained with more blood than phlegm.

'Chris, you don't know what you're asking me to do.'

'Roland, I know exactly what I'm asking you to do. Look around the ward. Look at all these poor souls. We all know there's only one way out of here. We're all waiting to die. The smart one's fake being in so much pain that the nurses let them overdose on morphine. The dumb ones wait until the pain is unbearable and the morphine doesn't cut through it anymore. They wait until their body is a fly trapped in a spider's web. There is nowhere to go until the HIV/AIDS spider comes and sucks the life out of your already exhausted body, leaving only a paper-thin shell, a dried-out exoskeleton with nothing left inside. I've given this a lot of thought Roland. I need your help.'

Roland should have known better. He should have just got up and walked out there and then. He was kidding himself if he thought he was still in love with Chris after all this time. Too many years had passed. There had clearly been too much water under the bridge in the intervening years. Look at where they found themselves now. Different lives on divergent paths. Neither could fully comprehend the journey that had resulted in them reaching their current destination. Roland was on his way to making his first million, and Chris was teetering on the razors-edge of death.

'Roland, you said you'd do anything for me. You know I have got so little time left. Help me go, before I lose everything? At least now I can go thinking someone loved me. Let me go on my terms, not in a stupor where it is the increasing doses of morphine that kill me. Look at the other people in this ward. Do you see any of them having a dignified end? Don't kid yourself to think that any of your clients end up going home?'

Roland put his face in his hands. His world was unravelling. Being a heartless prick devoid of emotion was so much easier. Just get the form signed and get out of there, he told himself. It was a simple formula. A formula that had already made him richer than he could have dreamed of being. It was silly to come back to see Chris. It was stupid to think he was still in love, but he couldn't help it. It wasn't just an adolescent memory that he had fabricated into something more in his head. He loved her. He loved the memory of her. He loved that he had held her in his heart for so long, despite not seeing her for years. He loved she had instantly recognised him, even if he was slow to recognise her. He loved that they had enjoyed talking about their school days. He couldn't believe they'd been able to talk about things so frankly. He loved her. He loved her back in school, and he loved her now. He'd loved her as a sixteen-year-old, as she was about to become a woman and now, he loved her on her deathbed, as she was about to become a corpse. He'd loved her sixteen-year-old skin that was so smooth and tanned and he loved her skin now, bruised and blemished. Now her skin was like the fabric of a bi-plane stretched and shrunk over a skeleton framework. How could she ask him such a thing?

'Roland, please. You know I wouldn't ask if there was any dignified alternative.'

'Christina, Chris, I can't.'

'I don't want to die any more than you do, but there is no alternative. I can die here today with my last remnants of dignity and with the pleasant memories we've shared, or I can let this disease determine when I go on its terms. I've seen how others around here go. It's not pretty. Don't you think they deserve better? Don't you think I deserve better? Some go blind, others go mad and others become vegetables until the morphine takes them away. There's already too many of us for the nurses to give us proper care. They're not grumpy, just overwhelmed. They do all they can, but they still leave some poor patients sitting in their shit or gurgling on their spew for hours, unable to help themselves. I don't want to go that way. Roland, you can't want me to go that way either. I wouldn't ask you if there was an alternative. I don't have anyone else I can ask. I wouldn't ask you if there was any hope. Any hope I had eroded long ago. Please, please, help me?' Chris closed her eyes as if the effort to speak was taking away all reserves of energy.

She stretched to the limit of her reach and placed her hand on his forearm. Roland looked into her eyes. He wasn't crying, but he was pretty close. Tears welled up in both of their eyes. There was no doubt in his mind that Chris was serious. They both knew what she said was logical. Harsh and cruel but correct.

The actuaries were rarely wrong in their predictions. If she was on his list, she was expected to live less than a month, two at best. The insurance vultures, like him, didn't waste time circling someone that was going to hang around. They were after clients that were soon-to-be-corpses.

'What do you want me to do?' Roland said with resolve.

A faint smile crossed Chris's face.

'Do you want me to see if I can get some more morphine? They must be swimming in it around here.'

'No. I wouldn't ask you to do that. The drugs might show up if they do an autopsy for some reason; even though the place seems to be swimming in it, they have to account for all of it. The easiest way is to take my pillow and hold it over my face for a while. It won't take long, my lung capacity is shot already. No one will ever know.'

'Really? You really want me to do that?'

'Your story about the pillow-fight last night gave me the idea. Just crimp this oxygen tube for a bit, put the pillow over my face, wait two minutes, and I'll be gone. It's just like going to sleep. I'll see you on the other side sometime.'

Now Roland regretted telling Chris about the pillow-fight story. He'd had no idea that it would turn into this.

'Just take the pillow, put it over my face, and I'll go happily,' she repeated.

Roland swallowed again. 'Okay.' He couldn't believe he was agreeing to this. It was as if she had cast a spell on him. The reality was that he loved her, so much that he couldn't deny her any request, however tragic it might be. 'Okay. How are we going to do this?'

'Roland, I've saved a few of the sleeping pills they give me to get me through the nights. There's a little box in my bedside drawer. I'll take a few just to relax. They won't show up as anything out of the ordinary even if they bother to do a blood test once I'm gone. Sit with me until you hear my breathing slow down. Then just crimp the oxygen line, put the pillow over my face and wait for two minutes.' She had apparently given this some thought. It sounded too simple.

He retrieved the sleeping tablets and placed them in her hand. As she opened her mouth to swallow them, the white of the candida that coated the inside of her mouth contrasted starkly with the blood seeping from her gums.

'Pass me some water, please.'

He filled the squat glass from the hospital jug and helped her to drink from it. As she gave it back to him, he could see tendrils of blood spiralling in the water. The glass had now become a vector for the deadly virus. He needed to avoid the risk of infection. He checked his thoughts; this wasn't about him.

She slid a pillow from under her head, lay flatter, then passed it to Roland. She looked up to his ashen face.

'Chris, I don't know how to tell you how I feel about you. You know I stumble when I try to put my feelings into words. But I've always felt this way. There are so many words that just swirl in my head. The words have always refused to come out. I've tried so many times to get the words that are in my head to come out of my mouth. That's why I quoted Mr Darcy all those years ago like a fool. I tried to tell you how I felt about you so many times. How I feel about you now. How I feel about us. The future we might have had. Maybe we were just too young, not old enough to cut through the superficial and focus on the things that really matter.

My dreams of what could have been ran ahead of reality. It was an idealised vision of what might have been. Where we find ourselves now rips apart my heart. The guilt I feel only telling you now overwhelms me. I don't know if I can tell you how I really feel without breaking down. I know I am weak, only telling you now. I should have searched you out years ago. But I have to tell you. I don't care if you think of me as a coward, but I am a coward that adores you. I only care that you know I love you. I'm telling you this now for you, but I'm also telling you for me. I have always known. I ache, I ache because I believe that you've always known too. I love you. I have always loved you. I don't care that you are ill. To me, you are beautiful. You will always be beautiful.

My only solace is I am going to take away your pain. No more guilt, no more struggling to breathe. No more yearning for what might have been. You don't have to endure this horrible disease anymore. The love I have for you transcends the now, and I know I'll see you again, when we can be together forever.' Roland hung his head, feeling broken and worthless.

Roland wasn't expecting a reply, but Chris gathered her strength, took a deep breath 'Roland, I am very touched by what you say, but there is no future here. There is no guarantee about anything that would give me hope for tomorrow, let alone anything beyond that.'

Roland jumped in when Chris started to wheeze again. 'I don't care that we are only together now. That it is this horrible disease that has finally brought us together. I don't care where we've been, what we have endured, what we are or who we've become. I don't care what you do or what my fate is. I only care about now. This moment. I've always believed life was a gift. A gift that could be squandered on the mundane or a gift that could be invested in the sublime. We are given a life to use it how we choose. What stops us living our lives to the fullest? Each of us is given a short time in this world. It is up to each of us to take what we are given and make the most of it. To exhaust what is given to us. To suck the fucking marrow out of every moment. Anything less is a waste.'

He was about to go on when Chris reached out and placed her hand on his.

'Roland, my illness and where I am now only reinforces how I feel about that. I know my time is over. I know this is a one-way journey. Each day I live, I thumb my nose at AIDS. This disease doesn't define me.' She paused, sucked heavily on the oxygen before continuing, 'Don't let AIDS define our brief time together. Don't get me wrong, I hate AIDS. But I also love it for bringing you to me and for giving me a way out. I've known many men, too many, and I know there are none I could ask what I am asking of you. I just want there to be no more pain. Please make the pain to go away.'

'I'm not sure if I can do it,' Roland said, sniffing as a tear rolled down his cheek. Chris's watery eyes focused on the tear. He was embarrassed to cry in front of her. '*Heaven knows we never need be ashamed of our tears, for they are the rain upon the blinding dust of the earth. Softening our hardened hearts*,' he said, stealing another quote.

'Toughen up, Roland! You're not the one with the death sentence. All I'm asking you to do is to hasten the inevitable. All you need to do is hold a pillow to my face. It really couldn't be easier.'

'Yeah sorry,' he sniffed. 'That was Dickens, you know Charles Dickens, from Great Expectations.'

'What. You're quoting Dickens to me now?'

'Yeah sorry. It's a silly habit I can't break. I'm always falling back on the words of the great writers. A quote about tears seemed to fit even if *Great Expectations* doesn't.'

'Roland, you're such a funny bugger.'

She closed her eyes, and held his hand. Her face became less strained. Her cheeks were still horribly sunken, the bruises along the line of her jaw were still there and a fleshy growth sprouted from her earlobe but despite all of this, he felt nothing but love. It was as if the resignation with which she approached her death transferred some of the calm to him. He wasn't happy about what she had asked him to do, but he was determined to give her this final token of his love for her.

'I was too cowardly to do what I knew was right as I have been too cowardly to avoid doing what I knew to be wrong,' he said to himself. It seemed too fitting not to continue stealing words from the great Dickens. He allowed himself a moment's indulgence of what a fascinating man Dickens must have been before the reality of the task before him slapped him back to reality.

He looked at her face one last time. The rasping of her breath eased, and he folded the oxygen line over onto itself, providing a temporary seal, the line held the pressure without bursting. He held her hand, and she squeezed it and patted it softly, each pat weaker than the one before and then laid her hand next to his, barely touching. He let go of her hand, placed the pillow over her face and held it to the contours of her.

'I love you Christina. I've always loved you.' He knew she couldn't hear him. The minutes he waited seemed like hours. One minute, two minutes, three minutes, four minutes. She'd said two minutes, but he didn't want to stuff it up. He uncrimped the oxygen, replaced the pillow under her head, brushed a wisp of hair from her face and bent over and kissed her forehead. He expected some sign of her passing. Not something as cliché as an angel ascending, but something, anything. She looked normal, serene. She looked like she was resting peacefully and would wake up again in a few moments. He knew she wouldn't.

He tenderly wiped the wet mark of his kiss from her forehead. He took the unsigned insurance documents from the pocket of his jacket, ripped them into quarters and threw them onto the end of her bed. Without thinking, the words of another writer entered his head in a Californian accent, the accent of movie stars, evangelists, and authors.

'Death is two people walking side by side in the mist, not a word between them. Death was empty, yet right and peaceful, dignified, if you like. Not a continuation of life, but a leap into the dark with no possibility of ever coming back. And it was right and beautiful, why would anyone want to come back. The poor human bastards that we are, we ought to be glad that somebody devised a way out.'

Then the accent of the words in his head turned into his own voice.

'Every day, we slaughter our finest impulses. That is why we get a heartache when we read the lines written by the hand of a master and recognize them as our own, as the tender shoots which we stifled because we lacked the faith to believe in our own powers, our own criterion of truth and beauty.'

It was Henry Miller, first with the voice he imagined belonged to the writer and then in his own. The words hit home, and he realised there was no mystery around the origin of life or death. It just was. Even with Chris's beautiful corpse before him, any man and woman could only understand divine mysteries by resorting to faith or blind, ovine belief. It was more profound to just admit you had no fucking idea. Perhaps none of us ever really expected to have any fucking idea.

Roland would have loved to have been Henry Miller. He would have loved to have been someone clever enough to come up with such memorable words. Phrases that aspiring writers would quote. The closest he could manage was to steal quotes from Dickens and Miller. Two great writers that could hardly be more different. He wasn't even sure when Miller's voice in his head became his own. It was an imagined version of what he thought a hedonistic, west-coast American with a fetish for living on the edge might be. And yet, his words seemed more appropriate than any he could string together. To take twenty-six characters, craft them into words and then form them into phrases in sentences that leapt off the pages into someone's head was an extraordinary gift. Great writers aren't mortal. They transcended time. Their words live on beyond them, saying as much, and even more to future generations than those of their own time. A great writer is a time traveller.

He stopped and caught himself. He had morphed from being a parasite that fed off the words of writers to someone who now heard them speaking in his head. He felt unhinged. 'Oh, no. What have I done? I've murdered an innocent person, someone I've loved, still love.' Was he quoting another writer, or were the words his own?

He left the room and passed by the nurse's station.

'Leaving early tonight, Roland?' the *Arpege* nurse asked sarcastically.

'Yes. You've seen the last of me. I think there is a patient down there who needs your attention.' He walked to the lift as the nurse slowly rose from her chair behind the counter. 'I'm done,' he said to no one but himself.

22

Roland

Roland was true to his word. After he left Chris in the hospital, he was determined to finish with ANP. He went back to his office, penned a brief letter of resignation, and put it in the mail to his supervisor. He didn't owe anyone anything. He couldn't stomach sticking around to explain himself to his colleagues. He took another sheet of ANP letterhead and wrote a letter to his landlord, giving him notice of his immediate departure, telling him to keep the bond and whatever he'd left in the apartment. He'd already paid his rent in advance, so the landlord was making money out of him. He tossed the letter on top of the resignation letter as he walked out of the office. Both letters would be in tomorrow's mail.

He went back to his soon to be vacant apartment, changed into more casual attire and caught a cab to The Ravensbrook Arms in the yet to be gentrified end of the Rocks. He was confident he wouldn't know a soul there and wouldn't need to answer any questions. The Ravensbrook was a dying breed of pub. Horse races were always playing noiselessly on a tiny TV perched above the barman's head for anyone who cared to watch.

Corporate amalgamations that had swallowed the licences of similar pubs all over the country had overlooked The Ravensbrook. Some pubs were closed, and the licences converted to suburban liquor stores—alcoholic supermarkets for corporate brewers to sell their product under restrictive, government licencing arrangements. The Ravensbrook stayed true to itself because it was not part of any liquor conglomerate. The current publican owned both the licence and premises. He wasn't going to sell out the legacy that had been in his family since the 1800s. If his father, grandfather and great grandfather had outlasted razor gangs, corrupt police and politicians by the carload and standover types from Italy, Vietnam and Lebanon, he couldn't bear the shame of folding to a team of spotty-faced, pin-striped accountants. He'd rather burn the place down than sell out to such money-grabbing little pricks. Roland knew none of this, of course, but The Ravensbrook served his current need for free-flowing, cold beer served without trite banter and a clientele that really couldn't give a shit about him or anything he might represent.

'Schooner of draught thanks, mate,' said Roland and put a crisp twenty on the bar.

The barman grabbed a schooner cooling in the rack below the height of the bar, deftly spun it in one hand, and nestled it below the tap that he flicked with the other hand. It was a move he could have performed with his eyes closed. He flicked the tap closed and put the glass onto the beer saturated bar runner in front of Roland as he scooped up the twenty without uttering a word. Conversation wasn't this barman's strong suite and that suited Roland just fine.

Roland downed half the schooner before the barman returned with his change. There was no way Roland was going to be leaving here sober.

The following day, Roland awoke face down on his own bed. He couldn't remember how he got there but remembered why he'd gone on the blinder. He felt shithouse, but he refused to allow himself any sympathy. He opened one eye at a time while he worked to produce enough saliva to unglue his tongue from the roof of his mouth. He rolled onto his back and wished he hadn't. His head spun. Any movement gave him the sensation that someone was banging a crowbar on a metal drum that contained his head.

He looked around the room through eyes that complained that they had to open into light that shone in shards of pain. After making a shitload of money, what did he have to show for it? The Rolex, jewellery and the Jaguar were nice, but what did they mean at the end of the day? Nothing would fill the void in his heart that Chris had left. He was a murderer. Sure, she'd asked him to, but he should have just said no. He could have just walked away. But if the taking of someone's life was less cruel than letting them live, was it still murder? Chris didn't deserve to die. She sure as hell didn't deserve to suffer an HIV/AIDS death. He tried to justify his role in her death as best he could, but it was still taking someone's life.

Roland gingerly lifted himself off the bed and walked slowly to the kitchen. He glanced at the clock's blinking red LED numbers showing 14:13 and decided to cook up a good, fatty, very late breakfast as a hangover cure. He recalled his father telling one of his mates that the best way to cure a hangover was to get some fat in your guts: 'it soaks up the alcohol and puts a lining on your stomach.' If anyone had a credible hangover cure after a blinder, it was his old man—he'd certainly had a few. Roland wasn't sure if there was any science in the belief, but it couldn't hurt. He lowered his head to the sink, cupped his hands, turned the tap on full and gulped down as much water as he could without fear that it would bounce back up.

He leaned on the fridge and opened the door. He rummaged up eggs and a couple of rashers of fatty bacon, complimented with toast smeared with a generous amount of butter and Vegemite. He didn't regret throwing in the towel on his ANP job. The money was fantastic, and he had earned more in those short few years than he could spend, so his bank account was fat. But it was fat with what he now knew was blood money. He had traded his soul for dollars. He resolved to find something meaningful to do, get far away from Sydney and start afresh. He would redress the ledger. He would make sure he did some good. He was long past believing in God, but he still subscribed to his own brand of karma. If his life had been undeserving to this point, he would make it his life's purpose to redress his past, so he left this world a better place.

While the frying eggs spat against the fat oozing from the bacon, a plan came together in his mind. Why couldn't he buy a coffee shop? He had told Chris it was possible. He had more than enough money. He could buy one outright. The money he'd accumulated from dying patients could readily fund a café, and so much more. Even after he left the money would continue to follow him, while the last of those that he had signed up passed away. But he needed to get away. Make a new start. Go where people didn't know his background, didn't ask questions or simply didn't care. He couldn't stomach staying in Sydney any longer than he had to. He couldn't face returning to questions in Perth. He needed to get far away. The size of his bank account meant he could go wherever he wanted. Like the little balls popping around in a bingo machine, he saw potential locations roll around in his mind: Melbourne, Thailand, Cambodia, Bali, Darwin, New Zealand. Melbourne and New Zealand seemed too close to Sydney, and Bali was full of people from Perth he'd rather avoid. Thailand and Cambodia were cheap, but people would put him in the rich Aussie ex-pat category with the deviants and paedophiles. So, Darwin, it was.

He finished his breakfast of fat and salt, showered, leaving the water to run over his head and neck while piecing the plan together in his mind. He dressed and then put what he thought he would need in Darwin into a suitcase. He left the apartment keys on the kitchen table for the landlord to find and then drove the Jaguar over The Bridge, in search of the nearest car dealership he could find. He gave little thought to his blood alcohol content which probably still exceeded the legal limit from the night before. He drove north until he saw the blue and white car dealership sign approaching. He pulled the Jag into the North Shore Ford.

'Good morning, sir, lovely day, isn't it? You looking to buy a little something for the missus, the girlfriend or perhaps a nice little vehicle for each?' Roland thought that only a used car salesman could sound more condescending than an insurance salesman.

'Good morning yourself,' Roland retorted, not bothering to acknowledge the question. 'I want to trade in the Jag for something sturdy, four-wheel-drive good for touring. I will be driving long distances.'

'Well, sir, you're in luck. We've got exactly the vehicle that fits your needs. A beautiful F250, a demo model all ready to go.'

Roland thought the guy was a tosser but reflected that he had probably sounded the same when he was working for ANP, but that was yesterday. Today, he was no longer 'the insurance guy'. He was going to be a coffee shop owner and barista.

'What sort of price are we looking at?' Roland asked.

'Well, the Jaguar is a lovely car, but we don't have many clients looking for a vehicle of that prestige, sir. The F250, big-block V8 has been the dealership manager's car, has only fifteen hundred kilometres on the clock, a factory-fitted canopy, long-range tanks, extended warranty and every accessory you could think of. It is a steal at $50,990, drive away. I'd need to speak to the manager about what we could give you for the Jaguar. We'd have to on-sell it to another yard, of course.'

Roland wondered who'd be doing the stealing at that price. It was apparent the salesman was talking up the sale and talking down the trade. 'What sort of dollars are you able to give me for the Jag? You can see it is a bloody good car, full logbooks, and it's got all the extras. Been looked after right. Low k's, still the current model.' Roland fed the salesman back the same language.

'Well, Sir, as I say, I'd have to check with the manager.'

Roland knew this meant the guy didn't have any idea. He would scurry off to see if there was an estimate in the *Red Book* and then offer something significantly less to start the negotiation.

'Okay. You run off and speak to your guy and let me know. I'm interested in the F250, but only if the price you give me for the Jag is reasonable.' Roland couldn't help playing along with the game, but he wouldn't fluff around. He wanted an answer now.

The salesman quickly trotted off, knowing the punter was a likely sale. He returned at a much slower pace, head down, trying to look pessimistic, but despite his charade of his overacting, he couldn't help wringing his hands, confident that he was on a winner.

'Well, what's it going to be? Are we going to have a sale or not?' Roland deliberately sounded impatient.

'Well, sir, the Jag is lovely, but our clients are seldom at that end of the market. I'd have to pass the Jag onto one of our associate businesses to sell. You'd appreciate that the more hands it has to go through, the longer we take to sell it, and the time to find a buyer for a prestige vehicle like this it is going to cost me—'

'Just cut the crap and tell me your figure,' Roland interrupted.

'The best I can do is $37,500 for the Jag, but I can knock $500 off the F250. After transfer and stamp duty, it will only cost you $12,990. That's less than 13 grand.'

Roland was pissed off. The Jag was worth $42,000 on an average day. He was sure he could get that if he shopped around himself. The $500 discount was bullshit. That would be the same discount if someone came in cold. Despite himself, he just wanted to make a new start. The F250 would suit his needs.

'Done. If I can drive it away now, write up the paperwork.'

The used car salesman was flustered. He wasn't expecting a result without the usual bluff, bluster and bullshit. Roland hadn't even taken the F250 for a drive. 'But, Sir, aren't you going to drive the F250 first? I'm sure it is satisfactory but have a drive. See how she goes.'

'You seem like a trustworthy guy,' Roland lied. 'You wouldn't rip me off, would you?'

'No, no, of course not. I just want you to be a happy customer.' The salesman regained his composure and went back to sales mode. 'I'll get the paperwork sorted at once.'

Roland extended his hand and shook the salesman's eager hand. With a shake, they sealed the deal. Roland waited while the salesman checked the papers and organised the bank transfer. He took his suitcase from the Jag's small boot and put it in the spacious passenger seat of the F250. Where he planned to go, the Jag wouldn't cut it. The F250 seemed huge, and the gas bill from the big V8 would be too, but he didn't care. Let the new life in the Top End begin.

23

Roland

Time is not absolute. It is something that manifests itself somewhere between the points of life and death. From the moment we leave the shelter of our mother's womb and scream for our first lung of air until our last dying gasp, reference points are needed to make sense of any of it. The days, the weeks, and the years between birth and death appear arbitrary. Some, perhaps arrogantly, believe some divine deity or holy being determines the period. I've never been convinced of such a thing.

Just as it is impossible to tell exactly when you will take your first gasp of air, it is equally impossible to predict precisely when you will take your last. The multitude of breaths that occur between these two markers are those that define a life. Who we are, what we have done, what we have built or destroyed and what legacy we have left for others? A fortune, words of wisdom or just a line of genes? Each of us has an opportunity to leave an endowment to those that follow. Some leave no trace, content to do nothing of significance or stick their head above the protective parapet of a quiet and sheltered life. Some are frightened to express themselves creatively, lest they be criticised. There is, however, a certainty that life, death and the events that play out in between will occur for all of us. Some will live, some will die, and some will leave little evidence they ever existed. Others will leave a legacy that lasts long after their physical being has ceased to exist. A legacy that spans generations and is passed to others to complete.

A stone tossed into a pool generates a wave, ripples that radiate further and further outward, dissipating as they progress to the edge. Most of our lives create waves that dissipate to nothing before they reach the pool's edge, while others leave ripples that radiate further and further outward.

Roland Redman's life created ripples that radiated far, leaving a legacy that continues to this day.

24

Paul

'Thank you for breakfast, Spiros,' I said, entering the hotel reception around ten o'clock. Spiros had resumed his position behind the counter, looking intently at the little TV again. I'd had a full meal, a shower and a shave and felt much better than I had done the previous day. 'How much do I owe you for breakfast?'

'No problem, Mr Ball . . . I mean, Mr Winter. Your friend Mr Redman, he pays for everything.'

'Spiros, I need to meet someone at a café in The Mall. Can you tell me the best way to get there?'

'Of course. Sergeant Yates tell me to get you a taxi when you wake up. It is not far, maybe you want to walk. I show you on the map.' Spiros pulled a tourist map off a pad of them. Advertising covered every border, attempting to lure tourists to whichever point of the compass they were heading. The Crocodile Park, fish feeding at the shorefront, Mindil Beach Markets, Laneway Coffee and Burgers, Litchfield National Park, The Magic Wok, souvenirs, and a bus tour to Kakadu all competed for turf around the map's border. The map was crested with a banner that proclaimed, 'Welcome to Darwin'.

'You walk down McMinn,' he said, pointing out the door. 'After 10 minutes, you turn left into Lindsay until you get to Smith, and then you 'bout halfway. The Mall is on Smith Street. So, you walk another ten minutes and you there. Sergeant Yates, he says the café is just past the bookshop. You can't miss her.'

'Yes. Thanks, Spiros; a walk would be much better.'

A walk is an excellent way to clear your head, and although mine was less jumbled than the previous night, it was still spinning with a whirlpool of thoughts, dredging up issues from the past and confused prospects about my immediate future. McMinn, Lindsay and Smith were easy directions. They sounded like a firm of old accountants.

Darwin's humidity was still yet to rise to its midday potential, so if I was to walk, this was the time of day to do it. What sort of mess had I walked into? Roland couldn't be involved in people smuggling, could he? He'd liked to push rules to their limit and would smile convincingly as he relieved a client of the cash that he'd judged them too dumb or lower on the evolutionary scale to deserve, but he'd never actually broken any law. At least not that I was aware of. While I questioned the morality of some things Roland had done in the early days, he had always stayed within the boundaries of the law when we had worked in insurance.

What Yates was accusing him of was totally different. People were dead. Lots of people. And what did Christina Brown have to do with any of this? My life in Perth was dull and boring, but I didn't want to be dragged into a crime and be questioned by the police. I'd answered Yates as honestly as I could, so I could get back to Perth without delay. I had committed no crime and had nothing to hide.

Smith Street Mall is a couple of hundred metres of cafés tourist shops and other small businesses. This time of year, many of them had Christmas decorations in their windows. Pine trees, cotton wool, draped to look like snow and oversized red and white candy canes, all looking strangely out of place. Only the snow-white kangaroos conceded a reference to where in the world they were located. I found The Bookshop Darwin easily. The Red Cross charity shop was on one side and the café on the other. I smirked at the irony of the sign hanging above the door of the Red Cross, extolling 'The Power of Humanity'. I wondered if Roland had seen the sign and had felt the humanity to be there for people in need. Did he think he was offering refugees a better option? Did he step in to play a role he thought others should have played?

I couldn't assemble the pieces into a picture that made any sense. The information Yates seemed to hold true didn't align with the Roland I thought I knew. Thoughts whirled through my head again. I paused in front of The Bookshop Darwin. Just inside the door, a stand of colourful, cobalt bordered books beckoned, 'Lonely Planet – On Sale'. Kakadu, Darwin and Northern Territory were at eye level, followed by Australia, New Zealand, California, Peru, South America and Iceland. The locations became more distant and exotic as my eye tracked down. I wondered how many Darwin travellers would make Iceland their next destination. To the other side of the doorway, a display advertised 'Literary Classics'. Ornately bound in burgundy leather, there were gilt editions by Dickens, Greene and Hemingway. Roland would have loved this place. I'm sure he would have read every book on the stand and he could probably quote passages from each of them. It seemed like they had assembled all of his favourite authors in the one display stand. If I were here longer than I planned, I'd come back and take a better look through the shop.

Yates sat at a little marble-topped table by the window of the café, watching me as I approached.

I walked up to his table. 'Morning,' I said and slumped into the chair opposite him.

'Not too early for you, I hope?'

I'm sure Yates wouldn't have cared if I said it was. 'No, I'm alright, just feeling strung out by that you've told me.'

'Can I get you a coffee?' Yates already had a large mug of black coffee steaming in front of him.

'Sure, I'll have a flat white. I don't intend to be long, though.'

Yates ignored my suggestion of the clock ticking and gestured to the waitress leaning on the front counter. She prised herself away from the counter where she was leaning and headed towards us, making it apparent that customers were an inconvenience she struggled to tolerate.

'Another coffee, Sergeant Yates?' the waitress asked, emphasising the sergeant and indicating she knew both Yates and his profession. I got the impression she was also letting me know. I appreciated it.

'A flat white for Mr Winter, please, Lorissa,' Yates said, letting the waitress know he knew who she was too.

Lorissa walked back to the coffee machine. She had long legs, a thin waist and a bust that impressed me and I'm sure many others. The café uniform made her figure even more spectacular—a short black skirt, inches from dignity, and a black t-shirt, at least two sizes too small, with bright green script rolling across her chest.

Yates said nothing as he stirred his coffee for longer than necessary. He was quiet until the waitress returned minutes later with my coffee. She placed the coffee in front of me without saying a thing and returned to the counter.

'Pretty, isn't she?' Yates enquired.

'I suppose she is.'

'I thought you were looking at her pretty intently.'

'I was admiring the uniform. She reminded me of someone I once knew,' I lied.

The waitress was pretty, spectacularly so. The uniform made it impossible not to notice her. Her youthful indifference embellished her prettiness. She was one of those young women who would be pretty until a certain age, and then nature kicked in, children were born, hips widened, waists disappeared, and the weight piled on. But for now, she was very pleasing to the eye. Attractive in an exotic way only Darwin could conjure. Her features suggested a gene pool that exemplified Darwin's diversity stretched across three continents, gathering the best elements from each. She had high cheekbones, long legs and a cheeky walk to go with the chest. The walk said, 'I don't give a shit if you look at me. But touch me, and I'll break your arm—unless I want you to.'

'Do you know who she is?' Yates asked.

'She is the waitress. You just called her Lorissa. How would I know her?'

'She was Roland's girlfriend once.'

'What? She's a bit young, isn't she?

'Roland was a lady's man. But I guess you already knew that.'

'Is that why we're here?'

'That's part of the reason we're here. Haven't you twigged to the name of this place?'

I looked at the sign above the coffee machine. I was the same as the script on the t-shirt. 'What, Chris' Café?'

'Yeah. Roland bought this place. He bought it outright with cash and spent a bomb refurbishing it with these marble tables and fancy chairs. I heard the coffee machine cost him more than twenty grand, alone.'

I looked over Yates' shoulder at the coffee machine. It was overly ornate with brass stainless-steel and chrome. An eagle with outstretched wings sat on top. It was something that would have been more at home in Lygon Street, Melbourne than Smith Street Mall, Darwin. The cash register was similarly ornate. Someone, Roland, had spent a lot of money on the place.

'I think Roland made this place a little shrine to Christina Brown. The place is named after her—Chris's Café. I'm surprised you didn't join the dots before now. Look on the wall behind the cash register.'

The colour drained from my face as my eyes focused on the gold-framed photo behind the cash register. It was a blow-up from our year eleven school formal. It was grainy and blurry, but even from this distance, it was obviously Christina Brown.

'Shit.'

'Is that all you've got to say?' asked Yates.

'Well, it's a lot to take in. Are you telling me this is Christina Brown's café?'

'No. It's Roland's café. Don't you get it? He left Sydney and bought this place. Fixed it up and named it 'Chris's Café' after Christina Brown. It used to be a bit of a greasy spoon. Now it is a mecca for all of Darwin's coffee lovers. This place is Roland's idea of a tribute to Christina Brown. His creepy little shrine to her.'

I prodded the foam on my coffee with the spoon. Now a few of the threads were coming together. Threads that once seemed just tangled were a Gordian knot, a puzzle infinitely more complex than it first appeared. How would the tangled mess unravel?

'So, you're telling me Roland was still hung up on Christina after all these years. What's wrong with that? If it was a crime, you'd have to arrest most of the male population from our school. I still don't understand what you're getting at and how any of this relates to me. Roland and I were once close, but we hadn't been in contact for years. I was meant to meet him in Darwin, but none of that is going to happen now, is it?'

Yates ignored my questions. 'The police down south have been interested in Mr Redman for a while. He came into a great deal of money via some insurance schemes he was involved in—money that is still flowing in.'

'Roland was working for ANP. I heard he was doing pretty well, but I didn't think there was any problem with any of it.'

'I suspect you're probably right, but the money we're talking about has had those office people and police down south asking a few questions ever since Roland came to Darwin. It sounds to me like he upset several families down south and left in a bit of a hurry. I don't think my colleagues down south have found anything substantial yet. I'm sure they would like to though. It strikes me as odd Christina Brown was his last known client before he came to Darwin.'

'Yates, I'm really tired of all of your insinuations. If you are going to accuse me or Roland, get on with it or leave me and the memory of Roland alone. None of it has anything to do with me.'

'Are you sure you're not involved with Roland's business interests?'

'As I said, I haven't seen Roland in years. I knew nothing about his business in Sydney or Darwin until he called me recently.'

'So, tell me about your job. I believe you're in marketing?' Yates had clearly done some checking since last night. 'I always thought that would be a pretty exciting profession.'

'Are you kidding! I worked for Perth Water. What could be more meaningless than marketing water? No one can do without the stuff, and there's a monopoly supplier in Western Australia, so what did I really have to do? I still stuffed it up.'

'So, when Roland called you out of the blue, you came running to Darwin? You must have really been a good friend.'

I had to give it to Yates; he was persistent in his questioning. 'I was Roland's oldest friend.'

'Nah, some barflies at The Criterion would have at least thirty years on you, even though it looks like they could have fifty.'

'I didn't mean his oldest friend in years. I meant I've known him for the longest time, more than anyone else, I expect. Now he has died, I'll head back to Perth.'

'I'd rather you delay that for a few days, maybe a week. You'll stay for the funeral, won't you? It won't hold you up for long; we're pushing it through; there's a bit of a backlog. The dead refugees from the wharf have complicated things.'

'Sure, I'll stay for the funeral, but we're done, Sergeant. I owe you nothing, and you're just tarnishing my friend's good name,' I said, even though I believed Roland's name was tarnished years ago. All Yates could do was add another layer of veneer. 'I don't know why the police are persisting with their investigation. Nothing they find will bring Roland back, and even if they do find something, who are they going to charge? The poor bugger's dead. Don't you have some real criminals to chase after? I don't know what you hope to achieve.

Roland might have been dodgy sometimes, but I've never known him to do anything illegal. I think you're barking up the wrong tree if you think he is involved in people smuggling or illegal things at his old insurance job. He might have had a funny way about him, but he always did the right thing by me. His folks, always looked after me too.'

'I'm not a betting man, but I'll give you a hundred to one that I'll find something dodgier about your mate Roland than you give him credit for. I might even find out something you'd rather I didn't.'

'What do you mean?' I shivered. He was clearly suggesting Roland had been doing something illegal, but it also sounded like he didn't think Roland's death was an accident.

'It was rather convenient for the police to find Roland was in an accident that made his body almost impossible to identify. And very convenient for Roland, it occurred immediately after the disaster on the docks, just as we were closing on him.'

Yates was behaving oddly now. His jaw stiffened, and he talked through clenched teeth. Was this a sign that he was wildly speculating, trying to see if I'd react in some way or was it that he detested that someone was callous enough to kill so many desperate people? If Yates was hoping I could shed any light on any of this, he was going to be disappointed. I couldn't believe that Roland was involved in the deaths on the docks. I knew nothing about his time in Sydney. It seemed I didn't know as much about Roland as I thought I had. What had I unwittingly become involved in? Why was it all so confusing? I didn't need any of this.

'Thanks for the coffee. I've had enough. Now I need some air,' I said, rising from the chair.

Yates peered at my half-finished coffee. 'I'll see you at the funeral, Mr Winter,' he said, but I had already turned and was walking away.

25

Paul

Two days later the taxi picked me up from the hotel, arriving almost 20 minutes late. Even later than I would have expected from a Perth taxi.

'Darwin Cemetery, thanks, mate. Can you make it quick? I'm running late.'

'Don't normally have customers rushin' to the cemetery,' the driver chuckled insensitively at his own humour.

I didn't bother replying. He was being a smart arse. Letting him get to me wouldn't get me there any quicker.

The drive to the cemetery took longer than I thought. I paid the driver and saw him park a little up the road, knowing he'd probably score a fare back to town from those who had attended the funeral.

There was a small group just inside the gates that I assumed were there for Roland. The Darwin 'uniform' of singlet and thongs was modified in reverence to the occasion, but not by much. Black shirts or t-shirt and jeans replaced the shorts and singlets. I wouldn't have looked out of place down south with my shirt and tie, but up here it was not the most sensible attire in the heat.

The small crowd seemed to be representative of Darwin's eclectic population. There were Asians, swarthy eastern Europeans and Anglo Saxons, the latter looking over-cooked and reddened by time in Darwin's sunshine. Strangely there didn't appear to be any Indigenous people. For someone who had, if Yates was correct gone into business with these people it struck me as odd.

While the funeral attendees had tried to comply with the customary black funeral attire, one woman stood out. She wore a red satin dress split to the thigh with a scooped back that was only just dignified. What was she thinking?

A classic Holden station wagon rumbled in. It had been modified with added height and length in its conversion to a hearse. The paint was well polished, and its chrome sparkled, but it belched grey smoke and sounded like major mechanical maintenance was overdue. It stopped just short of the gathered mourners and belched once more before it relaxed into inactivity. Two thin, funeral attendees exited and donned their top hats in a cartoon parody of their profession.

I scanned the mourners for any of Roland's family but couldn't recognise any in the crowd. Surely his brothers would be here? The attendees handed out little cards, ostensibly for you to put your name on so the family would know who to thank for attending, but in reality, a thinly veiled tout for business. If the family didn't show, were they really likely to thank us for attending? I wrote my name, together with my Perth address.

'Can I borrow ya' pen, mate?'

I turned to face the pen-scrounger, an elderly man who looked like he liked a drink. His nose had been broken so many times it couldn't decide which way to zig-zag down his face. The nose was held in place by a spider's web of thin veins that spilled across his cheeks. It was hard to tell if his yellow eyes were moist due to the occasion or because of his years of drinking. I guessed the booze was more likely.

'Sure.'

He then passed my pen down the line of mourners. Hadn't any of these people thought to bring a pen? I watched as my pen passed from hand to hand, including Spiros, the Greek hotel proprietor. He had put a dark shirt over his singlet. That he managed to arrive ahead of me when I'd passed him in reception as I departed made me realise the taxi driver had taken a longer route to stretch his fare. Finally, the pen passed to the woman in the red dress. She filled in the little card, spoke to Spiros, who then nodded in my direction. She stared at me for a moment, clicked the pen closed and walked towards me.

'I believe this is yours?' she said in an accent that I guessed was Indian.

'Yes. Thanks,' I said, taking the pen from her. She seemed to hold onto the pen a little longer than expected, resulting in us both holding the pen at the same time, as if exchanging a relay baton in slow motion.

'Thank you for that. I normally always have a pen with me, but I don't have any pockets in this dress,' she and brushed her hands down both hips to confirm the absence of pockets, and in doing so, highlighted her curves.

'It's a stunning dress,' I said genuinely, but also inviting that an explanation might be in order.

'It was Roland's favourite. I know it is unconventional on this sort of occasion, but I know Roland would have appreciated it this one last time.'

'I'm Paul, Paul Winter,' I said, holding out my hand for her to shake.

'Yes, I assumed you were. Roland asked me to keep an eye out for you while you were in town. I'm Kamahli,' she said, pausing and shaking my hand, again holding on longer than usual.

'How did you know Roland?' I asked, but as I did so, the small crowd lurched forward, following the coffin that had been unloaded from the hearse and was making its way to a freshly excavated site.

'Let's speak later.'

Kamahli walked on ahead of me, working her way back through the modest gathering of mourners and assumed a place directly behind the coffin.

There was a mound of dirt beside the hole in the ground covered with green felt. The sky had become pale grey with bright white clouds that piled on top of each other. Darker clouds accelerated towards us from the horizon suggesting that a thunderstorm was on the way. The changing light made the scene seem almost monochromatic, except for Kamahli's red satin and the red scar in earth, which appeared even more startling than they might have otherwise.

I tugged at my collar as the humidity made its presence felt. I wondered how long it was before out-of-towners adjusted to the humidity or adjusted what they wore to accommodate the heat. If I were to spend any length of time up here, I'd have to get some new clothes. Darwin's temperature would not be kind to anyone foolish enough to stay out in it for too long.

All I could see of Kamahli was her shoulders and back. The dress didn't appear to have a back. Her skin was flawless, the colour of fine chocolate.

I couldn't help staring at her. I know I should have been paying more attention to what the priest was saying. He was the only person more ridiculously dressed for the weather than I was. He wore black robes, white vestments with gold brocade and a brimless little hat with a pom-pom.

I looked at Kamahli again. I had thought she was simply out of place regarding the choice of dress, but this was amplified when I noticed she had glitter on her back. Who wore glitter to a funeral? The glitter covering her back caught in the sun's rays, sparkling between her shoulders. Had she put makeup on her back? Then I realised the glitter was growing in size. It wasn't glitter at all. The 'glitter' was sweat forming on her back in the heat of the sun. As I watched, the glitter grew and grew and eventually coalesced, catching more and more of the sun. Finally, the 'glitter' could no longer withstand gravity and streamed in rivulets down her back, accelerating as it travelled southwards. I realised I was sweating too. The heat and the thoughts I was having about where the rivulets were heading had contributed equally.

'This is your friend's funeral. What are you thinking?' I thought, stopping my inappropriate thoughts and glancing at the people beside me to check I had said nothing out loud.

At that point, the priest stopped whatever he had been saying, reached down and scooped up a handful of red earth and threw it onto the coffin. It made a dull thud, as if the coffin was empty. The funeral directors took the priest's queue, took hold of the ropes strung under the coffin, and lowered Roland into the ground. At that point some in the crowd turned and dispersed. Others shuffled forward and scooped a handful of earth and tossed it onto the now lowered coffin. Kamahli bent and picked up a handful of the dirt and threw it, and blew a kiss with the other hand. I turned to leave and saw Sergeant Yates a few metres behind the last of the crowd, heading directly for me.

'I see you've met Kamahli,' he said as he approached.

'Yes, she's hard to miss.'

'She was Roland's business partner, you know.'

'Nothing to do with me, Sergeant.'

'I thought you might have been interested, that's all.'

The funeral director was working his way back to the hearse—what a job. I couldn't stand to do that every day.

He approached and handed me another little card that said, 'Please join the friends and family for a small celebration of the life of Mr Roland Redman, formerly of Sydney and Perth, at The Criterion Hotel, Larrakeyah.'

'Can I give you a lift to The Criterion, Mr Winter?' Sergeant Yates asked.

I'm sure he wasn't expecting me to answer in the affirmative. 'Thanks, Sergeant. I'll make my own way there.'

'I'd be happy to give you a lift, Paul.'

That accent again. Not English, not Indian. I would have guessed Indian by the way she looked, but it was something else.

'Thanks, that would be great,' I said to Kamahli, smirking at Yates as I brushed past him and took up the better offer.

I was fully expecting Kamahli to be driving a little red sports car to match the dress. It seemed out of character when she ushered me towards a short-wheelbase Land Rover ute that had seen better days.

'It was a nice service,' I said, trying to make small talk as we began our journey.

'I hate funerals,' Kamahli replied, shutting that line of conversation down very quickly.

'I believe you and Roland knew each other well.'

'Who told you that?'

'The sergeant told me you and Roland were partners.' I'd deliberately left out 'business' to see how she reacted.

'We were lovers once but we have more recently been business partners. Both of those things seem like years ago now.' Kamahli said matter-of-factly as if both statements were of the same minor significance.

'What business were you partners in?' I asked, thinking Kamahli did not look the type to work in a café.

'Imports. Roland and I imported furniture from south-east Asia. We'd get it made in Indonesia and ship container loads of it to Darwin. Sometimes we'd send containers directly to Perth or Melbourne. Roland bought me out of the business a while ago. Let us see what this party is going to be like.'

I thought describing a wake as a party was a bit of a stretch. With only about forty people at the funeral and some of those clearly itching to leave as quickly as decorum permitted, describing a gathering of mourners as a 'party' was a stretch.

The Criterion didn't look like much of a venue for a party either. It had always amused me that the names for dero pubs seemed to be from a playlist that frequently contradicted the less glamorous reality: The Palace, The Royal and The Queen Victoria. Every second town had one or the other. The Criterion suggested it had passed some standard; by its appearance, it must have been a low one.

We crossed a carpark with its tarmac a filigree of potholes. The outside of The Criterion had seen better days; the paint was peeling, and the veranda posts struggled to hold up the sagging roof. Several posts were replaced by scaffolding jacks to retard the collapse. The Federation green and cream tiles on the outside walls to eye level were reminiscent of a Melbourne tram.

I approached the right half of the door to the front bar. Multiple posters were peeling from the door with the current top veneer advertising 'Hush. Bony Moroney Tour'. Even one-hit wonders have to end up somewhere eventually, I suppose. The door opened, and I was gobsmacked at the pumping crowd within.

'Roland liked to make a memorable entrance. I suppose he will make a memorable exit too,' Kamahli shouted in my ear to make herself heard above the noise of the crowd and the unintelligible music.

'Yeah, right. Where were these people at his funeral?'

'I suppose they didn't like the formalities. Some people really just don't like funerals. Roland's Indigenous friends would fit into that category. They have cultural issues with deceased people, despite that, they go to too many funerals for their own people. I think if they could find any reason not to go to a white-fella cemetery, they would. I heard Roland, or his estate, had put money on the bar. I suppose that buys you a few friends around here.'

'Geez. I sure could use a drink.'

I elbowed my way to the bar. If I thought the funeral service had been a microcosm of Darwin, I'd underestimated this city. This was like the bar scene from *Star Wars*, only with more outlandish patrons. Every possible demographic was here. Only barflies were overrepresented. Still, if you put five grand on the bar of a pub like The Criterion, it was hardly surprising.

The two employees working the bar were flat out.

'What'll it be, mate?' one of them asked.

'I'll have a schooner of draught, thanks,' I responded and turned around, thinking Kamahli would have traversed the maze to the bar and still be right behind me, but I could see her in the distance speaking to a young couple. The woman wore a hijab and held a bundle against her chest, clearly a small child. 'Thanks,' I shouted above the noise that was now increasing with the alcohol and pulled 20 dollars from my wallet.

The bartender frowned. 'If you're a friend of Roland's your money's no good here today.'

I suppose there was a tab running. It seemed strange to have an open bar at a wake, but judging by the size of the increasing crowd; it was a popular move. I couldn't guess how long this crowd would take to drink the dollars dry.

I took my beer and made my way across the room. The crowd wasn't making it easy. I took a couple of good swigs from the beer fearful I'd spill it in a collision with someone's elbow, if I left it full. It wasn't as though I needed to worry about damaging the carpet. The way that the floor grabbed at the soles of my shoes at every footfall advised me it had seen more than its share of spilt drinks and probably a few chunders over the years. I made a determined line to where I'd last seen Kamahli, oblivious that two hundred or so people had now gathered at the bar to see Roland off.

I reached Kamahli. 'I needed a drink. Can I get you one?'

'Thank you, Paul. Please, let me introduce you to Roland's friends, Hashani and Kahled, and their little boy, Roland. They are Hazara Muslims originally from Afghanistan. Now they are Australian citizens living just outside Darwin. It is nice of you to offer to get us a drink, but alcohol is strictly off-limits for them. I'll have a Champagne, though.'

I shook Kahled's hand.

He gripped my hand tightly and said, 'Very pleased to meet you, sir,' in a heavily accented but seemingly well-rehearsed line.

I returned his greeting and held out my hand to shake Hashani's. Kamahli stared at me and shook her head, just perceptibly. Clearly, shaking Hashani's hand wasn't a good idea. Hashani ignored my gesture and tugged her headscarf a little tighter.

'Can I get you something to drink, non-alcoholic, of course?'

'We are very happy, thank you. We are only here to pay our respect to Mr Roland. No beverages are necessary,' said Kahled.

I took another swig of beer and renegotiated my way back to the bar. The carpet was way beyond redemption, but I didn't feel like it was fair to add my slops to the ecosystem thriving within it. Kahled, Hashani, and baby Roland were quite a little family. What sort of influence had Roland had up here to have Afghans calling their children after him? I'm sure it wasn't just great coffee at Chris's Cafe.

I stood shoulder to shoulder with an Indigenous man also waiting to catch the eye of the busy barman. He looked like he could have been one hundred years old.

'G'day, how's it going?' I said.

'Well, mate, I've had better days. Lots of better days, I must say. I'm very sorry that my brother Roland has gone. How'd you know Roland?'

'I was his mate from school in Perth. I've only just come up here recently. Had you known Roland long yourself?'

'Not that long, I suppose. Roland and me were working on a program to get kids in the bush reading. Now he's gone. It'll be up to me to continue it.'

The barman, the same I'd seen earlier, returned and put two beers in front of the old man. He picked them up and headed back into the crowd. I would have loved to hear more from him. The barman looked at me, still nursing the only partially depleted beer and raised a single eyebrow.

'A Champagne for the lady, please,' I said, carefully making him aware that the Champagne wasn't for me.

'Any preference? I've got a sparkling from Tonon's in Carmel or French Veuve Clicquot. Just finished the last of the Dom, sorry,' the barman said to my surprise.

The last thing I was expecting was a selection of Champagne. 'Let's go with the Veuve; thanks, mate,' I replied, not knowing if he was taking the piss. He produced an orange labelled bottle, prised out the cork and poured a very nice-looking glass of real Champagne.

I traversed the front bar again, negotiating a zig-zag path through the noisy crowd and returned to Kamahli as Kahled and Hashani were leaving with Roland junior.

I passed the Champagne to Kamahli. 'What's the story with Roland junior?'

Kamahli paused before she responded. The sound of the crowd didn't make it easy to think clearly, so the visible effort wasn't unexpected.

'Kahled and Hashani had a great deal of respect for our friend, Roland. It is a great honour that they have acknowledged him in this way. In Afghani culture, the first-born son is very special. Kahled and Hashani feel,' she paused, choosing her words decidedly, 'very strongly, that Roland has blessed their life. I am aware of several other 'Roland juniors, as you say, here in Darwin.'

'I don't understand. How does someone who runs a coffee shop and a cheap furniture business have such a lot of impact around here?'

'So, I see you two are getting on okay.'

I turned to see Sergeant Yates with a squat glass in his hand, probably ice water. I took it as a sign that he was on duty.

'Yes. Kamahli was just telling me about her business with Roland.'

'I'd be pretty interested in that too,' Sergeant Yates said with an odd expression.

'I'm sorry, Sergeant, I need to refresh my drink,' Kamahli said, looking at her glass from which she had taken a solitary sip. Red lipstick, the same colour as her dress, marked the rim of the glass. She wasn't keen to hang around to converse with Sergeant Yates.

'So, what do I call you in this lovely setting, Sergeant or Yates? I suppose you have a first name too.'

'Yates is fine. Most of my mates call me Yates. My first name is Bill, as I've told you before, but nobody remembers it. Sergeant isn't appropriate here. Not sure if I've got too many mates here, anyway. Your new friend seemed pretty reluctant to stick around to talk with me.'

'Kamahli? She seems pretty intent on working the room. Looks as though she knows everyone here.'

'Yes, your Ms Kamahli is quite a social butterfly. She certainly seems to know everyone. She's done very well for herself here. She's come a long way from arriving in Darwin years ago as a Sri Lankan refugee,' said Yates pointing out that Kamahli had already moved from the first group to whom she was talking to the next group.

'I'm struggling to understand why Roland moved to Darwin. So far, I've heard he has a café and a furniture import business. I was just hearing about him and the reading program for kids too. He had a bloody lucrative position in Sydney. Why would he up and leave that to just become a café owner?' I then realised the alcohol that I had may have dulled the defences I would generally have employed in a conversation with the constabulary, even if Yates wasn't in uniform. Maybe I'd already said too much to him previously. Clearly, my beer was not an equal match to Yates's water. At least he had solved the accent question for me: Sri Lankan.

'We'd be pretty interested in knowing an answer to that question, too.'

I was then aware of a presence beside me.

'Excuse me, Paul, there are some people I'd like you to meet. Sorry, Sergeant.' Kamahli reappeared at my elbow, just as it was becoming interesting with Yates. She took me by the elbow and led me across to the other side of the bar, to no one in particular. She turned to me and said, 'I'm not sure if it is in anyone's best interests for you to be interrogated by Sergeant Yates.'

'I don't think you could call it an interrogation. He seems genuinely interested in Roland's departure.' I still couldn't call it death. It didn't seem real.

'Don't be naïve, Paul. Sergeant Yates couldn't care less about Roland. I am stunned he had the gall to turn up here. All he is interested in is finding someone to blame for what has happened on the docks.'

'What do you mean?'

'Paul! You're even wetter behind the ears than Roland warned me you were. Surely you've heard about the appalling situation down at the docks?'

'The strike? I thought that'd been sorted out.'

'Not the strike. The refugees who were found dead or dying in a shipping container. A shipping container with Roland's name on it.'

'Yeah, I know, what a terrible thing. But I don't get all this. I know Roland was involved in some stuff in Sydney that was a little dubious, and insurance companies are mongrels, but it was all above the law. What has this got to do with anything up here? Least of all refugees in a shipping container? Was there some sort of insurance scam going on?'

'Keep your voice down.'

A break in the blaring music made the volume of my voice appear like I was shouting.

Kamahli glanced over my shoulder. 'Roland was never what he appeared on the surface.'

'So, I'm expected to believe he was a shining knight that brought refugees to Australia?' I asked in a more subdued tone.

'I'm sure if you asked Kahled and Hashani, they would certainly see Roland as a 'shining knight'. They wouldn't be the only ones either.

There are many here that are genuinely mourning Roland. I'm sure even you can appreciate that teetotalling Muslims wouldn't normally be seen in a hotel, celebrating a Christian burial and the tradition of seeing off the dead in such a fashion, if they didn't truly honour and respect Roland.'

'Sorry. I'm not sure if this beer agrees with me. You're telling me that Roland and you, as his business partner, were involved in people smuggling?'

'I certainly didn't say that.' Kamahli turned on her heel and headed off to a conversation on the other side of the room, leaving me staring into my beer.

I turned as I heard someone clearing their throat next to me.

'Excuse me. You are a friend of Mr Roland?' a woman in a yellow sari asked, rather than stated.

'Yeah. Yes. I was, I am,' I stammered, not knowing what was coming next.

'Mr Redman was a wonderful person. It is with great sadness that he has so tragically passed. Please accept the condolences of my family.'

Before I could ascertain any details about what she meant, she disappeared into the crowd that was now becoming even noisier as it ate into the generous bar tab. Kamahli, too had disappeared.

This would have been remarkable, were it not for several others who delivered a similar short message of the same kind. Two separate women in hijabs, a man in cheese-cloth 'pyjamas' and a heavily-accented Middle Eastern guy in an *'I heart NT'* T-shirt, shorts and black thongs, seemingly trying too hard to fit in, passed on their respects.

What was going on? The Roland I knew didn't have any connection to the Middle East, migrants or anything that didn't feature Roland as the centre of attention.

I tried to locate Kamahli. Perhaps she could shed some light on what was going on. I scanned the bar and progressively raked my gaze through the crowd when she almost magically appeared and thrust a bar coaster into my hand.

'This is my address. We need to talk. Meet me there in forty minutes. Don't drink too much. And don't leave me waiting.' She then turned and left.

It seemed my once good friend Roland really was more complex than I had given him credit for. I sure as hell didn't want to get involved in any illegal stuff. I didn't need any complications in my life, but I could use another beer. I turned up in front of the barman once again.

'Another beer, thanks, mate.'

The barman poured the beer, as he had no doubt done so thousands of times before.

'So, how d'you know Roland?'

I turned to face a short, thin guy wearing a black AC/DC T-shirt, a greasy mullet and three days' stubble. He'd asked his question and then nuzzled his beer.

'I was his mate in school. How about you?'

He slurped and responded, 'I used to work for Roland. Real gentleman he was. Gave me a break when I got out, when no one else would.'

'What sort of job did you do?' I asked, deliberately avoiding the obvious question about from where he'd got out.

'Bits and pieces, here and there. Running around. Dishes, even peeling spuds at the café if they needed me. Unloading shit. Running the mail. Getting him the fish and crabs from the blackfellas when they'd catch some. But my main job was keeping his boat up to spec. I worked on a cray boat out of Geraldton for a while. I know my way around boats back to front, and I love being out of the water. Gonna miss him. Miss him a lot.'

'Seems Roland had quite a few friends in Darwin,' I said, knowing the answer if the still increasing numbers in the bar were anything to go by.

'Oh, shit yeah. Everybody loved him. He helped a shit-load of people out. Did you know he sponsored an orphanage?

Jesus, it sounded like Roland was the second coming, a bloke's version of Mother Teresa. 'Nah. He didn't mention that one to me.'

'Yeah. I don't think many people knew. Ol' Roland liked to keep most of his business to himself. I heard he'd made some dough down south, in computers or something. Came to Darwin to spread it around a bit.'

I didn't bother correcting him about what I thought Roland had done down south. To this guy, insurance and computers both would have sounded equally mysterious.

'He could've stayed down south and been just another tosser driving round in a flash car, going home to a flash house and going home to his skinny blonde missus with plastic tits. Up here, he could be somebody and make a difference. His orphanage was in Cambodia, Battabulla or some bloody thing. Every month I'd go to the post office to send them off more dough. He'd get a few drawings and stuff from the kids and that. He sponsored quite a few reffos too.'

'What? You mean refugees?'

'Yeah. You know, people from other places, running away from wars and stuff: Muslims, Christians, Hindus, the bloody lot. Hardly any of 'em could speak a word of English when they turned up. Roland helped out with that too. Gave 'em a job and got them doing English at night classes.

'Oh yeah,' I said, trying not to show my increasing astonishment but not wanting to stem the conversation. This guy was giving me more insight into Roland's last few years than anyone I'd spoken to since I'd arrive in Darwin.

'What do you know about Roland's businesses up here?'

'Well, there was the café, of course. Most days, you could find him there. He'd come in for breakfast every morning. Regular as clockwork he was. Six-thirty. Short black and Vegemite toast. Then there's the furniture import business he had with Ms Kamahli. He had a seafood export business going with the blackfellas. Made good money on that one too. He had the blackfellas catching those bloody big mangrove crabs and barramundi and sending it off to Hong Kong, Singapore and stuff. The Chinese pay shit-loads for them up there. Most of the money from that went into a cultural centre and school for the Indigenous kids. He built it with them himself, you know. He'd have 'em learning stuff from the elders. They'd do like dot paintings, dancing, bush tucker and stuff the tourists can't get enough of. I heard he signed over full ownership to the elders once it was up and running. Roland never made nothing off it, but the business gave 'em plenty of jobs. Kept 'em out of trouble with the coppers, off the grog and stuff. Kept 'em on country and gave 'em something of their own to be proud of, you know.'

The Saint Roland story just kept getting better and better. I took a sizable gulp of my beer. 'Sorry, mate, I should have introduced myself. Paul. Paul Winter,' I said, thrusting my hand towards him.

'Geoffrey. Geoffrey Taylor. Most of my friends call me Squizzy.'

'Geoffrey? I didn't know your name was Geoffrey, Squizzy.' A bloke appeared behind Squizzy. He was wearing a sleeveless blue and grey flannelette shirt that had probably seen more years than washes. He could have been Squizzy plus another thirty years. Thirty hard years.

'Piss off, Blue. You knew my real name was Geoffrey. I've told you a hundred times.'

It was even hard to believe Blue was called Blue. He was totally bald. Bushy white eyebrows and copious nostril hair were the only hair left on his head. He must have earned the nickname Blue at a time when he still had hair on his head.

'This here's Paul, an old school friend of Roland's.'

'Pleased to meet you, Blue,' I said, shaking his hand. Blue's face and forearms showed he'd seen too much Darwin sun over the years and was now paying the price. His face was a network of skin cancers and scars where they had once been. At some point, years ago, someone had had a go at fixing them, but I suspect there was just too many. The cancers had almost obliterated a tattoo on his forearm that had a resemblance to an anchor. Discoloured marks covered the backs of his hand up to where his turned-up shirt covered the rest of his arm. Bleached, white lesions and crusty old growths covered his skin.

'Likewise, Paul. A friend of Roland's is a friend of mine. Not sure if I'd say the same thing about some dodgy characters Squizzy sucks up too, though,' he said, giving Squizzy a light-hearted jab in the ribs.

'Leave it off, Blue. Paul sounds like a gentleman, like Roland. He doesn't want to hear any of your crap.'

'Fair enough. Time for another beer.' Blue banged his empty glass onto the bar. 'Hey, Jock, another three of the same mate!' he called to the barman.

'Sorry, Blue. I don't like to be rude, but I've got an appointment I need to be at. Can't keep the lady waiting,' I said as Blue looked genuinely disappointed. 'I'm sure Squizzy will keep you company. What do you say, Squizzy?

'Yeah. I could certainly go another one. I enjoyed your company, Paul, but I'm not averse to joining Blue here for another one or three. *Can't afford to keep the lady waiting*, hey. Anyone, we'd know?' Squizzy said, giving Blue a wink.

'Squizzy, Blue, I do apologise, but a gentleman never tells,' I said and headed for the door.

26

Paul

When I first entered the pub, it had been full daylight. In the interim, darkness had descended. It was amazing how quickly day turned to night in the tropics.

A column of taxis had accumulated across the road. I tapped on the window of the taxi at the head of the column. The driver woke with a start. I slumped into the back seat and handed the driver the crumpled bar coaster with Kamahli's address. He read the address and handed it back to me. I had no idea how far it was. The driver seemed to know without needing to look at a map. We were there in about fifteen minutes. It wasn't a fancy street or a desirable part of town. A few shops were clustered together across the road, a fish and chip shop and a laundromat. A liquor store, a 24-hour deli and a TAB were a little further along. They were probably the only businesses around here, legitimate businesses at least. The deli and the laundromat appeared to be the only places still open. The feeble light in the laundromat showed one bedraggled occupant, who I assumed was there to sleep the night, rather than to wash his clothes, though both he and his clothes looked well overdue for a wash.

The taxi dropped me in front of the fish and chip shop. It was closed, but the sign advertising its wares was left flashing on the roof. The sign was made from glass neon tubes bent into letters of a flowing script. It must have seemed modern when it was first installed. Now the best it could manage was an intermittent flash between "fish and ips" with the 'fish' flashing red within a fish shape and "ips" flashing green. The green was too bright, as if the truncated word was still receiving the quota of energy meant for the full word.

I paid the driver the $8.45 fare with a $10 note, which he quickly put into a cigar box that he pulled from under the seat, returning it as quickly as he'd taken it out and making a feeble effort to conceal within the folds of *Fannie Bay Race Guide*.

"Keep the change, mate," I said, knowing he had no intention of offering me any change.

"Thanks, mate." He looked over towards the apartment and said, "Do you want me to wait?"

I assume the people that visited this part of town were either chasing a fix or a cheap hooker. He would have been disappointed to find I was after neither. "Nah. She'll be right. Don't worry about waiting. I could be a while. You can go," I said as I got out and closed the door. He headed up the road and pulled over outside the long-closed bottle shop. I wondered how long the $10 would have lasted him if the TAB was open.

I took the crumpled coaster out of my pocket and reread the address. It was definitely the right place. I really didn't know what to expect. I was keen to talk to Kamahli. She seemed to be the link to what Roland had been up to, and I hoped she could answer the questions twirling around my brain.

I knocked furtively on her door. Kamahli opened it and reached out her hand, taking mine in hers and gently pulling me in without saying anything. She was still wearing that dress. She pulled me towards her and kissed me hard. I kissed her back, oblivious to anything other than her. Despite having had the beer, it was Kamahli that I was intoxicated by. She tasted great. I held her eagerly. Neither of us could deny it had been a weird introduction, but equally, I wasn't about to hold back the yearning she had suddenly awoken. Kamahli reached over my shoulder and flicked the door closed behind me. I felt her breath on my neck.

She led me towards the bed where the covers had been pulled back. She turned as we reached the bed and pushed me through 180 degrees and down, encouraging me to sit. She stepped back and slipped out of her dress. She was naked above the waist and only wore tantalisingly small, panties in a colour that matched the dress that now lay crumpled on the floor. She joined me on the bed. Her perfume saturated my senses. It was gardenia, sandalwood and cloves. It was everywhere. It was in the room, on her body and on the sheets. She seemed simultaneously fragile, lustful and assertive.

The lights from the "fish and ips" sign across the street flashed into the room, through gossamer curtains. The lights matched our rhythm, pulsating, alternating red then green. The red and green cast a hue over her dark skin, making her appear to be one moment a glowing caramel, the next moment radiant jade. The caramel was delicious. The jade was mysterious. We finally slumped, exhausted and fell asleep in each other's arms, emotionally and physically spent, still breathing hard. I'm sure neither of us was entirely sure what had just happened.

It must have been close to five when I woke. I deliberately tried not to wake Kamahli. I had an uneasy feeling that I had crossed an invisible line. A sensation of simultaneous loss and gain. Neither feeling felt entirely wrong, but neither felt fully right either. Kamahli remained asleep. She was resting in the crook of my arm, hard up against my body. She still smelled so good. The neon light continued to play its relentless rhythm across the room, bathing everything red then green, red then green, over and over in an endless loop. A dog barked in the distance.

Other than the complaining dog, everything else in that long moment was silent. Strangely, I thought of Roland. Had I betrayed a loyalty? Was it even possible to betray a dead man? I thought back to all those years ago when Roland and I went to parties and Roland went home with the girl and I went home alone. Roland would call me in the morning and ask me to come and pick him up from wherever he had ended up. I suppose I was jealous of never being the one that stayed the night with the girl, only to leave in the stillness of the morning. But it wasn't the case this time. I'd slept with Roland's lover or his former lover. Had I bested him even if he was dead? I felt guilty. Had Kamahli slept with me, for me, because I was a convenient replacement for Roland or in an effort to keep me away from Yates? Had I slept with her because she was Roland's former lover? Or had we both sought solace in each other's arms to get through this strange series of events? I finally fell asleep again, reeling from the recent events.

It was too hard to think of what the week had been, let alone the last few hours. I couldn't get my addled head to work things through to a logical conclusion. I tried, unsuccessfully to go back to sleep. As days went, this was one of the more bizarre that I'd ever experienced. I closed my eyes. I tried to sleep. Sometimes harder you try to go to sleep the harder sleep it is to find. Eventually, I drifted back off.

The alarm clock in my head went off at six. I woke with a start, not immediately knowing where I was. I eased my arm away from under Kamahli's neck. She turned, mumbled something unintelligible and continued to sleep. I swung my feet to the floor and silently crossed the room, retrieving my clothes from where I had discarded them on the floor. I dressed quickly and quietly, making sure to open the door as quietly as I could. The door offered a slight squeak, an exclamation mark, punctuating my guilt as I left.

I walked the five or six kilometres back to the Apollo Hotel, surprising myself that I found the way. Darwin was still asleep. There was no traffic on the road, and the humidity was yet to rise. I ruminated on the poor form I had just demonstrated in leaving without a word. I felt confused. Despite sleeping beside Kamahli, I still felt sleep-deprived, as if I needed another eight hours. I was still reeling from Roland's funeral and the events that had followed. At the same time, I was still strangely euphoric. Kamahli was beautiful. I couldn't wait to see her again.

27

Paul

I couldn't stop thinking about Kamahli. I was ashamed about how I'd silently slunk out the door without even having the conversation that I had gone there for. There hadn't been any opportunity for conversation.

Now that I'd endured Yates' questions, I was free to do as I liked. What I'd like was to see Kamahli again. I cleaned up my hotel room, grabbed some breakfast from Spiros and went searching for a taxi. It was after ten when I left my room.

I gave the taxi driver the address and headed off again. It wasn't as far as I thought it was the first time and it certainly felt shorter than when I'd walked it. Driving through the streets seemed different. The 'fish and ips' place still looked dead, its lights on but barely noticeable in the sun's glare. The TAB was doing a brisk trade. I suppose the races over east were already underway, even if it was early for the locals.

'Just up here thanks, mate.'

I saw Kamahli talking to some guy in a battered blue Datsun out the front of her place. She leaned in to the window and quickly kissed the driver. The driver gunned it towards my approaching taxi. Kamahli was left standing in the middle of the road. She stared after the rapidly departing car. What a way to leave someone like Kamahli, she was beautiful. I wrenched my eyes off Kamahli just as the Datsun and its occupant sped past.

'Fuck!' was all I could say. My jaw actually dropped.

'What, mate? I thought you said just up here,' said the taxi driver.

I struggled to close my mouth before replying, 'Yes, yes I did. Just up near the lady, thanks' I couldn't believe who I'd just seen barrelling past me in the Datsun. I'd seen a ghost. Or at least someone who should have been a ghost. I thought he was a dead man. I mean, I'd just been to his funeral. Roland!

I dropped a ten-dollar note over the front seat into the driver's lap and jumped out of the cab before it had come fully to a stop. I rushed to Kamahli as she walked towards the curb.

'Kamahli! What the hell is going on?' I screamed louder than I should have.

Kamahli spun around. 'Paul, I wasn't expecting you.'

'I can see that. Who was that just leaving?' I knew full well who it was, but I wanted to hear it from her.

'That was a good friend of mine,' she paused. 'Ah, Bob, Bob Smith. But I'm sure you don't know him.'

'Bob Smith? Surely you could come up with a better name than that.'

'What? What do you mean? It was Bob Smith. I'm not sure I like your tone, Paul. We didn't discuss anything last night or this morning, but you don't have the right to turn up here unannounced and tell me who I can or can't see. Bob's been a friend of mine for ages.' Kamahli was aggressive in her response.

'I'm not telling you who you can see or not unless they are my dead friend! I know Roland when I see him. What the hell's going on?'

'Paul, you need to calm down. Keep your voice down. You're talking nonsense.'

'Kamahli, last night meant more to me than you can imagine, but don't take me for a fool. I know it was Roland. You've got to appreciate I've known Roland most of my life. Longer than you have known him. Despite that silly looking moustache, I'd recognise him anywhere, so just level with me.'

'You'd better come inside.' Without waiting for a response, she turned and led the way back to her flat.

Like a puppy, I followed and entered the front door.

She turned to face me. 'I know this must be very confusing for you.'

'You bloody well got that right—' I was about to go on, but I complied when she lifted her palm to signal me to stop.

'Please let me try to explain what's going on. You're right. You did see Roland. The body at Roland's funeral wasn't his. Things are much more complicated than you could understand.'

It was my turn to interrupt. 'Complicated? Well that's a fucking understatement. I get a call out of the blue to come to Darwin from a mate I haven't seen in years; he dies, I fuck his girlfriend, and he comes back to life again. Roland, fucking 'Lazarus' Redman. Unbelievable.'

'Paul, I'd prefer it if you didn't describe things so crudely.'

'Crudely? What do you think the cops would make of all of this?' I said but instantly regretted it.

Kamahli's face hardened at the mention of the police. 'Sit down.' It was not a hospitable offer, but a directive. 'I don't think it is in anyone's best interest to run off to your new friend, Sergeant Yates.

'Right,' I said, following the order to sit. 'Explain it to me, so I don't have a reason to go to Yates, right now.'

'Roland was assisting immigrants to come to Australia, and things didn't go to plan.'

I dropped my head into my hands. 'Kamahli, are you telling me Roland *is* responsible for the deaths of those people on the docks?'

'Paul, things are never as simple as they first appear. Roland is a good man who has helped many people to a better life. People like me, people who didn't have the option of going through official channels.'

'So, Roland was responsible for all of those people dying?' I asked again.

'People died, that much is true, but Roland helped many more people than the authorities will ever know, to have meaningful lives in Australia. Lives where they work hard and can contribute to this country. Do you have any idea how many people Roland saved from death?'

'So, are you trying to tell me Roland is a bloody saint?'

'No. Paul, you of all people know Roland is no saint, but neither is he a murderer. Nobody is wholly responsible for who they are. Life sculpts all of us. Roland wasn't proud of some of the things he did down south, but he didn't shirk away from them either. He came to Darwin to make amends, to redeem himself. Did you know he built orphanages in Cambodia and charitable businesses in Indonesia? He brought almost two hundred people to this country, saving them from death and persecution in their own countries. Many of them are scarred from the torture they have endured. Even here in Darwin, Roland employed people who would otherwise have been left on the streets or worse. There's a very good reason you met mothers and fathers with children that they had proudly named Roland at the hotel yesterday.'

'So, Roland *was* a refugee trafficker. He went from taking money from dying AIDS patients to taking money off refugees?'

'Roland made money from people dying of AIDS. That much is true. He once worked for an insurance company where it was his job to do so. He did not make any money from refugees. You're not hearing what I am saying. Roland funded the travel of these people to Australia. Roland didn't take money from them; he sponsored them. He sponsored them because there was no legitimate way for them to get away from the hell in which they were living. If that meant paying people smugglers along the way. It was Roland who paid them.'

'You still haven't acknowledged those poor bastards in the container at the port. How do you or Roland intend to bullshit your way around the dead people?'

'I can't. I don't intend to 'bullshit' you about anything,' Kamahli said, using air quotes for 'bullshit' and then forming her hands into a prayer shape. 'Do you really think it is in anyone's best interest for you to speak to Yates? Surely you know by now that Roland came to Darwin to make amends.'

'Amends for what?'

'You know, restitution for the job that he had done in Sydney. He made a lot of money but he felt unworthy of it. He hated it. He moved to Darwin determined to start over. He wanted to make amends, to 'redress the ledger' as he would say. He felt that his time in Sydney was taking from humanity. In contrast, his time in Darwin was an opportunity to give back. Sydney demolished his soul. Roland was determined that whatever he did in Darwin would involve building it back again.'

'I know Sydney was tough. Ripping off the dying will knock anyone around. But he made a shitload of money in doing it,' I said, not appreciating just how aggressive it sounded until it came out.

'Paul, you only know parts of the whole story. Did you know about Roland and Christina?'

'Christina from school? Yates mentioned her too. What's that all about?'

'I know how confusing this must be for you. I think some of these questions are best asked of Roland.'

'I agree. If Roland wasn't a dead man, it would be so much easier to ask him. Where the fuck did he speed off to, anyway?'

'I can't tell you that.'

'Can't or won't?'

'Both, actually. I don't know where Roland is going, or what he is doing. But if I did, I wouldn't tell you. I know he doesn't need the police on his tail. He needs a friend who can stand by him when he is down. All I am asking of you is to not go to the police. But, if you really feel you need to, wait twenty-four hours—just one day. Even if you believe nothing, I've told you about the good Roland has done, just press the pause button. Wait. Wait one day. What harm could it do? Just give him a chance to sort himself out.'

'Don't you mean just give him a chance to get away? I don't need to be implicated in any of this.'

'That might be a consequence of your decision, Paul. But I ask you to focus on the Roland you once so obviously cared about, not the Roland you think you know now after the last few crazy days. Focus on the Roland you really know. You know in your heart he is a good man.'

'And where do you fit into all of this, Kamahli?'

'I know it is difficult for you to understand, but I love Roland. Not love in a sense you might think. Roland is the reason I'm here. Without Roland, I'd be dead or Kamahli Krishnamurthy living a far lesser life in Sri Lanka, not Kamahli in Darwin. I wouldn't be the Kamahli in front of you now. I wouldn't be the Kamahli that made love to you last night. I wouldn't be the Kamahli imploring you to not make a rash decision. Just think twice before rushing off to speak to Yates. Think twice before you make decisions that can't be reversed. Stop, Paul, and think about how many lives you will affect. Nothing will bring back the poor souls that died on the wharf. All you can do is search your heart and do the right thing. Don't do something that will make things worse. Think about the Roland you once thought so highly of. Think about the good that there is in this world, that can, at times appear to be so horrid, and about what you do next. Don't think just about how you might protect your own interests. Think about how Roland might have become entangled in something that is bigger than you and me. What do you owe Yates, anyway? You don't owe him anything. You don't owe anyone anything. All I'm asking of you is not to make a decision you'll regret.'

'Okay. Enough. I won't rush off to speak to Yates. I'll keep quiet. But I'm not going to lie. If I'm asked a question, I'll answer it. The truth is I'd tell them I loved Roland too. There was a time in years gone by we were closer than brothers. I couldn't turn him in, whatever he's done. What does it mean for us?'

'There really is no us. Last night was wonderful and you were great. Roland asked me to look after you, that's all.'

'So, last night meant nothing to you?'

'You've got to appreciate this is happening in a timeframe totally out of our control. Nothing in the last few days seems normal.'

I'd thought about how I felt last night. I had so hoped that it had meant that my shallow, meaningless life had finally turned a corner. To hear that Kamahli was merely playing out a role hurt. It hit me hard. Darwin wasn't working out how I had hoped it would. I just wanted to go back to my boring life in Perth. Everything associated with Roland got more and more complicated. I wouldn't run off to Yates and rat on a mate, even a mate I hadn't seen for years. The deaths at the docks were appalling, but there was nothing I could do or say to bring those poor people back to life. I needed to decide where my allegiances were. Was I a fool being manipulated by Kamahli? Sex could certainly make logical decisions harder. But I really did know Roland, and I knew he wouldn't deliberately hurt anyone. He wouldn't murder people. He wouldn't write off dead people in a container as an unfortunate side effect of business.

'Kamahli. I hear everything you're saying to me, but I just need some space. I can't deal with all that you're telling me. I wish we could just go back to last night. But I know that's just not possible. I know whatever has occurred between us has been influenced by what you feel for Roland.'

'Don't think that last night was trivial for me either. That's not who I am.'

'I thought you slept with me to provide a distraction for Roland.' Even as I said it, I could see the hurt it caused.

'Roland didn't ask me to sleep with you. Even if he had, do you think I would sleep with anyone so casually? Please don't think of me that way. I'm not some sort of whore. Last night wasn't what you think it was. Perhaps we were just two confused, lonely people who needed to forget about things for a while?'

'I'm sorry, Kamahli. All of this is just doing my head in. One minute Roland is calling me and is larger than life, like he always was, then I'm grieving over my friend only to find you and him are kissing in the middle of the road.'

'Paul, you need just stop. Cool down. Take a little time. If you need to go back to Perth go, I'm sure everyone will understand.'

'I just feel like I've been taken for a fool. I can't see how you and Roland expect to just walk away from this. How can you treat people, me, the refugees, like we are just bit-players in whatever your grand plan is?'

'That's not how it is at all, Paul. I was a refugee. I feel I am responsible for Roland helping people to come to Australia. He was just a café owner when I met him. But he was a café owner looking for a higher purpose. Roland feels terrible about the people on the docks. And he feels terrible about how things have turned out for you. He was just speaking about you as he left.'

'Really, what did he say?' Even I thought the condescending tone in my voice was a bit much.

'He said he was sorry he'd ever called you. That it wasn't fair to drag you into this without letting you know what was going on. That he'd like to tell you his side of the story.'

I was unsure if I was still being played. Some people seem to be able to tell you what you need to hear. Others you end up telling you more than you probably should. Kamahli was both of these people.

'Okay. If 'Saint Roland' wants to speak to me, he knows where to find me. All he's got to do is tell me where and when.'

'I'll see what I can do.'

'I'll stick around for a few days. Roland paid for a week at The Apollo. If you or he needs to contact me, you know where I'm staying.'

With that, I left. I crossed the road and walked down to the TAB where the cab I'd arrived in was still waiting.

'Not as long as you'd thought you'd be, mate?' the driver asked as I climbed into the back of his cab.

'No. I suppose not. Back to the Apollo Hotel where you picked me up, thanks, mate.'

28

Paul

'Hello, ah, Mr Winter,' Spiros said as I walked into the hotel a few minutes later. He smirked and was obviously pleased he hadn't slipped up and called me Ball-sack again. 'Are you in for the day now? Is there anything that I can get you?'

'I'm not sure. I might be going out again, Spiros,' I replied, returning the courtesy of remembering his name. 'Any chance you could get me a bottle of Johnny Walker?

'No problem, Mr Winter. I could get you lovely ouzo if you'd prefer, straight from my cousin in Thessaloniki. He makes it himself on the farm. The recipe she has been in my family for many, many generations. I can do you a good price.'

'Just the whisky if you could, thanks, Spiros.'

'No problem, Mr Winter.' Spiros left the front counter and returned with a bottle of Red Label and a small bucket of ice. 'You want any Coke, soda or something?'

'Nah, the ice will do just fine, thanks. If anyone calls for me, please let me know.'

'No problems, mate,' Spiros said in a way that sounded like he had been rehearsing his Aussie twang.

I passed the yellowing *'Not Working'* sign on the lift door and trudged to my room. I suppose Spiros could have organised a glass for me, but the coffee cup in the room would do fine. I poured a healthy, or perhaps an unhealthy, amount of whisky over a handful of ice in the coffee cup, filling it past halfway.

The amber liquid flowed smoothly over my lips and bloomed into a warm glow as it descended. The second and third sips were much the same. I was unsure if a midday Scotch was the customary thing in Darwin, but it took the edge off the turmoil my mind was in, and the confusion with which I was struggling. The Scotch felt warm on the way down, despite the ice. Beads of sweat broke out on my forehead. I was halfway through my second when the alcohol and Darwin's humidity combined to send me to sleep.

'Mr Winter. Mr Winter.' Spiros was thumping on the door.

I reluctantly opened my eyes. Surely, he wasn't bringing me breakfast again already. I looked out the window and then at my watch. I had only slept for a few hours.

'Mr Winter. Mr Winter.'

I prised myself up and opened the door. 'What is it, Spiros? Is there a fire or something?'

'No. No fire. A gentleman just dropped off this package. Said it is very important for you to get it immediately, right away. He said it couldn't wait for the morning. You need to open it now. The gentleman paid me fifty bucks just to get it to you immediately, so it must be important.'

'Who was this gentleman, Spiros?'

'I've never seen him before, Mr Winter. He didn't tell me his name. Please open the package right away. He said it's very important.'

I took the little cardboard box from Spiros. It felt empty, yet was encased in many layers of clear tape. No markings were on the box, not even a name. There was no hint to its contents. I took the box to the little table in the room where the morning's breakfast dishes were still waiting. I grabbed the knife, wiped it on the already soiled paper napkin and hacked at the packaging tape.

'Were you expecting something, Mr Winter? He said to let you know immediately,' Spiros repeated as he waited at the open door, clearly as curious as I was about the contents of the box.

I stopped hacking at the tape and walked towards the door. 'Thanks for getting this to me so quickly, Spiros,' I said and shut the door, clearly disappointing Spiros, but I didn't know what would be inside. The day was already one of the most bizarre that I'd experienced. There was no need to involve someone else unnecessarily.

I returned to hacking through the layers of tape on the box. Something other than a blunt hotel room knife would have been good, but the rest came away easily once the first layer of tape was removed. I lifted the top off the box. All that was inside was a folded piece of paper. Printed in block letters in blue pen: 'Stokes Hill Wharf, Port Side Grill, 6 pm. Ask for Yang.'

I didn't know what to make of the note. I suspected it was Roland, but I'd hoped it was Kamahli. It was already almost four-thirty. I went to the bathroom and splashed cold water on my face to freshen up and counteract the drowsiness that the Scotch had caused.

'I'm off again for a bit, Spiros,' I said when I went downstairs.

'No worries, Mr Winter. No problems in the box, I hope?'

'We'll have to wait and see, Spiros. We'll have to wait and see,' I repeated once for Spiros and once for myself. 'Can you organise a cab, please?'

'Sure thing, Mr Winter, mate. Where you off to?' said Spiros sounding like he was a trying a bit too hard.

'Just out, Spiros. I won't know till I get there.' There was no sense letting Spiros know where I was going. If, it was Roland, the fewer people who knew he was alive, the better.

The taxi to Stokes Hill Wharf didn't take long.

'Just drop me here, mate,' I said when we arrived and dropped a twenty over the seat. Darwin taxi fares and a lack of change would send me broke.

'Cheers, mate. Thanks. Have a good day.'

The taxi couldn't take me quite as far as I needed. The drive to the wharf was a big one-way loop, and it was necessary to walk the last fifty metres along the boardwalk to reach The Port Side Grill. It was a nice-looking place at the end of the wharf. What was Roland up to? I supposed if this was the venue for our 'last supper', it was a reasonable choice. The Darwin sunset began to splash pink and apricot across the horizon.

Since I arrived in Darwin my head hadn't stopped spinning. The Scotch, the sea air and now the umami of steaks charring on the grill. Kamahli, Roland and Yates. It was all too much in too little time. My boring-as-bat-shit life back in Perth seemed more appealing to me now. The confusion that I had experienced since first landing in Darwin was making me lose my grip on reality. Things were way too complicated. It was out of control. There was a time when I thought more of Roland than anyone I'd ever known. He was more than a brother. I'd once thought I would do anything for him, knowing he'd do the same for me, no questions asked. Now, whatever we once had was unravelling. There was too much going on. I yearned for a logical explanation that would make everything alright.

Did I really know who Roland was anymore? Orphanages, cafés, Kamahli, even the bloody blackfellas' fish and art businesses. But dead refugees, what a mess. He'd sure been busy since he tossed in his Sydney job. He'd told me nothing about any of this. He'd asked me to do some office admin job for him. The reality of what Roland was now didn't seem to fit what I had remembered of him. I'm sure he didn't remember me the same way either. I don't think I've changed so much. So many dead people from the docks were the last straw. Whatever we had once was now gone. I didn't know what I was doing heading out to meet him at a Darwin tourist spot. What could he say that could make any sense of this mess? What was with all the cloak and dagger? Why didn't he just hand himself in? And Jesus, if it wasn't Roland in the car wreck, who was it? The dead refugees were one thing, but the thought of him killing another person to fake his own death was too much.

I walked into the Port Side Grill and scanned the tables for him. It was a nice-looking place. Nothing seemed out of the ordinary. I half expected to see him sitting at a table in dark glasses and a trench coat, doing some corny impression of Bogart in *Casablanca*. A trench coat in Darwin would have really stuck out. This place would be a good place to have a farewell dinner. I realised that apart from Spiros's breakfasts, I'd eaten very little. I approached the 'Please wait here to be shown to your table' sign and obediently waited. A young man, decked out in the black and white of a maître d', gave me a disapproving look and asked, 'Can I ask the name of your booking please, sir?'

'No booking. I'm supposed to ask for Yang.'

The maître d' spun on his heel and headed off. I didn't know if I should follow him or not. I waited by the sign. He returned with a diminutive, young woman in a headscarf in tow. The maître d' didn't look pleased, and his eyes didn't leave me as he watched as Yang said, 'Please follow me, sir.'

She walked past me, out the door, to the outside area of the café. A line of tables edged the wharf, close to the water. Many of these tables were occupied. Tourists were gathering to take in the Darwin sunset.

'Please sit down, Mr Winter. You won't have long to wait,' Yang said, knowing my name although I hadn't given it to her. With that, she calmly headed back into the café.

The tables were oriented to look back over the harbour towards Darwin across the water. Sitting there, I could see the glorious sunset developing. I could also see the crowds on the white sandy beach across the inner lagoon. The little patch of sand seemed out of place against the backdrop of mangroves. The distant crowd was appreciating the gloaming as the temperature dropped enough to provide relief from another hot Darwin day. I glanced at my watch.

'They look just like insignificant dots from here, don't they?' I spun around in my chair as Roland sat down beside me. I immediately noticed that Roland had shaved off that silly looking moustache, leaving a white shadow above his top lip, contrasting with his 'top-end tan'.

'If God reached down, he could just squash one of them with his thumb. Do you think anyone would notice, or we'd be any worse off?' he continued. 'Thanks for coming, Paul. And thanks for coming alone. I'm sure you appreciate the sensitivity of the situation.'

'What do you mean squash them with his thumb? I'm sure they'd consider themselves worse off if God squashed them.'

"But really, collectively, what difference would just one or two make? What difference would ten or one hundred of them make for that matter?"

'Don't be such a prick; every life is a special thing. You sound like a serial killer.' I had thought about meeting Roland again on the way out in the taxi. Surely his opening discussion should have been an apology, an apology to me, to Kamahli or at the very least to the bloody corpses, half of who they'd put in the cold store.

'Don't piss me off. A serial killer is a lunatic. I couldn't be saner. But you don't think sacrificing a few could help the many? *'You know that it's said, thirty years under the Borgias and they had warfare, rape, murder, terror and bloodshed, but they produced Michelangelo, Leonardo da Vinci and the Renaissance.'* What have we done here? In Australia, we've got untold mineral wealth, prosperity, democracy and peace. Were one of the richest nations on earth. But what have we really contributed to humanity? The Hills Hoist and the Pavlova? Shit, they reckon we even stole the Pav' from the Kiwis. Australia squanders what it's got, so why shouldn't we share it around a little? I'm not talking about killing anybody. What I'm talking about is letting more people share in the wealth we have. I don't mean in a hippie or commie sense. All I mean is that giving desperate people who have nothing a chance to contribute to Australian society. How can that be a bad thing? Giving people a second chance to a better life made this country. Think what the Harbour Bridge, the Opera House or Snowy Hydro Scheme would look like without the migrants that helped build them.' Roland was on a roll now and had worked up a head of steam.

'Don't think I missed the Borgia quote from Graham Greene. I've read '*The Third Man*' too, you know.'

'I didn't think you'd remember '*The Third Man*'. It's a favourite of mine.'

'I was sitting next to you in Balzac's class, remember. What you're doing is human trafficking. You're talking about bringing people into this country illegally.'

'Give me a break. These people can't come in any other way. In their own country, they don't exist. They don't have citizenship. They don't have a passport. They don't get a vote. Fuck, if their own countrymen would prefer that they're dead, surely bringing them here where we desperately need people makes it better for everybody!'

'Why can't you let the politicians work it out? Then they can come over here properly.'

'The politicians are the ones that created this problem. They're the ones who use them to point score. Sri Lankan, Afghan, Iraqi, Australian politicians, they're all the same. They segregate people based on their language, religion or ethnicity. They think by getting the majority with power to pick on a minority, they'll have an easier job to rule the populace. The Aussies try to make themselves look big by 'send them back' campaigns that appeal to the rednecks who spout 'fuck off, we're full' bumper stickers. Full of shit, I'd say. The refugees have no legitimate way of getting out of the living hell into which they've been born. Even if they did, do you think we'd let them in? For Christ's sake, look at us: two privileged white boys arguing about who can and who can't come into this land. The land's not even ours. We're from migrant stock, the same as those you call refugees. Do you think our forebears asked the blackfellas if they could come in? You're standing on Larrakia land, mate. You travelled across thirty blackfella nations coming to Darwin from Perth. Did you get their permission? Did you ask them if it was okay? Of course not.'

'Surely you're not suggesting we give this land back to the blackfellas?'

'Are you listening to me Paul? That's not what I'm saying at all. Still, if I was, it would have a lot more credibility than a bunch of grey-haired, overpaid, white-fella politicians in Canberra saying who can make a go of it in Darwin or not. It's like we've been granted permission to join an exclusive club, and now we're in, we want to change the rules so no one else can join. We think that keeping everyone out will mean we get more of a share, as if wealth is limited to a privileged few. That's such a dumb argument. It assumes everything is static. It assumes our privileged life is a cake with just a few slices. If privilege is a cake, let's work to make a bigger cake. Then there's plenty to go around. What makes us rich is health, happiness and joy, not dollars. Happiness and health can't be measured in dollars. In fact, we don't even measure them at all. But health, happiness and joy grow with diversity. Happiness is like a diamond; adding more facets makes it shine brighter.'

'You sound like a socialist revolutionary.'

'Maybe I am. But think about it. Do you think the rednecks with their offensive bumper stickers are right?'

'No, but—'

'Of course not. Frankly, if we could swap just one redneck for a hundred migrants, we'd be better off. I say bring more grateful, hardworking migrants to this country. Sure, send people back to where they've come from if they're criminals. But one of Australia's biggest problems is that there aren't enough people. Here is an obvious and way to fix it.'

'But what you're doing is a criminal offence. You know the cops are looking for you.'

'Well, now, at last, you're making more sense. Of course, it is illegal. What do they have left when all the legal means of sharing this country are taken away? What sort of country do we become when the hate the rednecks espouse is tolerated and grows? Elected politicians support closing this country off. What are we left to do when humane, compassionate, sharing of abundant wealth is criminalised?'

'So, change the law. Protest, run for office.'

'Yeah, how long do you think that would take? Even if it were possible, the politicians wouldn't let it happen. They make big men and women of themselves by finding minorities, like illegal immigrants, to hate. Hell, they won't even call them what they are—refugees. In Australia, you get five or six years if you're found guilty of murder. If you arrive by boat, having committed no crime in the eyes of the United Nations no less, you're locked up in a concentration camp indefinitely. You don't even know how long you're going to be in prison. How cruel is that? Some of these poor bastards have been in detention for years with no indication of when or if they'll ever be let out or sent back. As a nation, we will be judged by how we treat these people, and at the moment, all we are doing is building a debt of shame to pass on to our future generations.

Mark my words, it's the same thing we did as a nation to the blackfellas with the stolen generation. It's a disgrace. The refugee situation is a festering sore. In years to come, our children and our grandchildren will look back on this generation with inherited shame. You and me and everyone else that has allowed this situation to fester create this shame. The country's almost bloody empty, for fuck's sake. You could put a few million more people between here and Perth, and nobody would even notice them. You travelled up here from Perth. Did you look out the window? Did it look like we're full?' Roland paused for a breath and continued before I could respond. 'Well? Of course not. There's nothing out there except sheep and cows and an occasional hole in the ground mine. The rednecks' stickers should read 'Come on in, we're almost fucking empty.''

'But don't you think it is evil to profit from these people?' I asked nervously.

'I'm not profiting from any of this! You've no idea what I've had to pay. Cash up front. Straight out of my pocket, no one else's.'

Roland's tone left me with no doubt he believed he was telling the truth. If anyone could pick up when he was bullshitting, it was me. I always could.

'I paid so many people in Indonesia it's criminal: boat captains, boat crews, crane drivers, bus drivers, wharfies, security, even the bloody taxi drivers over there want hush money, and the rate goes up at the Australian end. If anyone is profiting, it is those bloody parasites. It costs them nothing to look the other way. There's no risk for them. All the risk is mine.'

'What! How can you say all the risk is yours? People are dead.' I felt the discussion was about to unravel.

'Yes, I concede the last trip didn't go well. You don't know how bad I feel about the last lot.'

'I should fuckin' think so! Do you hear yourself? You're talking like the dead are an unfortunate side effect, collateral damage. It's an absolute tragedy. You know they're calling you a mass murderer. It's splashed across the papers. Roland, I was at your fucking funeral. Who did we bury there?' I asked, not sure I wanted to know.

'That just shows you what a corrupt system we've got here. When the unions called their strike, I knew things were going to turn to shit. There was no way I could get to those people already in transit. The port was closed. I was shitting myself about how long those self-righteous union pricks would shut things off. Don't think I didn't try to get those poor bastards out. The unions can be so bloody pig-headed when they want to be. They're happy to take the money and look the other way every time except when they're on strike. Who do they think they're fooling? They aren't guiltless in any of this either. They knew what was going on. I'm just glad it didn't last longer than it did. At least I got some of them out.'

'Yeah, but whose body was in the car crash?'

'Haven't you figured it out? I needed a way out. I couldn't just disappear. It would look like I was running away and guilty of something. I put a full load of fuel in the back of the F250, filled the long-range tanks and splashed fuel over the seats. I jammed a four by two under the dash to hold the accelerator down, crunched it into gear and slammed it straight into the sign for the highway turnoff.

You should have seen her go up.'

'Answer the question, Roland. Who was the body?'

Roland coughed as he spoke, as if the preceding rant had drained the insurance salesman's bluster and bullshit from him. 'The person in the car wreck was a refugee from the sea container who didn't make it. He was already dead. I paid the security guard at the wharf, where they had put bodies in the cold store, twenty thousand cash for him. He was just a poor unnamed corpse. With so many in there, they would hardly worry about losing one. I figured they'd just think they'd miscounted. I put my watch and ring on him and put him in my car. Fuck, he was already dead. I was just giving him an impromptu cremation.'

'Jesus, Roland! Is that what you think you were doing? Do you really think anyone would look at what you've done as an 'impromptu cremation'?'

'No, but it's what I tell myself so that I can live with myself. It was a shitty thing to do. A really shitty thing to do. But what choice did I have?'

'Roland, you should turn yourself in. Yates seems like a reasonable copper.'

'Paul, even if Yates was a reasonable copper, and I'm not sure that he is, what do you think they'd do? I'd be locked up for years. The coppers and the politicians would have a field day trolling through my stuff, trying to send good people who deserve a chance at a peaceful life back to where they came. I can't turn myself in. I'm sorry. I didn't mean for you to get involved in any of this. Tell Yates the full story, tell him everything. I'm sure even he will see you've had nothing to do with all of this.'

'What does any of this have to do with Christina?' The mention of Christina stopped Roland. 'Yates has brought her up a few times. What's going on with her?'

'Christina is dead.' Roland's eyes welled up. 'We met again in Sydney. She was dying when we crossed paths. I love her. I'll never love someone as I loved her. I never wanted to do anything to harm her, but she had HIV/AIDS and insisted. Her time had already run out when I found her again. I helped her to end it on her terms. I killed her. I did what she asked me to do. I've hated myself for being so weak ever since. Call me a murderer if you like, I am, but I never intended to harm any of the refugees. I am responsible for three hundred and seventeen refugees coming to Australia from previous container shipments. But the only murder I am guilty of is of Christina, who I loved more than you'll ever know. This thing with the refugees was meant to be a good thing. It had worked out okay before. It would have worked out okay this time, too, if not for the extra days they had to spend in the container. I never intended to harm those people, Paul. You know that's not me. I hated who I had become in Sydney. I became richer than you could have ever imagined. I'm still getting cheques from insurance companies. But I'd sold my soul to them and their parasitic job. I came to Darwin to leave all of that behind me. To atone for what I'd done to Christina. Until the incident on the wharf, I thought I was doing okay.'

'So, was Kamahli in on all of this refugee stuff with you?' I said and glanced at the time.

'Paul, Kamahli was a refugee once herself. Long before I met her. She knew firsthand what it was like.'

'She told me as much. She also told me you and her were lovers once too.'

'I've had too many lovers, Paul. I think I was trying to fuck Christina Brown out of my head. I know half of them wouldn't even look at me today now that my bank balance isn't what it once was. But no one, not even Kamahli, came close to what I felt for Christina. Paul, Kamahli's not anywhere as tough as she makes out. She likes you by the sound of things.'

'Don't keep trying to bullshit me, Roland. She told me you asked her to look after me.'

'Don't flatter me, Paul. I couldn't tell Kamahli to do anything she didn't want to do. But you could do a hell of a lot worse than spend some time with her. She's smart, she's kind, and she is going to be okay. None of this business has anything to do with her.'

I looked at my watch.

Roland looked back along the wharf. 'How much longer, Paul?'

'What do you mean?

'That's the third time you've looked at that crappy Pulsar watch you were once so proud of. When are the coppers arriving?

'Roland, I'm so sorry. I had no idea about Christina. I had no idea what you've been up to. I told Yates I was meeting you here at seven-thirty. That gave you and me an hour and a half together, before he arrives.'

'Shit, Paul, I thought you owed me more than that,' Roland said with an air of urgency. He stood and pulled a mobile phone from his jeans pocket and hurriedly punched numbers in to it. I stood too. He turned square on to me, inhaled and broadened his shoulders that seemed to make him larger. 'He'll be here in less than forty minutes; it'll be earlier if I know Yates. Just tell him I didn't show up.'

I thought Roland was shaping up to hit me. His left hand rose. Was I about to be strangled or punched? Instead, Roland embraced me. I reflexively returned the hug, then embraced him more intentionally as I realised, I had judged him so unfairly. If this was the last time, I saw my long-time friend, I wanted it to be positive, even under these extraordinary circumstances.

Roland rolled his wrist and looked at the time. He glanced over my shoulder toward the water, and then I heard the thumping sound of powerful motors. I turned around to see *Durendal,* Roland's oversized boat, pulling up to the wharf with Squizzy at the wheel. Six two-hundred litre fuel drums were lashed to the deck. Squizzy let the engines idle, and the boat nestled up to the wharf; he didn't tie it off.

'Roland, what are you doing?' I asked.

'I can't stay here.'

'Where will you go?'

'It is best for us both if I don't tell you that. But I need to get away from here now,' Roland said as he jumped onto the deck, clutching one of the fuel drums to stop himself from falling over the side and into the water. 'Look after Kamahli for me. She deserves to be happy. She deserves better than me. She's been through enough pain for many lifetimes.'

Squizzy gunned the engines, and the boat's prow leapt up as the twin engines bit into the water. My head was reeling from Roland's rant, the deaths on the docks, his admission to stealing and desecrating a body, Christina's death and the lingering thoughts of Kamahli. There were still so many more questions I needed him to answer. But it wasn't to be.

I stared after *Durendal* as the roar of her powerful motors diminished to a hum, leaving me on the wharf staring after him.

'Paul, you need to sit down.'

I spun to see that Kamahli had come up behind me.

'What's going on? Roland told me you didn't have anything to do with any of this.' I said.

'Paul, I think we've all got some level of involvement in this mess whether we like it or not. I followed you here. It wasn't hard; you could have made it a bit tougher. I knew Roland wanted a chance to explain some of the mess he'd put you in. He isn't the cold-hearted criminal that you and Yates seem convinced that he is.'

'Kamahli, I'm so sorry. I know that now. Maybe you should go. I've told Yates that I figured I was meeting Roland here. I don't want you getting in any strife.'

'So, Yates knows you were meeting Roland?'

'Well, I told him about the note. I guessed it was Roland who had sent it.'

'Paul, I sent the note. If Yates wants to check it out, he will only find my prints on it. I sent it for Roland, but only you and I know that. Just tell Yates you guessed wrong, that the note was from me.'

It seemed too simple, but simplicity that was convincing. There wasn't any actual link to Roland on the mysterious note. It might work.

'Okay, let's do this. Can I buy you dinner then?'

'Sure.'

I waved to the maître d', whose demeanour hadn't improved.

'We'll be staying for dinner. Can we see a menu, please? But before that, please wipe down this table, it seems dusty and bring us a chilled bottle of Verve.'

'Our Yellow Label Brut Non-Vintage is one-hundred and twenty-five-dollars, Sir. We have cheaper sparkling wine if you'd prefer.'

'The yellow label will be fine. This is a special occasion.'

'Certainly, Sir.' the maître d' replied, with a look that suggested he had just trodden in something he rather he hadn't.

The Champagne arrived in quick time, together with the menus. The maître d' deftly opened the Champagne with a muffled pop.

'Well, this looks very romantic. Are we toasting absent friends?' Yates appeared from behind the maître d'.

'Hello, Sergeant. Yes, will you join us for a glass of Champagne? I was just about to make a toast. Toasting absent friend seems very appropriate, but so too does a toast to new friends and new beginnings.'

'Thank you, Paul, but I'm on duty. As much as I'd like to join you and Kamahli, I can't drink while on duty. I was hoping I might run into another one of your friends.'

'Sorry, Sergeant, I may have inadvertently misled you. I was mistaken. The note I spoke to you about was from Kamahli.'

I raised my glass and kissed it against Kamahli's in a toast, and glanced toward the ocean, where *Durendal* now appeared as a diminishing dot on the horizon, leaving Darwin in her wake.

'To absent friends, to new friends and to new beginnings.'

Yates looked towards the horizon. There was no way I could tell if he knew we were staring at *Durendal's* wake as it headed west, carrying Roland towards the sunset.

'To new beginnings,' Yates repeated before he turned and left.

END

References

The following creative works have been referred to in the text and are used within the copyright context of 'fair use':

Austen, J. "Pride and Prejudice." First published 1813 by Thomas Egerton (England). 2003 paperback by Bantam Classics cited.

de Balzac, H. *"Letters of Two Brides."* First published 1842. 1923 edition by Willian Heineman Ltd. London, England.

Dickens, C. *"Great Expectations."* First edition (as a book from the serialised publication) 1861. Chapman and Hall. London, England.

Green, G. *"The Third Man."* 1949. Penguin Books. London, England.

Heine, H. *"Almansor"* (Play). 1821-1822. Berlin, Germany

Hemingway, E. *"The Old Man and the Sea."* (1952). Charles Scribner and Sons. New York, USA

Miller, H. *"Tropic of Capricorn."* First published.1939. Penguin Classics. New York, USA.

Miller, H. *"Tropic of Cancer."* First published 1934. Obelisk Press. Paris France.

Miller, H. *"Sexus"*. First published 1949. Grove Press Edition (1994). New York, USA.

About the Author

Pete Mitchell lives, as a guest of the Wadjuck Noongar people, in Boorloo (Perth). After publishing one non-fiction book and more than 50 scientific journal papers Darwin's Wake is his first work of fiction.

With a background in science and tertiary qualifications in chemistry and business his previous studies have provided him with a unique perspective on the environment in which he finds himself. Previous jobs have included roles in customer service, chicken farming, and door to door sales from which he has drawn experiences and inspiration for the unique character descriptions within his works. A love of travel, a keen sense of social justice and an eye for the intricacies of human behaviour are demonstrated in his writing.

Pete is a member of Writers Victoria and is expecting to have his first short story published in Azuria in mid-2023.

When he is not writing Pete enjoys getting out in the beautiful Australian bush, travelling and reading (as all writers should).

More details on the author and additional publications can be found on the authors website: petemitchell.com.au

CPSIA information can be obtained
at www.ICGtesting.com
Printed in the USA
BVHW042216041222
653455BV00001B/3